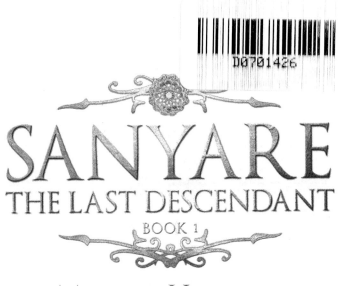

SANYARE

THE LAST DESCENDANT

BOOK 1

MEGAN HASKELL

Wonder Con 2023

TRABUCO RIDGE PRESS

ISBN-13: 978-0-9864083-0-4 (Kindle)
ISBN-13: 978-0-9864083-1-1 (ePub)
ISBN-13: 978-0-9864083-2-8 (Paperback)

Cover Designed by Deranged Doctor Design (http://www.derangeddoctordesign.com/)
Edited by Laura Taylor
Published by Trabuco Ridge Press

If you would like to be notified of new releases, events and giveaways, please sign up for Megan Haskell's newsletter mailing list at www.meganhaskell.com.

To my husband, Adam, for the unending support. You encouraged my writing before I even dreamed I could be an author. Thank you for believing in me.

Glossary

Nuriel (NOO-ree-el): Servant-Daughter
Our protagonist, she prefers the nickname Rie (REE-ay).
Human, raised by the high elves Curuthannor and
Lhéwen in the Upper Realm.

Aradae (AIR-a-day): Royal-Shadow
King of the Shadow Realm. Dark elf.

Blood Sidhe (Blood SHEE)
A race of greater fae that survives on the blood of
humans. They look human, but have the magical abilities
of glamour (illusion) and compulsion, which helps them
attract and entrap their prey.

Braegan (BRAY-gan)
The first person willing to help Rie navigate the Shadow
Realm. Blood sidhe (pronounced shee).

Curuthannor (koo-ROO-than-or): Skilled-Shield
Rie's foster father (a.k.a. warden) and martial trainer.
Lifemate to Lhéwen. He's the head of King Othin's
personal guard. High elf.

Daenor (DAY-nor): Shadow-Fire
Bastard son of King Aradae, Shadow Realm prince, and
Shadow Guard Commander. Dark elf and fire sidhe.

Dark Elf
The ruling species of greater fae in the Shadow Realm.
They have very dark black skin with bright white hair and
tall pointed ears. They are the masters of soul magic, able
to commune with the souls of the dead and see the past
and the future.

Fae (FAY)
A generic term used for any of the magical creatures that
live in the nine faerie (fairy) realms.

Faerleithril (fay-er-LEE-thrill): Spirit-Freer
Female heir to the Shadow Realm throne and Faernodir's
twin. Dark elf.

Faernodir (fay-er-NO-deer): Spirit-Binder
Male heir to the Shadow Realm throne and Faerleithril's
twin. Dark elf.

Garamaen (gare-a-May-en): Clever Wolf
A powerful Lord of the elves living in the Human Realm.
Origin Sidhe.

Gikl (GI-kill)
One of the pixies who has attached to Rie.

Greater Fae (Greater FAY)
A generic term for the fae species that can pass for
human; the elves and the sidhe. These species are
typically the ruling classes in the realms where they
reside.

High Elf
The ruling species of greater fae in the Upper Realm. Also called the glittering throng. They typically have very pale skin and hair that shimmers slightly in the light, and high pointed ears. They are the masters of spirit magic, able to drain or restore energy, heal, and manipulate emotion.

Hiinto (HIN-toe)
One of the pixies who has attached to Rie.

Lesser Fae (Lesser FAY)
A generic term for the more exotic fae species that would be unable to travel unnoticed in the Human Realm; the pixies, goblins, gremlins, trolls, etc. These species rarely hold political power in the realms where they reside.

Lhéwen (LAY-when): Thread-Maiden
Rie's foster mother, aka warden. She's the best seamstress in the Upper Realm. High elf.

Niinka (NIN-ka)
One of the pixies who has attached to Rie.

Othin (OH-thin)
King of the Upper Realm. High elf.

Pixie (Carnivorous)
The pixies are tiny creatures, just two to three inches tall. Like a chameleon, they have the ability to camouflage their skin to match the surrounding area. They are hairless, have translucent wings like a dragonfly, and avoid clothing or accessories that would hinder their abilities to hide. They eat raw flesh and can strip a small creature of all its meat in a matter of minutes.

Plink

An imp who becomes Rie's handmaiden. She looks like cross between a giant rat and a tiny goat, and has the ability to translocate in an instant.

Possn (POSS-in)

One of the pixies who has attached to Rie.

Ragnar (RAG-nawr)

Prince Daenor's friend and executive assistant. Goblin.

Rolimdornoron (roll-im-DOOR-nor-on): Most Swift Realm Runner

Rie's boss in the High Court messenger service. High elf with questionable lineage.

Sidhe (SHEE)

A generic term used for some races of the greater fae who identify by their abilities; blood sidhe, fire sidhe, frost sidhe, etc.

Tharbatiron (thar-ba-TEER-on)

Proprietor of the renowned and extremely popular Crossroads Inn in the Shadow Realm. Ancient dark elf.

Tiik (TEAK)

One of the pixies who has attached to Rie.

Tryg (TRIG, like in trigonometry)

Bartender and bodyguard for Tharbatiron

Turant (tour-AUNT)

A longma (dragon-horse) telepathically connected to Daenor.

Whixle (WICK-sell)
Renowned Shadow Realm bladesmith. Gremlin.

CHAPTER ONE

With a deep breath, Rie left the pretensions of the High Court and its glittering throng behind her. The portal stretched and squeezed, drawing her cell by cell from the hard marble hall onto soft sand touched by gentle waves. She rested her hand on the cool sandstone that arched above her head, gathering her bearings as her heart rate calmed.

Centering herself, Rie pulled the salty stink of fish deep into her lungs before beginning the two-mile walk to Lord Garamaen's beachfront estate. The beach was hushed, as if setting the stage for the first appearance of the sun above the hills. Even the birds held their breath. It was too early for the tourists and dog-walkers to be out, and only a few surfers lounged on the calm waves in the distance. Rie savored the quiet, even if her two tiny companions didn't.

"The human realm is so boring," Hiinto said, spittle landing on Rie's cheek.

She wiped it away, careful not to swat the two-inch pixie holding onto her ear, but made a show of flinging the spit off to the side.

"Why can't we go somewhere new and fun?" he continued.

"Please. You wouldn't know what to do with yourself. You'd hide in Rie's hair the whole time," Niinka replied from her makeshift swing at Rie's belt. She lounged upside down, appearing as nothing more than a trinket on a chain hanging out of Rie's pocket, while she sharpened her claws to a precise point.

"Not true!"

Rie clenched her jaw, biting back her irritation. They were her friends, but sometimes she wished they would act like adults, rather than siblings.

"It is true, and you know it," Niinka said.

"Quiet," Rie snapped, patience gone. A headache throbbed behind her forehead. She needed to focus.

Two men stood on the beach, directly in her path. Still at least fifty yards away, they seemed out of place without the surfboards or exercise attire of the usual early morning crowd. Rie paused, assessing. The blond one crouched, taking something out of a bag in the sand. He flipped it once, a shard of light glinting into Rie's eyes. The throbbing in her brain burst in white-hot light, leaving her blind to the real world as she entered a vision.

***

The blond man stands, facing her. He pulls his arm back, a knife whistles toward her. Blood streams from her belly, her shirt soaked in seconds, the sand absorbing the overflow. The sky is all she sees, expansive gray-blue dotted with thin wispy clouds. A small hand taps her face. Niinka's wide black eyes float into view. Then darkness.

***

Rie gasped, coming out of the premonition. The blond man rose from his crouch, facing her. His arm pulled back.

Sending her thanks to the gods for the warning, Rie spun left as a knife passed through the air where she had stood. Dropping into a crouch, she scuttled behind a large rocky outcropping, just as another knife hit the sand at her feet. She picked it up, testing the weight as adrenaline surged and her heart rate sped. Fear twisted a knot of dread in her gut.

Curuthannor's training kicked in. This might be her first life or death fight, but he had prepared her well. She took a cleansing breath, washed away the fear and replaced it with determination. The pixies let go of their hiding spots, chattering in the clicks and whistles of their native tongue. Rie ignored them, focusing instead on her surroundings, and her options. Stairs wound up the cliff to her left, heading toward the street above, but a hundred feet of open space stretched between her rock and the first step. No matter how fast she moved, she'd be an easy target. If she ran back toward the arch, she'd be similarly open to attack.

Rie grabbed a handful of sand with her left hand, while her right hand reached behind and traded the unfamiliar throwing knife for one of two eight-inch khukuri blades in the horizontal sheath at her lower back.

"What are they doing?" she asked Hiinto.

The little pixie crawled atop the rock, his translucent wings pulled back and naked skin camouflaged to match the color and texture of the sandstone. "They've split up, one on each side. They're creeping along now, not sure what you're doing, I think. What *are* you doing?"

"Which one is closer?"

"The one near the cliffs."

"How close?"

"Fifty feet, coming closer."

"Are you two hungry?"

Hiinto grinned, revealing a mouth full of sharp, serrated teeth, while Niinka rubbed her hands together. "Humans taste almost as good as the elves and greater fae," she whispered.

"Wait until they are close. I will deal with the cliff-side man. You two take a bite out of the one on the ocean-side."

"Yum." Hiinto licked his lips.

Sliding a foot or two to the left, closer to the cliffs, Rie listened for the man's footsteps in the dry seaweed. When she guessed he was within a few feet, Rie lunged sideways out from behind the rock and threw the sand into his face. He sputtered, dropping his weapons and scrubbing at his eyes. Rie dodged into range. Her right arm snapped out and up across the man's body, drawing a horizontal figure eight across his torso, the razor-edged khukuri knife sliding through the soft tissue of his unprotected belly like a spoon through pudding. She pulled back and away, but not before a loud pop echoed off the cliff face.

Rie's right leg crumpled beneath her. She fell to the ground, blood saturating the cloth around a hole in her upper thigh. She rolled away from the dying assassin. Sand exploded from the impact of another round. Rie tucked in behind a driftwood log, waiting for the second assassin to make another move. Blood seeped into her leggings, staining the blue denim a dark burgundy. The wound wasn't fatal, but the blood-loss was already making her feel faint.

Rie peeked out from behind the log. The pixies were nowhere in sight. The man drew closer, carrying his gun out and away from his body, held loose as if he had all the time in the world to deal with his target.

"Thanks for taking care of Grant," he said, a wicked grin on his face. "I hated his constant bragging, and now the bounty's all mine."

Rie kept silent, thoughts frantic for a plan.

He took a deep breath, exhaling on a groan. "You smell

delicious. I can't wait for my first taste." His tongue slicked out across an extended fang. Blood sidhe, otherwise known as vampire. Shadow Realm hunters of humans.

Ten yards, and closing. There was no way out, nowhere to go, not with a wounded leg and open beach. She crouched, body weight centered on her good leg, the assassin's throwing knife drawn and ready. She would have to be fast, stand up and flick the blade end over end to hit her target.

The man screamed, gun firing two rounds in quick succession. Rie flattened against the log, but the rounds weren't aimed at her. Poking her head above the wood again, Rie gagged, the contents of her stomach threatening to spill onto the sand.

The pixies were hard at work. A fine red mist gathered like a cloud around the assassin's head. He swatted at empty air, turning in circles, but never close to touching Rie's friends. His cheeks disappeared first, hollowing out as the pixies stole chunks of soft tissue. Only visible as a flash when they paused to strike, the pixies made fast work of the man's face. With little meat left on his cheeks and Hiinto harassing his eyes, Niinka tunneled into the skin beneath his jaw. His scream abruptly cut off, Rie assumed when Niinka bit through his vocal cords.

The assassin faced her, mouth gaping like a fish. Lidless eyes glared, whites showing all the way around the chocolate colored iris. He stepped forward, lifted his gun for a final attempt on Rie's life. Hiinto landed hard on his wrist, clawing his way into the tendons and veins, sending the weapon to the ground along with a hard spray of arterial blood. Having eaten most of the man's tongue, Niinka crawled out through his mouth. Rie stood, aimed. A flick of her wrist sent the knife spinning through the air, once, twice. The third round connected the pointed blade deep into the man's neck.

The pixies continued to feed as the assassin fell face first into the sand. Blood arced from multiple wounds, slowing along with his heart rate. The pixies, bloated with blood and flesh, flew to Rie's side, bobbing drunkenly from side to side.

"Sorry we were late," Hiinto said, his head tilted to the side. Blood and gore streaked his face and body from eyes to bellybutton. "We got a little distracted when you cut the first one."

"They were blood sidhe, not human. A more complex flavor, more depth to savor," Niinka added, dragging her fingers one by one through her mouth, licking off every drop of red liquid she could find. Despite her trip through the gunman's throat, she was already clean, only a few spots of red marring her smooth white complexion.

"We survived. That's all that matters."

Adrenaline long gone, Rie's limbs hung heavy with fatigue. She shivered, whether from shock or dread, she didn't know. Her leg was still bleeding. Making a tourniquet out of a strip of her shirt, Rie tied a knot above the hole in her leg. The blood loss slowed, but she knew it was a temporary measure.

"We'll have to take their heads." Rie leaned heavily against the driftwood log. As badly damaged as they were, the assassins might find a way to feed and heal. Decapitation was the only way to ensure they didn't rise again.

Using the driftwood for support, Rie dragged herself to the gunman. Niinka's work, plus the knife protruding from his throat, made it easy to take his head. It was nearly detached already. The second assassin was harder, in part because she kept having to chase off the seagulls that wanted his guts for lunch.

Through it all, Rie existed in a cloud of detachment, as

if the entire incident had happened to someone else. She didn't even regret killing the blood sidhe, the first sentient lives she'd taken. She hoped it was the shock, and not some sign of a malfunctioning conscience, but she didn't have the energy to worry about it. It was all she could do to finish her assignment and get home.

"Lord Garamaen will send someone to take care of the bodies," Niinka said. A deep yawn cracked her jaw. She climbed her way up Rie's shoulder to cuddle in the crook of her neck. Hiinto tucked himself into the pocket of her shirt.

Using the last of her waning strength, Rie hid the bodies as best she could under some loose driftwood, and stumbled in the direction of Lord Garamaen's hall. Salt and sand coated her mouth and throat, the gritty texture grinding between her teeth. She spit to the side. With a dry mouth, it didn't do much good. She prayed for enough strength to make it to his door.

***

Lord Garamaen's estate sat high atop a cliff, the creamy white house known for expansive views captured by floor to ceiling windows. It was plain compared to the ornate edifices in the Upper Realm, with their spires and arches and filigreed railings, instead focusing on simple lines and asymmetrical angles that maximized the beach exposure. That its owner was not human was a well-guarded secret.

"What sadistic bastard put 52 uneven steps from his house to the beach?" Rie asked no one in particular as she dragged her battered body up the last few punishing wooden boards.

"That would be me," a man said from the paved stone patio that led to the mansion's back door.

Rie's head snapped up. Recovering as quickly as possible from the surprise, she straightened and donned her court persona, the neutral facial expression her high elf warden, Curuthannor, had drilled into her.

Lord Garamaen didn't resemble the high elves she knew in the Upper Realm. He hardly looked like an elf at all. He was more muscular, and far too casual for the High Court. He kept his dirty blond hair trimmed short, just brushing the tips of barely pointed ears, and he wore the cotton shorts and thin shirts native to the area. He was taller than the average human, she supposed, well over six feet, but nothing extraordinary by greater fae standards. Worse, his right hand had been severed at the wrist, the handicap setting him apart from his flawless brethren.

She wondered, not for the first time, whether Garamaen maintained a personal glamour to help him blend with the humans he loved so dearly. She didn't think so, but then she was only human.

"Lord Garamaen, I am Nuriel Lhethannien, from the High Court messenger service. I have come with a message from High King Othin." Rie held out her messenger pendant for inspection, pulling it from beneath her shirt on its long satin cord. This was not the first time she had visited Lord Garamaen, not by a long shot, but protocol required the same introduction with each missive.

"Looks to me like you've had a bit of trouble getting here. And I prefer to be called Greg in this realm, if you recall," Lord Garamaen said, not even glancing at the badge.

Rie's thumb twitched, but she was sure no pain or anxiety showed on her face. She returned the medallion to its place.

"I remember, but I have to follow protocol. The King sends his regards and requests the honor of your presence at the High Court in three human days time."

Her voice stayed steady, but her heart raced and her right leg trembled. She locked her knees and hoped Lord Garamaen wouldn't notice.

"Come in and let me look at you. We can't have a king's messenger returning to service in such a state."

Rie shivered. It would be nice to get warm, if nothing else, since the sun had apparently decided to take its heat elsewhere.

"I appreciate the offer." Rie's vision swam. She could barely feel her right leg below the tourniquet. She was forced to admit she wouldn't make it back to the portal without passing out.

"If you hurt her, you'll regret it," Niinka snarled from her hiding spot behind Rie's left ear.

"Who do we have here?" Garamaen asked, not quite covering the twitch that gave away his surprise. "A pixie? Two? How would you like a reward for helping me with your messenger friend?"

"What have you got?" Hiinto asked. He poked his head out of her shirt pocket, resting his arms on the edge of the fabric, and his chin on his arms. He must still be too full to move, since he wasn't already swarming Lord Garamaen for his prize. The pixies were suckers for a shiny trinket or length of satin ribbon, Hiinto the greediest of them all. Like tiny dragons, they hoarded their treasures in personal nests, keeping them hidden from everyone, even the other members of the swarm.

"Be careful," Niinka hissed. "He will help, but he's a tricky one."

Rie took a step forward. Her leg buckled. Lord Garamaen caught her before she hit the floor. Pulling her arm over his shoulder, he half-carried her through the doorway and into the sunken living area.

"Have a seat, I'll be back in just a minute." Lord Garamaen eased her down into an ivory leather chair without giving her the opportunity to protest making a bloody mess on his furniture, and sped out of the room.

"Don't forget our rewards!" Hiinto called out after him.

Unable to resist, Rie's head drifted back to relax in the supple leather support. Snuggling her entire body deep into the cushions, she sighed in pleasure. The comforts in this home were far removed from her sparse quarters in the messenger barracks. Even her room at the estate was stiff and cold compared to the cushioned warmth of Garamaen's — Greg's — living room. Decorated in creamy ivory accented with soft blues and greens, every seat had an unobstructed view of the beach, ocean, or both.

When he returned, Lord Garamaen carried a red box with a white cross on the top and a bowl of loose change, buttons, and other assorted baubles.

"Pixies, you can have whatever you like out of this bowl, including the bowl itself, if you can carry it." He placed the bowl on the slate ledge surrounding the fireplace, then turned to Rie and opened the red box. He withdrew a pair of scissors and using the stump of his right hand to hold the fabric in place, positioned them in the hole created by the bullet. "I'm going to cut away your jeans, so I can see the wound. Alright?"

Rie nodded, her head getting woozier by the second. The pixies, meanwhile, were busy searching through Lord Garamaen's offering.

"My name is Hiinto, and I will take three silver coins and a pearl, plus this ribbon to tie them up in." He selected three dimes and a round white button, wrapping them carefully in the bright red satin ribbon and strapping the entire collection around his waist.

"You can call me Niinka. Rather than anything in the bowl, I would like a strand of your golden hair, if that would be acceptable?"

"That is a very personal request, Niinka," Lord Garamaen replied, his tone low and serious. He paused his ministrations to Rie's leg and held Niinka's gaze for a few seconds before continuing. "I will grant this request, but you will owe me one personal favor of my choosing, and to be completed at the time of my choosing."

"Done!" Niinka zipped to his head and plucked a single strand of hair, wrapping it around her wrist until it made a thick bracelet, which she tied into a knot. "It's so beautiful," she whispered, stroking her new jewelry.

Hiinto hissed and clicked, clearly yelling at Niinka in their native Pixl. She turned her back, ignoring his protests while admiring the bracelet.

"The bullet went all the way through, which is good. It means I don't have to dig around in there. But now I have to clean it, and this could hurt a bit." Lord Garamaen used a pair of tweezers to dip a swab in alcohol, then began to wipe away the blood and dirt from the perimeter of the bullet hole. Rie gasped when the swab pulled across the wound, the stinging pain making her jump and squirm.

"You don't have a healer, by any chance, do you?" she asked, eyes tearing.

"If you mean a magical healer, I can close the wound and repair some of the damage, but first I have to get it clean. Just hold on for a few more minutes. Then I'll take you up to your room where you and the pixies can take a bath and rest."

Rie clenched her hands on the cushioned armrests and glanced wildly about the room, looking for something, anything, to take her mind off the pain. A large painted portrait of a dark-haired woman sat in place of honor on the wall behind the couch. She was beautiful and exotic looking, with almond shaped brown eyes and flawless golden skin. Her hair hung loose around her shoulders, with the exception of a single braid that carried a large white feather.

"Who is the woman in the painting?" Rie asked,

"She was my wife, long ago," Lord Garamaen replied.

"She was human?"

"Yes, we lived together with her tribe in what is now known as the Ohio Valley. She was a shaman of her people."

The warmth and passion in his voice overwhelmed Rie. Her heart ached for the woman she had never met. She couldn't help but meet his gaze as he paused his ministrations to examine her face.

"You look a bit like her, you know," Lord Garamaen said before returning to his task. "Your hair is almost the exact same color, but your eyes throw it off. The violet is rare in humans, and uncommon even in elves."

Rie didn't know how to respond, unused to compliments of any kind. The high elves had such perfect beauty, there was no way he could compare her favorably to his brethren. Yet he'd bonded with a human woman and chosen to live in the human world instead of amongst the glittering throng. His preferences must be a little warped, but she couldn't mention that.

Rie watched the pixies dart about the room. They were everywhere, examining objects, opening cupboards, and generally causing mischief.

"Get out of there, you pesky little beasts," a gravelly voice said from beneath the kitchen sink. The cabinet door was open a crack and four knobby fingers gripped the edge. "You're going to muck up my house."

"Hilgor, they are guests. They are free to move about the house and grounds, but if they try to take anything without my permission, you can go ahead and swat them. Until then, leave them be."

"Hey!" the pixies protested in unison.

"We know how to behave." Hiinto returned a silver toothpick to its place by the stove.

"We were just looking," Niinka added, a guilty expression crossing her face.

Rie smiled. There was no reforming a pixie.

"At least make them wash up. I'll have enough trouble cleaning that chair. I'd rather not have to clean the whole house." Hilgor's hand disappeared, then reemerged, waving an old stained rag in the air. Without protest, the pixies dashed to take the rag from his outstretched hand and scrub themselves clean.

"You have a nisse living here?"

"Hilgor came with me when I decided to live here on a permanent basis."

"Who else would take care of him?" Hilgor said from his hiding spot. "He has no woman, and little family left."

Rie had never heard of a nisse so dedicated to an individual. They were notoriously shy, and typically only cared for a particular house or property. That Hilgor chose to follow Lord Garamaen was a sign of his power and respectability, especially since he lived in the Human Realm.

"Why don't you tell me what happened on the beach?" Garamaen asked, changing the subject.

"Two men attacked me. I survived, they didn't."

"Come on, spill the details. Why were they after you?"

Rie clenched her teeth as Lord Garamaen tugged on something in her leg.

"I don't know. They were blood sidhe, but I wasn't just a breakfast target. They wanted me dead."

"And you know that because?"

Rie hesitated. Only her wardens and the pixies knew of her abilities. Curuthannor had encouraged her to keep her premonitions secret, to use them as a tactical advantage. He had tried to teach her to bring them on at will, but she had never been able to manage that kind of control. With almost seventy-five years of practice, she didn't think it was going to get any better. "I have a minor gift, a small premonition. It's the only thing that saved me from a thrown knife to the gut."

"You're also skilled with a blade, and quite fast."

"You were watching?"

Lord Garamaen nodded. "I know everything that goes on, on this beach."

"And you let them attack me?" Rie held her expression and kept her tone controlled, but not without effort. It was typical elven superiority, unwilling to help the so-called 'lesser' races.

"You handled yourself well." A flash of warmth in her leg drew Rie's attention downward. "All done," Lord Garamaen announced, removing his hand from the air above the wound. "Let's get you up to your room to rest."

"My room? While I appreciate your help, I need to get back to the Upper Realm before sunset." Without the magic of a faerie realm surrounding her at the fading of the sun, she would wither and die, gaining the physical age that had been suppressed for so long.

"Yeah, yeah. I know you're a changeling, but my estate holds a piece of faerie. You'll be fine."

The pixies giggled. "Of course, she'll be fine," Niinka said as Hiinto elbowed her in the ribs.

"I really must insist." Rie ignored the two-inch pests. "I need to get back to the messenger barracks and report in."

"In your condition? I don't think so. You need to rest that leg, and I believe I still outrank a messenger. It's not going to be a problem. Trust me." Lord Garamaen extended his hand.

CHAPTER TWO

Rie rested in the guest bed of Garamaen's estate, waiting for sunset to determine her fate. The mattress was so deep with feathers, she felt like she was floating in the warm water of the salt springs, but she couldn't enjoy it with the anxiety roiling in her stomach. She had lived in the Upper Realm for more than one hundred years, the magic of faerie keeping her young and whole. If Garamaen was wrong, if his home was too human, she would immediately progress to her physical age, probably dying in agony as her skin shriveled, teeth and hair fell out, and muscles atrophied. She clutched the golden twelve-hundred thread count duvet and shivered. It wouldn't be long now.

"You're going to be fine, you know. There's nothing to worry about. Nothing at all," Niinka said, hanging upside down from the delicate wrought iron chandelier above the fourposter bed.

It was true that the pixies seemed to know things that others didn't, but Rie's nerves wouldn't allow her to believe them, this time. "What do you mean, there's nothing to worry about? I could end up a mummy!" She pulled the blanket tighter around her shoulders.

"Not a chance. See, there goes the sun," Niinka said.

"There goes the sun, do do do do," Hiinto sang from his perch on one of the intricately carved whorls of celtic knots that capped the bedposts. "There goes the sun, and I say, it's all right, ba dum dum dum dum dum."

"What's that from?" Rie squinted to distract herself from the imminent pain and misery.

"Wow, really? You need to brush up on your human culture if you don't know that song. It's by a band called the Beatles."

"I must have skipped that decade."

"You can open your eyes now," Niinka said.

Rie slowly opened her left eye and gasped. She had never seen a more beautiful sunset. The purple sky was dotted with soft pink-tinged clouds, slowly blending into the orange and yellow horizon, a rainbow of color that covered the entire skyline. The ocean waves gently crested onto the beach, glistening in the reflected colors of the sky. Palm trees rose high above the cliffs in the distance, absorbing the last dying rays of the sun like pilgrims with arms raised in supplication to their god.

Rie watched and waited. Nothing happened. Her body remained whole, unmarred by the change in the world around her. She laughed, throwing back the covers and jumping out of bed, forgetting for a moment the residual pain in her leg. She wiggled her toes in the thick fur rug, thrilling in the sensation of the soft strands against her still-young skin. She held out her hands, admiring the strength in her arms. "I'm still alive, I'm still me!" she shouted.

"I told you so!" Niinka said.

"Knock-knock," Garamaen said from the doorway. "How's it going?"

"Knock-knock, knock-knock," the pixies echoed, laughing and bouncing around the room.

Rie laughed, unable to contain her jubilation. "I

survived sunset. I can't ask for anything more right now."
Rie bowed, her formal training rising to the surface. She
was still angry that he had forced her to stay, despite her
changeling nature, but she couldn't afford to offend him
if she wanted to remain a messenger. As a changeling,
the alternative was serving the court as a cleaning woman
or entertainer, neither of which appealed.

Lord Garamaen — she really would have to remember
to call him Greg, even mentally — entered the room and
sprawled into the blue and gold striped cushioned chair
near the glass wall overlooking the beach.

"You look much better. How's your leg holding up?"

"I feel much better. Some pain, but I can support my
weight. You are a better healer than you let on."

"Not really," Greg shrugged. "And the clothes are okay?
How was your lunch?"

"Lunch was wonderful. I ate far more than I should
have. And the clothes are comfortable, if a bit big." Rie
pulled on the hem of the oversized red shirt Hilgor had
insisted she wear to replace her own bloody tunic. It
covered her knives, but made it nearly impossible to
reach them quickly.

Greg grinned. "No need to frown. Or worry about
accessing your weapons. You're safe here."

It was like he could read her mind. His grin widened,
stretching across his entire face. Could he read her mind?

"No, I can't read your mind, just your body language,"
he chuckled. "Now, I have some news for you, if you're
interested." He crossed his right ankle over his left knee,
stretching his arms across the back of the wide chair.
"About your assassins."

Rie sat back down on the bed, placing her hands
carefully in her lap and schooling her face to its most
neutral expression. She must be slipping if he could read
her that easily. The pixies' constant squeaks and clicks

went silent.

"I went down to the beach to clean up the mess of the fight and ensure that the humans didn't see anything."

"I apologize for the disruption."

"Not to worry, it's not the first battle I've seen or contained. In nearly six thousand years, I've dealt with my fair share of bloodshed. But do you want to know what I found?"

Rie felt her eyes widen. Lord Garamaen was powerful, but she hadn't realized how old he was. He might be the oldest fae she'd ever met. It was no wonder he had barely reacted to the fight on the beach. To him, it must seem like a common problem. She mentally shook herself, bringing her thoughts back around to his question.

"I am curious why I was attacked," Rie said, carefully.

"That, I can't answer," Greg said, "but I do know where the attackers were from."

"Oh?"

Greg raised an eyebrow, but maintained his casual pose. "You already know that the attackers were blood sidhe, therefore from the Shadow Realm."

Rie froze. Of course the blood sidhe were from the Shadow Realm. It was their home world. But she hadn't considered the implications. The Shadow Realm was off-limits to anyone from the upperworlds, and vice versa, as decreed by the treaty of the Great War. She had never had any kind of contact with anyone from the underworlds, but if anyone thought she had, her life would be forfeit. King Othin's hate was so profound, he would have her executed on the spot just for being on the same beach with them.

"The throwing knives used in the attack were made by a master smith in Nalakadr, capital city and home of the Shadow King, Aradae." Greg tossed the blade on the bed next to Rie. She lifted it from the covers and held it up in the light of the chandelier. About eight inches long, the knife was black powder coated to prevent reflection, except for three engraved slashes on the balance point of the blade.

"That's the maker's mark. He's a gremlin, known for making custom swords and knives unique to each client's fighting style. He doesn't usually make throwing knives, but when he does, it's for a very high price. The assassin must have been good to afford his fee. Do you have any idea why someone from the Shadow Realm would want you dead?"

"Not at all. I've never crossed paths with anyone from either of the underworlds," Rie stated, allowing no emotion to show on her face or find its way into her voice, not that it mattered. King Othin had written the law. Anyone in contact with the Shadow Realm, in any way, would be executed. A noble might be pardoned, or face a diminished sentence, but as a changeling, the best Rie could hope for was a swift beheading. But she wouldn't let her dread get the best of her.

"You can drop the act, Nuriel. I'm not out to get you, and you can relax here. Think of this as your home away from home."

"I'm not sure what you mean."

"You don't need to hide what you're thinking or feeling from me. I don't align myself with either side of that idiotic argument. I'm a neutral party. Take a deep breath, relax, and let's think this thing through together."

Rie released a ragged breath. "I have no idea why I was targeted. I'm loyal to King Othin and the High Court of the Upper Realm. As far as I know, I have never even met anyone from the underworlds."

Greg tapped his fingertips on the armrest of his chair. "You're a human messenger, sent with a message for me, a self-exiled sidhe lord who prefers to spend time with lowly humans to his own kind."

"So you think someone wanted me dead because of you? I don't understand."

"Your death had nothing to do with you, not really. Your death was the real message someone was sending me, someone who wanted me to get involved in politics. I crafted the treaty and insisted on the clause that made the Human Realm neutral territory. I like humans, I think they're fun, with their short, emotion-driven lives. Someone knows I would take your death seriously."

"I still don't understand."

"The attempt on your life had two possible outcomes. One: the assassination is successful and the Shadow Court is implicated in the death of a High Court messenger, violating the truce and bringing me back to court. Two: you survive, but it doesn't matter because of King Othin's stupid rule that any contact equals execution. He's been looking for an excuse to eliminate the Shadow Realm completely, so can easily be led to believe there's a larger plot in the works. The end result is the same. You're dead and the realms get ready for war."

"I'd rather not die."

Greg chuckled, lips quirking in a wry smile. "Glad to hear it."

"So you'll tell King Othin I had no connection to the assassins, and convince him there's no threat. Since I survived, how would anyone even know?"

"If you show up in the messenger barracks wounded and wearing ill-fitting clothing, or worse, your own tattered outfit, there will be questions. The truth will come out, your reputation and that of your adoptive parents — your wardens — will be ruined, and you will most likely be executed for breaking Othin's ridiculous law."

Rie's thoughts whirled as she struggled to comprehend

Greg's logic. Having never been involved in anything close to politics, she was beyond confused.

Greg leaned forward, resting his elbows on his knees. "I need to find out who hired the assassins. But I can't investigate, or I'll draw attention to the situation, potentially escalating the threat."

"What are you saying?"

"So far, no one knows what happened but me and your friends, the pixies. I want you to investigate for me. Find out who hired the hit men. You can go places I can't right now."

"I'm already in enough trouble. I don't want to make things worse. Plus, I've never been to the Shadow Realm. I have no experience with any of this. I can't go off on some hare-brained scheme. I should just report back to the messenger barracks and explain what happened."

"And be executed for something that's clearly not your fault?"

"I'll explain..."

"Right, because Othin is known for his patience and tolerance."

He wasn't. King Othin was known to torture and execute servants for no better reason than that they had spilled his wine and he was bored. But she was an oath-bound citizen of the Upper Realm. Fleeing punishment would be held against her as proof of treason.

"That sounds great, and all, but I swore an oath as a messenger to King Othin, that I would perform my duties and abide by the laws of the High Court. If I go to the Shadow Realm, I will be an oathbreaker. I can't do that."

"You wouldn't be breaking your oath if you were performing a service in loyalty to the High Court. In fact, you'd be protecting Othin from his own short fuse. But you don't have to decide anything now." Lord Garamaen rose from his chair, heading for the door. "Tomorrow I'll open the portal directly to Curuthannor's hall. The portal Watchers won't be able to track you, and no one will know what has happened for at least a day. Talk it over with your adoptive parents, and think through your options. One word of caution; avoid the High Court and messenger barracks until you've made a decision, or it will probably be made for you."

***

Curuthannor opened the door to a cloaked servant, dripping wet from the deluge outside. He was short and squat, but the cloak hid the fae completely. The servant kept his face hidden, but a four-fingered hand emerged from the dark gray fabric, holding out a medallion with the image of a sword backed by the sun.

"Please come in," Curuthannor said, holding the door open wide to allow the servant into the entry and out of the rain. "May I take your cloak?"

"No, I stay but a moment. The patron sends his regards, and praises your work with Nuriel. He is pleased with her knife skills, and is happy to see her developing foresight. He sends me to deliver a gift for her," the gravelly voice replied.

"Nuriel isn't here. She maintains quarters at the messenger barracks at the High Court."

"Yes. She ran into some trouble. The patron will send her here tomorrow. The patron asks that you give this to her at some point during her visit, and imply that the gift is from you."

The servant held out an oilskin wrapped box tied with waxed twine. Curuthannor accepted the parcel, handling it with care. Any gift from the patron would be powerful and precious.

"What is the gift?"

"I was told they are matching blades. You may look at them."

Curuthannor pulled apart the twine and removed the oilskin wrapping to reveal an intricate red and black enameled box. The top of the box was inlaid with the patron's sigil of a sword backed by the sun in white. He unhooked the silver clasp on the front and slowly lifted the lid to reveal the gifted blades.

The blades were unlike anything Curuthannor had seen in his fifteen hundred years. Eight inches of razor-sharp curved solid steel with a bulbous tip, the enchanted khukuri blades were deadly beautiful, designed to strengthen and protect their handler. Identical red jasper grips were inlaid with a long stripe of white aventurine; elements of fire and air to promote mental fortitude, heal, and improve perception. The center of the grip was studded with a deep black jet palm ring, set with sparkling red garnets; earth and fire to aid on a journey and repel negative energies while increasing physical strength and magic. The copper bolsters at front and rear were perfectly balanced and engraved with four sacred runes: Ansuz for insight and communication, Perthro for seeing the future and knowing one's path, Tiwaz for honor, justice, and leadership, and Uruz for physical strength and speed.

"These are beautiful, and priceless," Curuthannor said, glancing down at the servant.

"They have been custom designed for Nuriel, measured, weighted and balanced for her hand. The runes were cast by a tenth-level rune-master, and the blades have been blessed by an elemental from each realm. It took ten years to craft them to the patron's standards. They will serve her well and awaken many of her skills."

"Please reassure the patron that I will follow his instructions to the letter. Nuriel will not know about him until he chooses to reveal himself. However, I would also like to suggest that she may be ready to accept her heritage. She is coming into her powers and will soon be unable to ignore them."

"I will pass along your message."

Without another word, the servant turned and left, disappearing into the shadows. Curuthannor carefully returned the blades to their case and re-wrapped the box. He stood for several minutes, listening to the rain pound on the roof of the vestibule. The weave of Nuriel's destiny grew tighter.

***

Rie entered her wardens' home as surreptitiously as possible, treading barefoot on the marble floors to avoid detection. The pixies had gone on ahead to meet up with the rest of the swarm and show off their new treasures, rubbing it in to the others who had chosen to stay. Unfortunately, even without the pixies, Rie was too loud to sneak past Curuthannor. He met her at the end of the long arched hallway that led from the dining room to her personal quarters.

"Nuriel," Curuthannor said, using her full name. Nuriel meant servant-daughter in the low-tongue, and was a sign of her status as a changeling. She preferred 'Rie', but Curuthannor had never called her by her chosen nickname.

"Curuthannor," Rie replied. She made a deep curtsy, her loose black hair brushing the floor as she bent toward the ground. She would remain in that position until Curuthannor gave her leave to stand. Throughout her life, Curuthannor had insisted upon adhering to the strictest court etiquette.

"You may stand," he said, emotionless, no hint of his thoughts or intentions. Rie couldn't even tell whether he was surprised to find her home. She did as instructed and moved into a relaxed warrior's stance, feet hip-width apart and arms held loose by her side. Curuthannor's storm gray eyes traveled the length of her body and back, assessing her condition. Rie locked her gaze straight forward, staring at the center button of the brown leather vest that covered his torso from neck to waist.

Standing over seven and a half feet, Curuthannor was tall, even for a high elf. When she had still been little, the corded muscles that wrapped his wiry frame had seemed protective, but as her private trainer, they were intimidating.

"You wear ill-fitting Human Realm clothing, unsuitable for a confrontation," he said.

Rie felt the sting in his words. Curuthannor insisted on being ready for attack at all times. He preferred combat-ready clothing over the more fashionable court robes that most nobles wore, and insisted that Rie find ways to incorporate weapons and defensive garments into her uniform. Even at home, Curuthannor carried twelve-inch tactical knives on each thigh and likely had others stashed elsewhere on his person.

"Apologies," Rie replied, keeping her chin up. "I did not have an opportunity to return to my quarters at the messenger barracks to change into more suitable attire after my recent delivery. I had hoped to change here before meeting with you."

"I see. Are you injured?" Curuthannor's tone remained bland and unreadable, but Rie sensed a surprising depth of emotion beneath the words.

"I sustained a gunshot wound to the leg. Lord Garamaen healed the majority of the damage. I remain sore, but otherwise functional."

"And the attackers?"

"Dead."

"Good." Curuthannor's mouth twitched, nearly rising into a smile. For one brief moment, Rie thought she saw pride in his eyes, but it vanished before she could be sure. "Lhéwen will be pleased to see you," he said.

"And I her. It has been too long since my last visit."

"Dinner will begin shortly. You may join us, and afterward, you and I will talk in more detail."

"Yes, sir." Rie exhaled a sigh of relief as Curuthannor passed her in the hall and strolled away.

CHAPTER THREE

Rie stood behind her chair in the family dining room, waiting for her wardens. Her eyes traced the family sigil inlaid in the tabletop. After decades of meals taken in this room, she knew each curve of the clematis vine that wrapped the ebony shield, and could tell you exactly how many flowers bloomed in the wood.

Lhéwen arrived after a few minutes, arms spread to embrace Rie, a broad smile on her face.

"Rie, my dear, I am so happy you've come to dinner. I desperately need a break from the gown I've been creating for Lady Demeth," she gave Rie a kiss on each cheek, a harried expression creasing her unlined forehead. "Her daughter is taking a lifemate next month, you know. It will be a huge event, with all of the high nobles in attendance to honor her family, so you'd think she would finally be happy. But no, she's cried at every fitting, at least once, and I have to sit there the entire time, holding a towel under her chin to catch the tears and protect the gown from saltwater. She is lucky that her beauty outweighs her crying spells."

"I can only imagine how tired you must be," Rie replied, returning Lhéwen's embrace. Lhéwen was a brilliant and much sought after seamstress. As a result, she often had to deal with the eccentricities and whims of the nobles of the High Court. She was always patient when working with them, but the family often had the dubious pleasure of hearing about the episodes over dinner.

"Yes, well, it's nothing, really." Lhéwen brushed the fine tendrils of hair out of her face, tucking them into the twisted braid that flowed down her back. Her gown was functional, but fashionable, with tight sleeves and a fitted waist in a shimmering golden hue that almost precisely matched her hair. She tugged on the sleeves, pulling them back into place after a day in the workshop.

Curuthannor arrived, giving his lifemate an affectionate kiss on the cheek. His hand brushed across her shoulders, an embrace that wasn't. He nodded to Rie, then moved to sit at the head of the table, Lhéwen following suit. Rie waited until both were settled before seating herself.

"Business is good, then?" Rie arranged the creased white napkin in her lap, protecting the pale violet silk of one of her best gowns. Her thumb twitched, nerves jangling while she waited for an appropriate moment to discuss her predicament. Maybe it would all just go away if she procrastinated long enough.

Wishful thinking never got anyone anywhere.

"Yes, quite. Practically the entire High Court is invited to Lady Demeth's daughter's wedding, so I have more work than I can handle. I may have to find another assistant to help."

Rie's response was interrupted by the presentation of the first course.

"Good to see you, good to see you," the house nisse, Grmelda, said to Rie as she ladled out the thin creamy soup that was one of Rie's favorites. "You are not looking well. You eat up today, yes?" Grmelda had been an active part of Rie's life for as long as she could remember. At less than three feet tall, Grmelda barely reached above the table, yet never spilled a drop or crumb.

"Grmelda's right." Lhéwen sounded shocked, and she probably was. She was not the most observant individual when she was involved with a new design, and she might have completely ignored Rie's condition if Grmelda hadn't pointed it out. "Your face is scratched. Did something happen?"

The last thing Rie wanted to do was worry Lhéwen, but it couldn't be helped. Curuthannor needed all of the information to help her sort out a plan, and Lhéwen wouldn't want to be excluded from the discussion. She would have to tone it down, lay out the facts without too much description. She took a deep breath, and organized her thoughts.

"Lhéwen, before I start, I want you to know that it's not as bad as it sounds, so please don't get upset." Rie faced Curuthannor, directing the rest of her speech to the warrior of the family. "I was given a job yesterday. It was supposed to be a simple message to Lord Garamaen in the Human Realm, but after passing through the portal, I had a premonition of an attack. Assassins were waiting to kill me on the path to Lord Garamaen's estate."

Lhéwen's spoon clattered to the table. Her hand covered her mouth while her pale blue eyes grew wide and frightened. Curuthannor remained stoic, but stopped eating, his hand curled in a fist on the table.

"I killed one of them without a problem, but the second managed a shot with a human pistol, a through and through wound to the thigh. I scrambled away, and with the pixies help, killed the second attacker. Lord Garamaen healed my leg and let me stay in his hall over night. I returned here this afternoon."

"You haven't visited the messenger barracks or made a

report to your supervisor." Curuthannor made it a statement, but it was really a question.

"No. Because of my injuries, I didn't report in on time. That, combined with the physical evidence of an incident, means there will be an inquiry, and the attackers were blood sidhe."

Lhéwen gasped, her hand trembling at her lips.

Rie kept her voice controlled and even. She held her chin level and made eye contact with Curuthannor. She could do this. Logic would dictate her next steps. "Lord Garamaen has asked me to travel to the Shadow Realm and investigate for him. In return, he will use the information I find to vouch for me to King Othin. I was going to speak with you about it after dinner, Curuthannor. I need your advice."

Lhéwen's voice could barely be heard, even in the silence of the room. "Lord Garamaen asks too much." Curuthannor kept his eyes trained on Rie, studying her. At his lack of response, Lhéwen's voice rose, firm and demanding. "Rie can not be expected to go to the Shadow Realm. For one, it is against the law, but it is also too dangerous. She has no contacts, no knowledge of the underworlds."

"Nuriel can handle herself, of that I am unconcerned. However, this is not a task to take on lightly."

Rie hid her pride behind her spoon.

"You face an impossible task. If you are caught, you will be called an oathbreaker and executed for treason. Why won't he vouch for you to the king?"

"He agrees that I am not to blame, and believes that I have no dealings with the underworlds, but he can't prove anything. Plus, he says that I can investigate without drawing attention to the situation, where he cannot."

A deep furrow crept between Curuthannor's eyebrows.

He took a bite of soup.

Lhéwen's face scrunched and her jaw clenched. "This is his job, his task!" Rie had never seen her so angry.

Curuthannor retained his composure. "True, Lord Garamaen's word should be enough to convince the king, but perhaps he fears Othin's prejudices will prevent him from taking honorable action. I suppose, if you can identify the real traitor and provide proof of his or her culpability, then Lord Garamaen will be able to ensure his ability to be heard." He took another spoonful.

"But if she goes to the Shadow Realm, there will be incontrovertible proof that she's violated the law. She cannot go," Lhéwen said.

Curuthannor nodded, but continued as if he hadn't been interrupted. "As far as I can see, you have two options. You can return to the messenger service and hope for leniency. Or, you can heed Lord Garamaen's request and travel to the Shadow Realm. The first case will most likely end in your death."

"The king surely wouldn't execute her for *surviving*, would he?"

Curuthannor turned to his lifemate, his expression cold and serious. "He might. I've heard rumors of unrest, certain factions wanting to reestablish economic relations with the Shadow Realm. Nothing concrete has been discovered, but King Othin is looking for a way to reinforce his edict. And there's precedent. Remember the executions in the palace square?"

Rie had never heard any of this. "What happened?"

"Shortly after the Great War, when the direct portals were closed, a few enterprising merchants decided to run a black market in Shadow Realm goods. King Othin had them publicly beheaded, and their bodies burned. That's also when he established the Watchers to monitor traffic through the portals. He takes the law seriously."

Lhéwen's face turned gray, her skin losing its usual luster while her bottom lip trembled. "But she's a messenger. That must count for something."

Curuthannor reached out, squeezing her hand on top of the table. "Rie's worked hard to gain some level of respect, but you and I both know that outside of these halls she is barely more than a servant. King Othin will want to make an example of her, instill a little fear in the hearts of the lesser fae and even the nobles, especially those who might consider the law antiquated and unnecessary."

They twined their fingers together before Curuthannor returned his attention to Rie. "I can try to use my influence to convince him to spare your life, but I'm afraid it won't be enough," he said.

"Then let her hide here. She used Lord Garamaen's signature to get here, so they don't know she's returned to the Upper Realm. They might assume she's dead."

Rie shook her head, her brain throbbing a slow beat within her skull. "They'll come looking for me. They've probably been called to investigate already, or will be soon. And if they find me, you will be branded accomplices. Your reputation and your business would be ruined. I can't let you take that risk."

Curuthannor flashed her a sad smile and continued with his analysis.

"You have a better chance of survival with Lord Garamaen. You would be working with a powerful man, helping him calm political tension and avoid war by finding the real traitor. He will be able to get you in and out of the Shadow Realm without detection, so there's a chance you could stay hidden there, even if you don't find the answers you need. But if you choose that path, you must understand that you may never be able to return to the Upper Realm."

Curuthannor held Rie's gaze for several seconds, waiting, watching. The throbbing intensified, a premonition bursting to life.

***

The High Court throne room, light glinting off a double-headed axe on the upswing. Dozens of warriors charging, faces grim and determined. Twelve statues arranged in a circle, the smell of rosemary thick in the air. An imp, tears in its eyes, wrapped in a towel. A hand on her back, comforting and familiar...no...family. A man with mocha skin, golden eyes, laughing. Fire blazing up a sword. A platinum ring with a sparkling blue stone.

***

Rie shook her head, clearing away the last vestiges of the vision. It was an incoherent mess, dark and chaotic.

Lhéwen scanned Rie's face. Her forehead creased, furrows forming between her brows. "What did you see?"

"I don't know. It was a jumble, confusing." The images were barely discernible flashes, not the single scenes she was used to, and she couldn't tell whether it would happen in the near or distant future. "I don't know what to do. I swore an oath to abide the laws of the Upper Realm and faithfully serve the High Court messengers. I have done both to the best of my ability, and yet I find myself in an indefensible position. I didn't report back to headquarters on time. By now, the messengers know something happened. It won't take long for the story to reach Rolimdornoron's ears, and he won't hesitate to forward it on to the King's Counsel. This will be the first place they look to find me."

Lhéwen's voice rang with determination. "Lord Garamaen should be your shield, your protector in this. He should not leave you to fend for yourself."

Rie sighed. "He isn't letting me fend for myself. He has

given me an option. It's just not an easy option to take."

"So you have made up your mind, then?" Curuthannor asked.

Rie paused, taking a deep breath and holding it for a few heartbeats before answering, resigned. "Yes. I must follow Lord Garamaen, give him what he wants in order to save myself. I will go to the Shadow Realm."

Lhéwen pressed her eyes closed and hung her head, but Curuthannor nodded, his expression unsurprised. "If you are going to go forward with this, you will need to be prepared. Please excuse us, Lhéwen. Nuriel, come with me."

Rie rose from her chair and followed Curuthannor. She wouldn't have been able to finish Grmelda's wonderful meal anyway, not with the nervous knots tying up her stomach. She buried her thoughts before entering Curuthannor's office.

The hexagonal room had been one of Rie's favorite places to study during her childhood in the estate. It was spacious, but not overly large, with comfortable chairs for reading the books that lined the walls. Curuthannor stopped in front of one of four large windows and gazed out at the manicured rose garden in full bloom behind a decorative willow branch fence. A gnome trundled by with a wheelbarrow full of weeds, finishing his day's work.

"So far, your experience has been limited to the Upper Realm and the Human Realm, correct?" Curuthannor began.

"I was granted one mission to the Winter Court, as well," Rie replied.

Curuthannor nodded, his face impassive. He rarely spoke more than a few precise words to Rie, but it appeared that this conference might be an exception. He seemed to be thinking, perhaps gathering his thoughts.

Rie waited patiently. Whatever he had to say, whatever advice he had to give, would be valuable beyond measure.

"The underworlds are similar, yet also very different from any of your experience thus far," Curuthannor began, finally breaking the silence. "The dark elves and blood sidhe in the Shadow Realm are powerful, but no more so than the greater fae of the upperworlds. Nor are they any more dangerous, at least not from the perspective of their abilities. Just like each of the upperworld races, they have their strengths and weaknesses. Some individuals are extremely powerful, but most have unremarkable abilities. However, the underworlds are more openly violent and vicious. You must always be on guard, watch for attack out of any corner, and be wary of offending anyone in any way."

Curuthannor faced Rie, his hands clasped behind his back, feet wide, legs balanced. He pinned her with a stare.

"Though you've been in faerie since you were a baby, you are still of the human race. Blood sidhe require human blood for sustenance. There are laws in the Shadow Realm about taking blood from unwilling donors, but you are outworld and it is unlikely that anyone would come to your aid. You are well trained, but you are still at a disadvantage against even a weak blood sidhe. They will enthrall you and use glamour to make you see anything they wish. Be cautious, therefore, and do not put yourself in a situation where you might be at risk."

"Yes, sir," Rie answered, with a slight nod.

Curuthannor was even more intense than usual, if that were possible. Then again, he had fought the Shadow Realm at King Othin's side and would have made a detailed study of his enemy.

"The dark elves are masters of soul magic. They won't be drawn to you the way the blood sidhe are, but they are still dangerous. Do not offend them. The powerful ones can strip you of your soul, or control the screaming banshees that will deafen and drive a warrior insane."

Curuthannor rolled forward on the balls of his feet, as if preparing for a fight. Rie carefully eyed him, waiting for the tiniest detail that would predict his intent. "Before the Great War, I frequently traveled to the Shadow Realm on business for my father. He preferred the iron ore found in the black hills for his steel blades."

"Your father was a bladesmith?" Rie asked. Curuthannor had rarely spoken of his parents, who died in the war.

"The best in the Upper Realm. He was a great swordsman as well, and taught me all that I know."

"Did he die fighting?"

"No. He died in his smithy, when it was overrun by red caps from the Shadow Realm." With a severe glance, Curuthannor put an end to that line of questioning.

Reaching into one of four narrow drawers in his mahogany desk, he continued, "As I was saying, I used to travel to the Shadow Realm quite frequently to purchase the iron ore, and I would stay at the same inn each time. I became friends with the proprietor, Tharbatiron. If he still runs the inn — and unless he is dead, I can't imagine he would do anything else — he will help you. Just give him this." Curuthannor removed a silver medallion from a drawer and handed it to Rie. It was stamped with Curuthannor's shield on one side, and a celtic cross on the other. "It's the Crossroads Inn, at the center of the capital city, Nalakadr, near the outdoor market. The Nalakadr public portal opens outside the city walls, or it used to, but all major roads lead to the center of the city, so it shouldn't be too difficult to find."

Curuthannor strode to his personal bookshelf, a locked cabinet to the left of the windows. The cabinet held Curuthannor's most valuable and powerful possessions. He had never opened it in front of Rie, let alone allowed her to look inside.

"I have one other gift for you, which will aid you on your path," Curuthannor said, pressing his right thumb to the door and unlocking the cabinet with a whispered word. He removed a black and red enameled box, then closed and locked the cabinet before returning to Rie. Holding the box with both hands, he cautiously held it out, as if the contents might burst into flame. Rie handled the box with equal care.

"What is it?" she asked.

"Open it."

Rie set the box on the desk, pulled apart the clasp and carefully opened the lid, turning her head slightly in case something dangerous or explosive lay inside. It wouldn't be the first time that Curuthannor had tested her abilities without notice. She was astonished at the priceless gift before her. Two matching red handled khukuri blades were cushioned in black velvet inside the box, their dragon scale sheaths nestled beneath. Rie's court mask fell and her mouth hung open in shock. She'd never seen blades half as precious or deadly, and she had certainly never been allowed to touch anything so valuable.

"May I hold them?" she asked, hesitantly.

"They are yours. You may do with them as you wish," Curuthannor replied.

Rie drew her fingers along the flat of each blade, feeling the cold steel warm to her touch. They began to vibrate and hum, as if excited, until she wrapped her fingers around the grip, when they burst forth with a single clear note and went silent. She removed the blades, testing their weight and balance. She spun them in a circle, feeling their movement. They were like extensions of her body.

"These are incredible, Curuthannor. You honor me. Thank you for this priceless gift." The heartfelt words tumbled from her mouth. If ever there was a sign of Curuthannor's love, this was it.

"You know better than to thank the fae," Curuthannor admonished, not meeting her gaze.

"I am in your debt, regardless," Rie replied. "It matters little whether I thank you or not. But these blades are the most beautiful things I've ever seen."

"I am glad you value them. They were the work of many years, and your skills are deserving of better blades than you currently carry. They will serve you well."

Rie set the knives back in their case, wistfully running her finger across the metal before shutting the lid. She couldn't wait to practice with them, to feel their power as she moved through the forms.

"May I come in?" Lhéwen called from the doorway.

"Of course," Curuthannor replied, his severe face softening as his lifemate entered the room. The love they shared was a palpable thing, almost painful to watch. Rie quickly looked away.

Lhéwen set large a bundle of fabric on the desk, her expression composed of uncompromising lines.

"If you have to go, you'll go prepared." She shook out a soft gray gown with a subtle shimmer that made it come alive in the waning daylight. "I've been working on this for awhile, intending to give it to you at your nameday next month, but I think it is better served now. It's made of spider silk, strong but elegant and light as air. It will keep you warm on cool nights, and cool on hot days. I've cut the skirt high on each thigh so you can wear your blades hidden beneath but still have quick access when necessary."

Rie held the dress in front of her, watching the light catch the fabric. The collar and cap-sleeved bodice were edged with delicate hand-embroidered clematis vines, the heart of each purple flower sparkling with a single crystal. Matching fabric covered buttons fastened the top across the chest and down the right side, from the point of the deep v-neck down to the waist. Rie was speechless, in awe of the sheer number of hours that must have been put into the dress.

"The color isn't ideal for the High Court, but with your warm skin tone and dark hair...well, I thought it would be lovely on you regardless. I think it will be perfect for the Shadow Realm. And the flowers will bring out your eyes, especially if you wear just a touch of kohl."

"It's beautiful." They both knew Rie was too practical to bother with the makeup. It didn't matter what she wore or how hard she tried, she would never be able to draw any complementary attention to herself from the high elves of the Upper Realm. Lhéwen's advice was well-intentioned, but futile.

"The Shadow Realm will be reasonably warm, but you want to hide your identity as much as possible," Lhéwen continued, shaking her head. "You'll need this." She held up a cropped jacket with a hood made out of a thicker version of the same gray silk.

"And Curuthannor helped me with this piece," Lhéwen set aside the jacket and picked up a black leather corset. Rie gingerly draped the dress over the desk before examining the mildly embarrassing undergarment. "It's lightly reinforced and will provide support and some protection." The leather was thick, but had been worked into a flexible form that would — as Lhéwen would say — 'hold her up and tuck her in'. It laced up the side instead of the back, allowing Rie to easily dress herself, and since it had no boning, she would still be able to bend and move.

"Minimum protection from glancing blows only," Curuthannor added.

Lhéwen's eyes twinkled, silently laughing at her lifemate. "Unfortunately, hardened leather is both uncomfortable and unflattering; inappropriate for underwear."

Curuthannor crossed his arms, but there was a subtle smile flickering around the edges of his mouth.

Rie had no idea what to say, no words came to mind.

"I..." she began. "This is more than I could ever ask for. More than I need."

"Well, then, you'd better try everything on. I want time to make adjustments before you go. And then you should pack. I'll ask Grmelda to put together some travel cakes."

"I'm sure it will all fit perfectly."

"Don't even think about running off in the middle of the night without saying goodbye, either."

"She will leave before first light," Curuthannor interrupted. "She needs to remain unseen for as long as possible."

Lhéwen sighed. "All the same, I will see you off." She rushed out of the room, quickly brushing her right hand across her cheek.

"She will miss you." Curuthannor stood stoic, arms still crossed over his chest. "Be careful."

CHAPTER FOUR

The sun was setting when Rie entered the city of Nalakadr, the sky lit with an entire spectrum of blues and purples. The moon rose high and full overhead, sending deep shadows dancing in the corners and alleyways. As darkness took hold, lights began to appear beneath archways and bridges, giving the entire cityscape a warm glow that softly moved from light to shadow and back again.

Curuthannor and Lhéwen had seen her off before daybreak, as promised, riding with her to the center of Etsiramun. Following Lord Garamaen's instructions, she used his personal code to evade the Watchers that monitored public portal travel. She traveled light and fast, carrying only the bare minimum essentials, including a good-sized bag of gold coins that Lhéwen had pressed into her hands at the last second. The women clung to each other as they said goodbye, knowing that it might be their last meeting in this life. Curuthannor kept it simple with a warrior's handshake and a nod, before turning back to the horses.

The Shadow Realm, so named because the longest day lasted only 6 hours, was warm and humid, thanks to the lava that flowed beneath the streets. Here and there, steam vents blew the smell of sweetened ash in clouds above the skyline. As soon as she felt confident no one noted her presence and followed her into the city, Rie took off the jacket with its heavy hood. Sweat still ran in rivulets down her spine.

Unlike the ostentatious High Court, with its heavy white marble pillars and gold plated halls, the Shadow Realm capital of Nalakadr was crafted in sinuous wood and delicate carved stone. The buildings were multi-storied, but graceful, flowing from one form to another and highlighting the natural structure, rather than forcing form and order on the materials. Archways rose high and twisted, bending up as if searching for the light. The streets were paved with smooth worn stone and crowded with fae of all races. Even the dwarves, blind and allergic to the sun, made their presence known as they hawked their wares.

People bustled about their business, all seeming to know precisely where they should be and what they should be doing. As the light diminished, Rie expected the streets to clear. If anything, they became more crowded.

A troll the size of a human bus lumbered into Rie, sending her careening into a stand filled with some kind of purple hard-skinned fruit that smelled like rotting fish.

"Watch it." The stand owner, a portly goblin with four eyes and four arms, glared as Rie picked herself up and returned the fallen merchandise. "Damaged goods are your responsibility."

Rie averted her gaze and bowed slightly, apologizing as she backed away, stepping on the foot of a green-skinned gremlin in the process.

"What do you think you're doing, girl?" the gremlin growled.

Rie bowed, plastering a conciliatory smile on her face.

"I'm looking for the Crossroads Inn. Can you point me in the right direction?"

"Damn tourists," the gremlin grunted. "See that spire?" She pointed to a narrow tower barely visible above the surrounding buildings. "Head that direction and you'll find it." Without another word or a backward glance, the gremlin continued on her way.

Following the gremlin's advice, Rie tried to keep the spire in sight, but she kept losing it behind buildings. Curuthannor said that all roads lead to the center of the city, but the one she walked was forked and turned several times. She wished she'd thought to ask for a map.

"You should go left this time," Niinka said. "Last time you went right, so it's time to go left."

All five of Rie's primary pixie cohorts had decided to travel with her to the Shadow Realm. None could resist the temptation of new treasures from a restricted world. Plus, who knew what kind of mischief might be made? Niinka and Hiinto took places of honor hidden in Rie's hair behind each of her ears, while Possn and Gikl found space in her pack. Tiik preferred to ride on her sleeve and had tied himself a seat with a ribbon around her arm.

"Aren't you supposed to stick with the same direction each time?" Tiik swung his foot back and forth, rocking himself in his swing. "That's what they say about mazes."

"True! That's true!" Hiinto chimed in. "Maybe that's why you're lost. We should go back to the beginning and try again."

"We don't know where the beginning is," hissed Niinka.

"We can just retrace our steps," Tiik offered.

"Shh, all of you," Rie said. It was nice to have friends with her, and she was honored that they had chosen to come, considering it might be a permanent exile, but sometimes she wished they would just stay hidden and quiet. "I need to think. Going back is out of the question. We have to be closer to the center than the edge." Rie looked around. No one looked friendly enough to ask for directions, and everyone seemed to be in a hurry.

"There." Rie pointed to an elegantly carved wooden sign with a red goblet hanging above an open door. "That must be a tavern of some kind. I can ask the bartender."

Rie hurried across the street and into the bar before the pixies could protest.

As soon as she entered, Rie came to a halt. The bar was not what she had expected. Decorated in shades of black, white and red, the dim space was filled with couches and cushioned chairs, even a few beds could be seen in the dark recesses of the room. A faint coppery odor hung in the air. The bar itself lined the right side of the room, but no bottles could be seen anywhere. Instead, a sidhe woman dressed in a tight black bodysuit ushered men and women — *human* men and women — to the few seated customers. A woman groaned in sensual pleasure while a sidhe man sucked on her wrist.

It was a blood bar. Rie needed to leave, and fast.

She turned to go, but bumped into the broad chest of a man standing behind her. "Now, now, now," the man said. "Where are you rushing off to tonight? The evening's just getting started." His voice was smooth and seductive, sinking barbed tendrils of compulsion into Rie's heart and mind. He wore a simple pale blue vest over an ivory collared shirt with the sleeves neatly rolled up above his elbow. The undone buttons at his throat revealed a soft golden tan. Her gaze drifted upward to meet his, several inches above her own. His eyes were warm and dark, pulling her in under heavy lashes, his hair the color of burnt cinnamon. His ears were slightly pointed, and the teeth that glistened between parted lips showed pointed canines.

"I am on an errand," she said, dragging her mind back from the brink of giving him anything and everything. His gaze called to her, daring her to say yes to anything he asked, but she shook off the impulse. "I must be going."

He placed a hand on her shoulder, attempting to turn her body back toward the bar. "It's just one little drink," he urged. Every word twisted the compulsion tighter, willing her to relent. The pixies tittered and chirped, but their warnings were barely heard.

"I suppose one drink," Rie began, but caught herself after a step. She closed her eyes, momentarily cutting off the pull. "No, I have to go. Sorry."

The man's eyebrows lifted a fraction, surprise evident in his wide eyes, but his voice remained soothing and melodic.

"Come on, sit with me for awhile." His hand slid down her arm, his fingertips raising goosebumps. He took her hand and drew her forward, leading Rie into the dark room like a horse trainer with a skittish yearling. A stray lock of hair fell forward into his eyes. Rie yearned to brush it away. Her hand rose a few inches to follow the thought before she caught herself, pulling back.

"I..." Rie forgot what she was going to say. She licked her lips, glancing at his mouth and away. The man was being so kind, she really should sit with him for a few minutes. She could get to know him a little. It couldn't hurt, right?

Something bit her behind her ear.

"Ouch!" she said, swatting at the irritation.

"Stop that and get out of here," Niinka screamed in her ear. Rie's head snapped up.

Hiinto gripped her earlobe, pulling her head around to the side. "Plug your ears. He's ensnaring you. Let's go, let's go, let's go!"

Rie yanked her arm from the man's grasp and unsheathed her blades in the same motion. Her eyes cleared and she looked around. He had brought her all the way inside the room and nearly to the back wall. How had she gotten pulled so far into the bar without realizing? She stepped back, relaxing down into a wide fighter's stance, her legs balanced and ready for action.

"I am not your plaything. I will not be coerced," Rie said, her mind once again her own. She spun her blades, first one, then the other, willing to do whatever it took to avoid being the blood sidhe's next meal. His lips lifted, his teeth flashed in the lamplight. Using peripheral vision she assessed the rest of the bar. The bartender was watching from a distance, but everyone else was too absorbed in their own feedings to take notice. Rie took another step back. Her heart pounded. She stared at the man's broad chest and willed him to be slow enough for her to escape. She wanted his muscles to weaken, his energy to lag. She bounced on her toes, adrenaline flooding her system with new reserves as she prepared to flee. His eyes widened.

"You're a drainer," he whispered. His voice no longer held any power over her.

"Hold it," the bodysuit woman intervened, sliding forward from the bar and cocking her left hip to the side. "Braegan, baby, you know better. There's to be no violence in the Red Chalice. All donors are willing, all feeders are paying."

"I'm neither willing, nor a donor," Rie spat.

"I am so sorry." The man, Braegan, held out a hand, palm up. "I thought she was an ordinary human, leaving early. I had no idea. It will never happen again," he said, face stricken.

"Well, then, that settles that. No harm, no foul. And certainly no need to have naked blades in my reputable establishment."

Rie's thumb twitched on the khukuri's grip. She had been too close to being a predator's meal. She shook her head. "No offense, but they stay out until I leave. I'm sure you understand."

"I suppose I do. But I swear you'll come to no harm. Poaching is strongly discouraged."

"I'd rather just leave."

Braegan tilted his head to the side, a wolfish gesture that drew Rie's attention away from the woman. "Why are you here, then?"

"I need directions, and I didn't realize this was a blood bar," Rie admitted.

Braegan stepped forward, pushing into the edge of Rie's comfort zone. His eyes narrowed in a calculating glance, and a smile that never reached his eyes pulled up at the corners of his lips. "Directions to where, exactly?"

Rie paused. She needed information, but the man had tried to enthrall her. Could she trust him not to chase after her when she left the restrictions of the bar? Deciding it was worth the risk, she answered. "The Crossroads Inn."

"Well that's perfect then," the woman interrupted. "No one knows the city better than Braegan, and he can be trusted, if he gives his word."

Braegan spoke before the bartender had finished her sentence. "I'd be happy to be your guide." The woman raised an eyebrow, but smiled with an indulgent twist of her lips.

Rie stepped back, away from the pushy blood sidhe. "Thank you for the offer, but I'll be fine, if you can just point the way."

"I know we got off on the wrong foot, but let me make it up to you. I swear, I will get you to the inn, free from harm. I'm really not a bad guy." His molten chocolate eyes grew wide, and his bottom lip pushed out in a soft pout. He clutched his hands beneath his chin. "Please?" he whined. Rie couldn't help but laugh, his face was so comically sad.

"Fine," she relented. "If you swear under solemn oath, I'll go with you."

"Deal. I, Braegan Sangrresen, give solemn oath to bring," he paused, raising an eyebrow at Rie.

"Nuriel Lhethannien."

"Nuriel Lhethannien to the Crossroads Inn free from harm."

"And as quickly as possible," Rie added.

"And as quickly as possible," Braegan confirmed.

"Now that that's settled, let's get back to business, shall we?" bodysuit woman said. "I'm Allana, by the way. If you need anything, well, I'll give you a good price." She winked and quirked her lip up in a half smile.

"I'm fine, for now," Rie replied, sheathing her khukuris.

"Suit yourself." Allana shrugged. "If you change your mind, you know where to find me," she said over her shoulder as she slithered back to her post at the bar.

Rie turned to face Braegan, her new guide. He looked strong enough, but he must be young and relatively weak to have caved so quickly to a human.

"Before we go, do you mind if I have a sip?" Rie's head snapped to the side, her hands dropping to her knives without conscious thought. Braegan grimaced in apology. "From a willing donor, of course, not from you."

"I suppose that's okay." Rie relaxed her guard a fraction. She wouldn't be entirely comfortable so long as she was in his company, but she couldn't deny a man his lunch. Together they walked to the bar and leaned against the polished ebony wood. Rie turned to the side, facing Braegan and the front door. She would stay vigilant, even with a sworn oath of safety.

"What did you mean, when you said I'm a drainer?" she asked, while Braegan waited for his meal.

He leaned closer, as if to tell her a secret. "You don't know what a drainer is?" Rie shook her head. "Spirit magic, you know?"

Rie shook her head again, the mention of spirit magic — the magic of the Upper Realm — making her heart beat faster. "I have no idea."

"You stole my energy, drained it right out of me. And you did it fast, too. The stories say the Upper Realm has powerful master drainers that sent entire armies to their knees during the Great War." Rie kept her expression under control, but it wasn't without effort.

In the Upper Realm, they were called enervators, people with the ability to absorb the energy of others. And Braegan was right, the strongest of the enervators could pull the energy from entire crowds of people, using it to fuel their own power in a giant feedback loop.

"You don't by chance have some high elf ancestry, do you?"

Rie avoided making eye contact with Braegan, choosing instead to look out across the room with its shadowy alcoves and gasping sounds of pain and pleasure. He was too close to the mark. "Not that I'm aware of." She wasn't even sure she agreed she had taken his energy. It had never happened before, and after one hundred years, she thought any magical talents would have expressed themselves by now.

"Huh." Braegan slid a sideways glance her direction. "Well, it's a rare ability, anyway. Where did you say you were from?"

A shrill voice called out from the end of the bar. "Pixies? Who let pixies in here?" Rie's head snapped around as she searched for her friends. Perfect timing.

Her backstory wouldn't hold up to close scrutiny, and Braegan seemed a little too interested. "Out, out, out. Damn pests. Talking bugs. Get out!" Allana shouted, swatting at Gikl, who laughed hysterically.

"Well, that's our cue." Rie stood and made her way to the exit.

"But I haven't eaten yet. The donor will be here any minute, I'm sure."

"You'll have to hurry. I'll meet you outside." Rie walked to the exit without looking back.

CHAPTER FIVE

Rie stood outside the door of the Red Chalice, watching the pixies frolic. She took a deep breath, relishing the cool night air. Now that she knew what it was, the coppery stench of blood emanating from the room was obvious. She would not make the same mistake twice.

Hiinto hovered in front of her face. "You'd think the blood sidhe would be more accepting of us," he began, his eerie solid black eyes reflecting spots of light from the street. "Sure, we take a little meat with our blood now and then, and we're not so picky with the source, but we're practically cousins. You should complain."

"I think I'd rather we just moved on," Rie said. "Let's not create trouble where we don't need to, especially when my kind are on the menu."

With a huff, Hiinto flew off to join the swarm. Unable to snag a bite in the bar, they were hunting a furry creature that resembled a house cat, but bigger and without the tail. Rie watched, amused by their antics. Sometimes it was hard to believe they'd been with her for over eighty years.

"I hate to interrupt such deep thoughts, but are you ready to go?" Braegan asked, coming to stand next to Rie under one of the wisp lights.

"Yes." Rie was ready for this whole ordeal to be over. She knew it was a long shot, but she wanted to go home, back to her job, back to a place where she knew the rules.

"What brings you to Nalakadr?" Braegan asked as they moved down the street, the pixies trailing behind or flittering ahead, but leaving them to walk alone. Rie glanced at him from the side, watching as he maneuvered through the crowd with smooth grace, without letting any of the other pedestrians step between them.

Rie controlled the urge to flee, and held eye contact with Braegan, hoping he wouldn't sense the lie. "My parents sent me to Tharbatiron, to find a position as a waitress or maid at the inn." She and Curuthannor had developed the story on the ride to Etsiramun. It wasn't great, but it should be believable, at least on the surface.

"Where are you from?" Braegan moved a fraction closer. It put Rie on edge. She stepped away, not wanting to give him the opportunity to try to enthrall her again. Despite his oath, she wasn't convinced he could be trusted. "You're obviously not from Nalakadr, so where did you grow up?"

"A human conclave in the outer district."

"Really? I thought they were all abandoned. What's the name?"

Rie stepped sideways, avoiding a steaming pile of goop, and putting some distance between herself and Braegan. He was asking too many questions and her instincts were urging caution. "Why so interested?"

Braegan's resonant chuckle sounded forced and lifted the hair on the back of her neck. "Can't a man be interested in a beautiful woman?" She didn't quite know how she knew it, but he was avoiding the truth. She masked her suspicion with a coy smile.

"How long have you lived in Nalakadr?" She watched Braegan for any hint of evasion.

"My whole life." It seemed to be the truth. "My parents have a shop specializing in all things Human Realm, and I do most of the grunt work for them."

"Do you enjoy it?"

"I love traveling, but it can be a pain in the ass sometimes, too. There are too many rules and restrictions." Braegan winked and leaned in to whisper. "I would think you of all people would appreciate open travel."

Rie sputtered. "What? Why?"

Braegan pushed closer, his head only a few inches from her shoulder. "Come on, you're not really from a human conclave. Even if they hadn't been abandoned centuries ago, you wouldn't be wearing a fancy dress like that if you were from there. And given your reaction to my approach at the bar, I'm guessing you're not a personal donor or mistress. So...I'd bet money that you're on the run, fleeing one of the up..."

"Quiet," Rie hissed. She grabbed his arm in the pressure point above his elbow and scanned the crowd to ensure they weren't being overheard. No one was paying any attention that she could see. She shoved Braegan out of the street and into an alley, trying to be as discreet as possible without giving him the opportunity to escape. "Do you want to get me killed?"

"No one was listening." Braegan laughed. "It's not as if you're from the High Court."

Rie shoved him against a stone wall, pinning him in place with her body weight. "There's always someone listening. Always."

"Oh, shit. You *are* from the High Court!" Braegan's eyes grew wide with excitement, but he kept his voice low. He shifted, one thigh pressed close against her hip, the other braced between her legs. The heat of his body seeped into the fabric of her dress and her breathing sped along with her pulse. He slid a fraction of an inch to the side and rocked his leg against her. Slow heat pooled in her belly.

"I've always wanted to meet someone from the Upper Realm." He lowered his head, chocolate eyes boring into her from under thick black lashes. His lips brushed against Rie's in a soft caress, then trailed up her jaw to gently pull on her earlobe. Shivers traveled down her spine while she leaned in, tilting her head to the side to give him better access. Her arm relaxed and her hand slid down his chest, across the taut expanse of his abs, and around to cup his ass.

Her forearm brushed the blunt end of her khukuri. Her mind cleared, the glamour vanished, and sense returned. Unsheathing her blade, Rie retreated from the seductive pull of Braegan's mouth and held the edge across his throat.

"Give me one good reason why I shouldn't kill you now."

Braegan slid warm fingers down Rie's bare arm and up again, the look in his eyes a heated invitation. "You're beautiful and off-limits. You might be the first person from the Upper Realm to travel to the Shadow Realm in a thousand years. Let me show you everything we have to offer here." Compulsion battered against her willpower.

Shuddering, Rie clenched her teeth against his caress. She thrust her knee up against his testicles. "Try again."

The white of Braegan's eyes showed all the way around the iris and his voice sounded strained. "You need a guide." Braegan's throat bobbed against the razor-sharp blade, slicing a thin line of red that slowly dripped down his neck. "I know the city. I can help you."

He was right, at least theoretically. Rie pulled the knife back far enough to let him talk freely. "Why should I trust you, after you've tried to enthrall me not once, but twice?"

"I swear, it won't happen again. No human woman has ever resisted me before. I had to try again, just to see if I could." He lifted his hands. "Obviously, you're stronger than you seem. I won't push it. You can trust me."

Rie shook her head. What was the old line? *Trick me once, shame on you, trick me twice, shame on me...* She shouldn't even consider giving him a third chance.

"Let me make it up to you. I'll get you to the Crossroads as agreed, but in addition, I'll teach you how to act like a Nalakadr native."

"I'm that obvious?"

Braegan quirked an eyebrow in disbelief at her question. "You dress and carry yourself like royalty. There's not a person in the city who couldn't pick you out of a crowd."

Rie didn't know how to react to the compliment. In the Upper Realm, no one spared a single glance in her direction. It made her suspicious, but she didn't really want to murder a man in an alley. She would have to keep an eye on him, make sure he didn't talk, but the pixies could help with that.

Rie stepped away and sheathed her blade. "Okay, I believe you. But if you tell *anyone* about me, I *will* kill you."

Braegan wiped the blood at his throat with his hand. "Got it." He sucked the red off of a finger and winked.

"Since you're still alive — for now —and still my guide, why don't you lead the way."

"My pleasure." Braegan held out his left arm, a gentleman escorting a lady. Yeah, right.

"Thanks for the offer, but no thanks," Rie said. She wasn't going to accept a position that left her defenseless, unable to move quickly and react independently. Especially when she wasn't confident in the man next to her.

"Come on, loosen up a little. A human woman alone will draw attention. If you're with me, no one will bother you. They'll have to get through me, first."

Rie rolled her eyes. Men and their egos. "Fine, but I'm not wrapping my arm through yours."

"How about this?" Braegan took her hand and placed it on his bicep. The position pulled Rie's body into and slightly behind his shoulder, but left her free to move. Rie synched her steps with his as they once again merged with the crowd heading into the center of the city.

Braegan's arm flexed under her touch as they slid around one particularly rambunctious group of young goblins playing some kind of ball game in the street. Without thinking, she let her hand squeeze his bicep with gentle pressure, feeling solid muscle beneath the fabric of his shirt. The best glamour in the nine realms couldn't alter the feel of an object, and there wasn't a spare ounce of fat on his frame. He had the kind of wiry strength Rie could admire on a man; not bulky to indicate narcissism, but strong enough to prove that, at a minimum, he took care of himself. Her gaze drifted across the broad shoulders and trim waist under the pale blue vest. If she were a gambling woman, she would bet on Braegan having some martial training, perhaps a close-combat specialty. It looked good on him. Realizing the drift in focus, Rie snapped her attention back to her surroundings.

This section of the city was dedicated to evening entertainment, with bars, restaurants, dancing halls, and even some less savory pleasure outlets. Dark elves predominated the sidewalks, traveling in pairs or trios, looking like the haughty nobility that they were, while a few blood sidhe trolled for available humans. Rie thought she caught Braegan warning away a competitor with a silent snarl once or twice, but it happened so fast she couldn't be sure. What she did know, was that even though she drew a few eyes, those eyes glanced away without a hint of suspicion.

"Braegan!" A young blond woman separated from a group of people lounging against a wall about 20 yards ahead, and dashed toward them, flinging herself into Braegan's arms. Rie removed her hands from the grips of her khukuris and stepped away from the tangle of limbs.

"Darling, it's been far too long! Where have you been? What have you been doing?" The woman spoke so fast Rie had a hard time understanding her words.

"I've been around. You know — here, there..."

"Everywhere," the woman finished, the accompanying laugh sounded bright and joyful, free in a way Rie had never experienced. The woman kissed Braegan, wrapping her legs around his waist and rubbing her body against him. His eyes closed and bliss crossed his face as he returned her caress and hauled her against his chest. Rie's hands returned to the security of her blades. She clenched her teeth, the desire to draw steel near overwhelming.

Disturbed by her own jealous reaction, Rie looked away. She couldn't believe she was feeling possessive over a man she had just met. Worse, he'd tried to take advantage of her twice already. She shook her head. She could admit he was attractive, but lust would have to be repressed until her life wasn't in danger.

A faint buzzing announced the arrival of Niinka and Possn. They came in fast, landing hard on Rie's shoulders before wrapping themselves in her hair.

"Gag me," Niinka whispered. "If you ever behave like that in public, I'll have to claw my own eyes out."

"So says the woman wearing no clothes." Rie kept her voice low, pitched for the pixies alone to hear. It was ironic really, that the blond woman's scanty clothing bothered her, when the pixies nakedness never had.

Niinka huffed. "If we wore clothes, we couldn't hide. Obviously."

Rie's lip twitched with a suppressed smile, but she let the conversation drop. It had been enough of a distraction to regain her composure; any more would draw attention.

Braegan ended the kiss and set the woman on her feet. He met Rie's gaze across the short distance and smiled, looking a bit embarrassed or maybe apologetic. He held out an arm, motioning Rie to come closer. With a quick shake of her head, Rie declined.

The woman leaned into Braegan's side and ran a hand down his arm. Blue eyes examined Rie with interest, and Rie returned the favor. On closer inspection, the woman was older than she appeared, several decades older than Braegan, if Rie had to guess. Her face was tiny and heart shaped, her hair cropped into a messy pixie cut. The top of her head barely reached Rie's shoulder, but her legs — bare but for strappy sandals and black shorts that barely covered her butt — seemed to stretch on for miles. Her midriff was also bare, her bouncy breasts tucked into a tight pink top that wrapped around her ribs and neck. The theme of her outfit, if it could be described in one word, was 'skin'.

"She looks tasty. I hope you're planning to share." The woman flicked her tongue between extended fangs. Rie tried not to let her disgust show.

Stepping away from the woman, Braegan grabbed Rie. He hauled her into his side and draped his arm across her shoulders. "'Fraid not."

The woman placed a delicate hand on Braegan's chest, running hot pink nails across the fabric of his vest. Her voice dropped several notches, a husky murmur. "We could break her in together, just you and me. For old times."

The woman's nails drifted closer, her body sliding in to striking distance. Rie unsheathed the knife at her thigh, keeping it out of the woman's line of sight even as Braegan's embrace tightened a fraction. "I've got it under control." He maneuvered Rie further out of the woman's reach.

"Really? From where I'm standing, she smells untouched. The three of us could have so much fun together." Rie sensed a push of compulsion, but it was far weaker than Braegan's had been, and she easily ignored it. The woman reached across Braegan's body to run a finger along Rie's cheek. She failed to notice the pixies, who took it as an invitation to feast.

Niinka launched herself onto the woman's hand, tearing away the offending fingernail, while Possn bit into the exposed flesh between her thumb and forefinger. The woman screamed, flicking her hand from side to side and flinging the laughing pixies into the air. The high-pitched wails brought her friends over at a run.

There were four of them, all male, and all blood sidhe. Rie pulled her second knife and stepped away from Braegan. The pixies, all five of them, hovered around her, clicking and squeaking in Pixl.

Braegan audibly sighed, rubbing his hand across his face. "Fuck me," he mumbled under his breath before addressing the group. "Stay the fuck back. Jean had it coming, and deserves what she got."

"My nail! Look at my fucking nail." The woman, Jean, extended her hand. Blood seeped down her finger from the raw nail bed, and a good sized chunk had been torn from her hand. The shallow wounds were already healing, the blood drying on fresh pink skin, but the claw was probably gone for good. As a group they turned and hissed, eyes flashing in the lamplight.

There was a time for diplomacy, but now it was time for strategic bravado. Jean wouldn't see her as anything but a meal and a plaything unless Rie stood her ground. "My friends thought you were threatening me. I can't say I'm sorry, but next time you might open your eyes before thrusting your hand where it isn't wanted."

"Bitch! I'm gonna drain you dry."

Gikl, the silent marauder, darted in and tore off a second nail. It was nice to have friends, but sometimes the most well-meaning gesture could spark more trouble. Jean's face contorted into a savage grimace and a harsh growl emanated from deep within her throat. Her lips receded from too sharp teeth, the skin of her face seeming to fold back as her jaw unhinged in preparation for attack. Her friends moved to flank her, coming up on either side. Teeth and claws glistened, ready for action.

Rie's pulse sped. Her thumb twitched. She shifted back and forth, balanced on the balls of her feet. Keeping her eyes on Jean, Rie watched for the first indication of intent. The odds weren't in her favor. Even with the pixies help, it was unlikely she would survive against five blood sidhe. Worse, even though Braegan had sworn to get her to the inn unharmed, she still couldn't trust him.

CHAPTER SIX

Braegan stepped in front of Rie, his arms stretched wide to either side. The nails of his hands lengthened into claws.

"Nuriel is under my protection." His voice sounded odd, gravelly. His head tilted to the side in a serpentine movement, and his right hand flipped over to display a large gold ring. It looked like a family sigil of some kind, worn on his index finger. Whatever it meant, fangs retracted and the group stepped back with uncertain movements. Everyone but Jean.

"You would protect a human blood whore?"

"I swore an oath. Even *you* can't ignore that." Braegan's voice was implacable, and Rie was relieved to discover that a solemn oath carried weight even in the Shadow Realm. "Find a healer and fix your claws. But move your ass out of our way, or you'll have to deal with me."

Jean's eyes narrowed, but she stepped back and her face returned to its original delicate facade. "I won't forget this."

Rie gripped her blades, unable to stand down until she was confident the threat was past. "Nor will I."

The pixies gathered, finding their hiding spots on Rie's

clothing as Braegan led the way past the still snarling woman. Rie followed, armed, but cautiously optimistic that no one would try anything.

Out of earshot, but still in sight of the group, Braegan pulled Rie back under his arm. "Sorry about that," he said, leaning his mouth close to her ear. "Jean's what you might call a succubus. She's not used to being turned down, least of all by a human."

"Is that supposed to explain why the two of you practically had carnal relations in the street?"

Braegan huffed, a wry smile twisting his lips. "Jealous?"

Rie watched Braegan out of the corner of her eyes. "I would prefer a guide who didn't get distracted."

"Her kiss is addictive. She was my mentor back in my school days, and I was completely under her thrall."

"Doesn't seem like much has changed."

"Ah, so you *were* jealous!"

Rie huffed and rolled her eyes. "How much farther to the inn?"

"We're already there." Braegan patted the twelve foot stacked stone wall beside him. "But it's about a half mile to the entrance."

Rie blew out a breath. If the wall was anything to go by, the inn was more a compound than hotel. She hoped she carried enough coin to cover the cost, though she could probably find a cheaper place to stay, if needed.

Braegan glanced at her, his mouth opening and closing a few times. Rie stayed silent, amused at his discomfort until he finally spoke up. "I have to ask, how did you get here?"

Rie balked. "Why do you want to know?"

"It must be a spectacular story. As far as I know, there haven't been any Upper Realm visitors since the Great War." He paused. "At least, none that weren't here on official king's business."

"Who?"

"I don't know the guy's name. It's not as if I'm involved in court politics."

"Then how do you know he's from the Upper Realm?"

"'Cause there's a big stink every time he's here. The city guard shows up in full force, wearing battle armor, and you can't go anywhere without being accosted and questioned."

"Huh." Rie would never have guessed there was communication between the courts. She would have thought there would be at least rumors in the messenger barracks, but she hadn't heard a word.

"Back to the question at hand, how *did* you get here? The curiosity is eating me alive." Braegan grinned, fangs retracted. For a moment, Rie debated what to tell him. He had been helpful, stuck up for her with Jean and the others, but she couldn't reveal too much or attach anything to Lord Garamaen.

"The logistics weren't difficult. I double ported, first to the Human Realm, then through the public portal outside the city."

"But how did you get through the portal? Every time I go to the Human Realm, I need to file a request with the Watchers and get a timed gate key."

"I had help." At Braegan's sharp glance, Rie added, "I'm not giving you a name."

"There are smugglers in our midst."

Braegan looked thoughtful, but Rie didn't respond. Technically, Greg wasn't a smuggler — he was exempt from the portal restrictions — but it was best to let Braegan make his own assumptions.

"Here we are," he said after a few moments of silence.

There was no sign, nothing to indicate a business, except the noise emanating from the entrance. If Rie had been alone, she might have missed it.

"Before we go in, I should probably warn you, The Crossroads is more than geography. It's a meeting place for all fae, an equal opportunity establishment."

"Meaning?"

"It gets a bit rowdy." Braegan grinned, a teasing light in his eyes. "Try not to piss anyone off, okay?"

Pushing her forward with his arm, Braegan ushered her through the heavy wood gates. A pea gravel path led the way into a natural bowl amphitheater filled with fae of every description. The pixies dashed ahead into the crowd while Rie struggled to gather her bearings. She had never seen so many different creatures gathered in one place. The noise and smells crowded into her brain, clamoring for attention.

Groups of dark elves, mostly women, sprawled on the grassy hills surrounding the center courtyard, lounging on blankets and looking bored. Two trolls wearing nothing but leather leggings drank beer out of gallon jugs and pounded their fists on a flat rock while shouting profanities at one another. One of them burped as Rie passed by, the stench of sour milk sending her stomach into her throat. A half dozen leprechauns huddled together on the next small rise, smoking long pipes that reeked of something that wasn't tobacco.

The crowd grew thicker and angrier the closer she got to the center. Braegan seemed to have no trouble navigating his way through the crush of people, but Rie clutched his arm like a lifeline while trying to watch everyone and everything around her. Nearing the bowl of the amphitheater, Rie caught sight of the horde's focus. Two men fought inside a dirt ring with fists and magic.

"Fight night!" Braegan's eyes were wide with excitement, his teeth bared in a gleeful snarl. "And the Commander's fighting Cendir. That explains the crowd."

On the left, a dark elf with mocha skin and uncharacteristic strawberry red highlights in his white hair pulled his arm back and threw a fireball the size of a small goblin at his opponent. The crowd gasped, watching the dark elf with the more typical black skin and silvery hair face down the flame. A fraction of a second before impact, the fireball spread out in a wide shield, forcing the dark elf to dodge to the right. The fire-thrower charged after his creation, but the dark elf was ready, blocking several punches and landing a few of his own. The crowd cheered every hit.

As they walked around the edge of the ring, Braegan continued his animated explanation. "The fire elf is Prince Daenor, Commander of the Shadow Guard, and the dark elf is Cendir, the Queen's brother and Daenor's technical second in command. They don't get along too well."

"Why not?"

"Prince Daenor fought and defeated Cendir in a fight just like this one about twenty years ago, taking over as Commander. Cendir's been trying to take it back ever since."

Rie pursed her lips, considering. In the High Court, leadership positions were chosen by the king, usually granted to his toadies. She wondered if this system wasn't a little more fair, even if it still didn't seem to grant power to the people that truly deserved it.

Rie couldn't take her eyes off the mocha-skinned elf. Wearing only black trousers, the man was a master at hand-to-hand combat. Wiry muscles glinted in the blue wisp-light, his abs bunched and contracted as he lunged into a whirling series of kicks aimed at the silver-haired elf's head.

"Why fight here?" Rie asked.

"Entertainment. Once a month, give or take, the

Shadow Guard holds a fight night here at the Crossroads. Fighters interested in joining use it as an audition, and there are hierarchy fights for those already under contract. They used to do it at guard headquarters, but as it turns out, people like to watch, and the crowds got too big to fit into their practice arena, especially on nights when Daenor has a match."

Catching the prince's leg, Cendir threw him to the ground. The fire-thrower rolled, coming up to his feet near the barrier as Rie and Braegan walked by. He caught her gaze and held it for a moment, just long enough for Rie's heartbeat to race and for Cendir to land a kick to Daenor's head. Rebounding off the barrier, the prince flicked a small missile at Cendir, who dodged to the side and out of the way. The two came together in a vicious tangle of limbs until the prince pushed Cendir into the opposite edge of the arena.

Rie couldn't take her eyes off the fight. Even injured, with blood slicking down his face, the fire-thrower moved with grace and speed that could only be honed by centuries of practice. His technique was perfect, his speed and agility superior to anything she'd seen before. His body flowed from one form to another, incorporating multiple fighting styles with precision. Overwhelmed, the silver-haired elf finally fell to the ground. He breathed, but would require a powerful healer.

Tearing her attention away from the arena, Rie followed Braegan to a covered patio that housed a massive stacked stone bar, serving customers of every description. Six bartenders of different races — including a troll and two leprechauns, who carried stools to reach the bottles and serve customers — served the guests who pushed and shoved against each other in an attempt to get a drink. Accent lighting under the shelves and along the edge of the bar provided a soft glow that illuminated the area without damaging the customer's night vision.

Keeping Rie tucked into his side, Braegan squeezed into an empty space near the troll. At Braegan's wave, the troll nodded, finished unloading the tray of drinks and food, and lumbered over.

"What'll ye be having?"

"I'd like to speak with Tharbatiron," Rie said, looking the thickset troll directly in the eyes. It wasn't generally considered a good idea to stare down a troll, but Rie was too tired to waste time playing nice.

"What d'ye want with 'im?" The troll rumbled, his voice thick with the sound of boulders rolling down a mountain. He wiped the counter, waiting for an answer without breaking eye contact.

"That's for his ears alone." She took Curuthannor's medallion from her pack and placed it on the table. "Please give him this."

The troll grunted, a look of surprise softening his face. "I'll be right back with Tharbatiron." He thumped away on broad feet, taking the medallion with him. As he moved, his girth bounced off of the other bartenders, the shelving, and anything else that was stupid enough to get in his way. Luckily, the shelves had been built to withstand the barrage and protect the bottles and glasses within.

Rie turned her back to the bar, gazing out across the courtyard. She refused to admit she was looking for the prince, but it didn't take her long to find him. He sat on a grassy hillside to her right, while a three-eyed goblin cleaned a gash above his eye. He had gotten dressed in the few minutes Rie had been at the bar, and now wore a simple gray sleeveless tunic over black pants. He'd added weapons — a shoulder holster held two human handguns, and Rie could see the hilt of a sword sticking up over his shoulder.

Rie cocked her head to the side, carefully examining the man. He was obviously a powerful fire sidhe, but he was also the prince of the Shadow Realm.

"How is it that a fire sidhe is the prince of the Shadow Realm?" she asked Braegan.

He turned, following Rie's gaze. "That's a Shadow Court scandal that refuses to die. The dark elves call him The Bastard."

Rie glanced at Braegan, feeling her eyebrows lift.

"Never to his face, of course, unless you want to end up worse than Cendir."

"Bastard?"

"He's the son of King Aradae, but his mother was a fire sidhe captive from the war."

"I thought the war was fought over a woman."

"It was."

Rie scoffed. "You'll fight wars for love, and then waste it for one night with a pretty face."

"We're not all bad. And the current king wasn't king at the start of the war. His father died in battle. It's the only reason King Othin agreed to the truce."

"What happened to the captive?"

"No one really knows. She got pregnant, then disappeared once Prince Daenor was born. Some say she was raped, and couldn't bear the sight of her child. Others say she loved the king but died in childbirth." Braegan shrugged. "In the end, it doesn't matter. The king claimed him, but Daenor has always lived on the outside. Not pure enough for the dark elf royalty, but too much an elf to be accepted outside court."

Before Rie could ask more about Daenor, the troll returned, following behind a tall dark elf with perfect military posture. He was wearing a deep blue traditional robe embroidered with silver thread, and occasionally accented with a sparkling white crystal gemstone. His long white hair was pulled back in braids at the sides. All in all, a very conservative dark elf, and likely much older than even Curuthannor's fifteen-hundred years.

The elf approached, his lips pulled upward just enough to give the hint of welcome without committing to an actual smile. He inclined his head ever so slightly, the only greeting Rie could expect from an elder.

"I'm Tharbatiron," he said, introducing himself. "Perhaps we should move to a more private location. Please come with me."

They followed Tharbatiron down the length of the bar and around the back, continuing along a smooth pea gravel path lined with torches toward another squat building with a tiled roof. The troll brought up the rear, closing the door behind them after they entered the single room of what was apparently Tharbatiron's office. A heavy, granite-topped desk occupied the majority of the space, with two floor-to-ceiling cabinets lining the wall behind. A ledger stood open on the desk, but Tharbatiron closed the cover before Rie could see the details inside. He sat in the high backed chair, waving Rie and Braegan toward small guest chairs positioned before the desk.

No one spoke. Tharbatiron steepled his hands in front of his mouth, and examined Rie with a thoughtful expression. Braegan shifted in his seat, impatient or uncomfortable, Rie couldn't tell. The troll, meanwhile, took up a position at the door, crossing his arms and leaning against the wall.

Rie's hands began to sweat a little and her thumb twitched before Tharbatiron finally broke the silence. "So tell me, how is my old friend?"

"Curuthannor is well. I left him just yesterday."

"Did he ever take a lifemate?"

Rie nodded. "He and Lhéwen bonded more than seven

hundred years ago."

"But they took a ward, so I'm guessing no children of their own?" That was a very personal question, not one normally considered appropriate for general conversation.

"They don't have any children, no. I was orphaned as a baby and they took me in." Rie replied. "There is still time for them to bear their own."

"Yet Curuthannor sent you to me. Did he tell you of our past?"

Rie nodded. "He told me that he knew you before the war, that he used to stay here when he was traveling on business for his father."

"Yes, that's all true." Tharbatiron leaned forward, resting his elbows on the granite and relaxing his posture. "I introduced the two of them," he said, whispering out of the side of his mouth, as if telling Rie a great secret. The tension left Rie's shoulders as she relaxed and leaned forward in response. "They were both staying here on business. In those days many of the high elves had business in the Shadow Realm, but it was still rare to have more than one in the inn at a time. But those two were here so frequently, they couldn't help but cross paths. Soon it became clear that they were planning their trips to *make sure* their paths crossed. They were young and in love. But then the war broke out, so I never got to hear the end of the story. I do hope you'll tell it to me over a glass of honey wine someday."

"I would enjoy that." Rie smiled, genuinely pleased at the invitation. After a hundred years, she felt like she knew her wardens well, but they never talked about the time before the war. None of the high elves did. It would be fascinating to learn what they were like in their youth.

Tharbatiron leaned back again, still relaxed, but professional. "Well then, go on and tell me why you've broken every law to come here to my humble establishment."

Braegan snorted, and Rie mentally agreed. The Crossroads was a grand establishment, not humble in the slightest.

"I'm looking for information. Curuthannor thought you might be able to assist me, and trusts that you will keep my presence to yourself."

"I will tell no one, I give you my word. And do you trust him?" Tharbatiron nodded his head toward Braegan, who put a hand on his chest and gave a good show of looking offended.

"He's been helpful." Rie shrugged. "As much as I can trust anyone here, yes, I trust him. And he already knows I'm from the Upper Realm. If he had wanted to turn me in, he could have taken me directly to the city guard."

Braegan sat back in his chair, a self-satisfied smile plastered on his face.

Tharbatiron nodded, pursing his lips. "Alright. Then what information are you looking for, that you couldn't find in the High Court?"

"I am looking for the maker of these knives." Rie removed one of the throwing knives from her pack and placed it carefully on the table, the hilt pointing toward Tharbatiron, blade directed at herself.

Braegan leaned forward to get a better look at the blade, but Tharbatiron placed a hand on it, blocking it from view. "What's your interest?"

"Assassins were sent to kill me. They carried these knives."

"Assassins?" Braegan looked shocked. "And you think they're from here? Why?"

"I was told the knives were crafted by a master bladesmith here in Nalakadr."

Tharbatiron chuckled, a wry smile twisting his lips.

"Since you are alive, I'm guessing Curuthannor passed on some of his skill with a blade."

"As much as a human can master, yes."

"My dear, you are no mere human."

Rie paused. For the second time that day, someone was questioning her humanity. In the Upper Realm, it was taken for granted, but not here. Here she was constantly on the defensive. If she were more than human, it would have come out by now. "I'm well-trained, but I'm still a changeling."

"Any assassin carrying a blade forged by Master Whixle would not be easy to kill. If you killed them, then there's more to you than meets the eye." His words were spoken without inflection, stated as simple fact.

Braegan turned his entire upper body to face her, eyes wide. Rie shrugged away from his gaze and stayed focused on Tharbatiron. "So you know the maker's mark?"

"Yes. He only takes commissions from warriors that will truly appreciate the blade, and use it to its best advantage. Well, and royalty, I suppose, though even they have a difficult time acquiring his weapons."

"Where can I find him?"

"Unfortunately, he's well-guarded and only takes clients by appointment, usually booked years in advance."

"But I'm not a client, I just need information."

"If you go in saying that, there's no chance he'll see you. He *only* sees clients. However, he may allow you to accompany someone who already has an appointment, and I think I know who can help."

CHAPTER SEVEN

"Tryg, could you please go find Prince Daenor and bring him here?" Tharbatiron asked. The troll nodded, and lumbered out the door. "The prince commissioned a new blade from Master Whixle several months ago, and he's due to pick it up soon. He may be willing to take you with him."

Rie shook her head. "No. If he finds out I'm from the Upper Realm, he's bound to arrest me. It's too big a risk."

"If you want to talk to Whixle, you have to have an invitation. It's the only option. You'll just have to be careful what you say and do."

"I don't think it's a good idea," Braegan said. "An idiot could tell she's outworld. I figured it out in minutes."

"You're supposed to be helping me with that," Rie said.

"And I am, but it's not gonna happen overnight."

"You'll have some time," Tharbatiron cut in. "At least a day or two."

"It doesn't matter how well I can or can't act. I need information, but I can't ask a bunch of questions without the prince becoming suspicious. There must be another way."

"There's not." Tharbatiron held firm.

"I will make my own appointment."

SANYARE: THE LAST DESCENDANT

"That could take years. Time you don't have, if you ever want to return to the upperworlds. I promise, this is your only option, unless you have another lead?"

Rie shook her head. The assassins had carried nothing with them. There was no way to identify them, or discover where they were from, except those knives. She had to see Whixle.

"Then you'll have to deal with Daenor."

Rie's shoulders slumped, defeated. A breath later and the door opened. The prince strode into the room, an aura of command surrounding him. He tipped his head in greeting.

He didn't appear to be the worse for wear from his fight. A faint pink line cut across his forehead, the only indication he had been in a fight at all. The gray sleeveless tunic turned out to be a belted vest that crossed at the waist, revealing well-defined pectorals beneath the sturdy fabric. He crossed his arms and stood, feet placed wide. Rie responded to his greeting with her own, lower, bow.

Braegan nudged her with an elbow, and she straightened to see Daenor giving her an odd look.

"What's this all about?" His gaze raked Rie from head to toe. Rie stood tall, chin up, staring ahead without meeting his eyes, as if she were under Curuthannor's inspection. After a heartbeat of silence, Daenor glanced at Tharbatiron and lifted an eyebrow.

Rie glanced at the innkeeper from the corner of her eye. It was his plan, so he needed to provide the cover story. He sat back, relaxed in his cushioned desk chair, a light smile playing around his lips. "A close friend of mine sent his ward here to commission a blade from Master Whixle, but he didn't realize she needed an appointment to see him. I heard you have one coming up."

"And you want me to take her."

Tharbatiron shrugged one shoulder. "I would consider it a favor."

"No. Master Whixle doesn't like unexpected guests. He barely tolerates expected ones." Daenor shook his head. "I commissioned the sword almost a year ago. I won't risk it."

"I will vouch for her. All you have to do is get her in front of Master Whixle."

"She can make her own appointment. If you vouch for her, I'm sure Master Whixle will agree to a meeting."

"Daenor's right," Braegan interrupted, drawing a baleful stare from the prince. "We don't need his help."

"I don't have time to wait around for his next opening." The prince's gaze sharpened at her words. Rie needed to make this meeting happen, and Daenor was too astute to be misled by a weak story. Some truth was better than none. "Tharbatiron is being discreet, and I appreciate it, but the truth is, I only need to ask Master Whixle a few questions about a blade that carries his mark. It won't take long."

"What blade?"

Rie nodded to Tharbatiron, who still held the throwing knife. He presented it to the prince on the palm of his hand. "It was used in an attempted murder. I've been tasked with finding out who ordered the assassination."

Daenor glanced at the knife without touching it, then concentrated his full attention on Rie. He paced around her and pursed his lips, considering. "What's your name?"

"I'm Rie, Your Highness." The words left her mouth without thought, but she didn't have a chance to correct the error and give her true name.

"Rie." The prince's smile made Rie's breath hitch, and her heart caught in her throat. "Call me Daenor."

Rie hid a smile, pleased to have been given the familiarity of his name. In her experience, royalty didn't allow lesser fae, let alone humans, to use anything but their title. It suddenly seemed appropriate that he use her preferred nickname rather than the reminder of the low position that the High Court forced on her.

Daenor paused in front of Rie, his head tilting to one side. His hand reached out to brush a loose hair behind her ear. Gentle heat warmed her skin, following the path of his fingers.

"Why would a beautiful woman carry the burden of catching a killer? I doubt you even know how to use the blades you carry."

Rie felt her eyes narrow a fraction before she caught herself. "I'll make you a bet. If I can score a point on you in under two minutes, you'll take me to see the master smith. If not," she shrugged, "I'll find another way to see him."

"This is not a good idea." Braegan put a hand on Rie's shoulder, forcing her around to face him. "You don't have anything to prove, and if he's unwilling to take you, so be it."

"You presume too much, Braegan," she growled, while she quickly braided her loose hair back into a tight queue. "I'll admit you've been helpful, but I need to do this. Don't get in my way." Braegan scowled, but said no more.

Daenor chuckled, the sound bringing Rie's attention back to her opponent. "Okay, then. Sparring rules, no blood drawn."

"Deal."

"Stop." Tharbatiron moved around the desk and ushered everyone toward the door. "Outside, please. I'd rather not watch the two of you destroy my office."

The group headed out into the torchlit night, pea

gravel shushing under their feet. Tharbatiron sat at a small table beneath an arbor covered in thick vines, Tryg standing guard a few feet away.

"Shouldn't we go to the arena?" Rie asked, surprised that Tharbatiron would kick everyone out of his office, only to have a fight in his yard.

"Daenor?" Tharbatiron asked.

"Nah, this is just a quick baseline trial. We won't need the barrier."

Rie bristled at his dismissal of her abilities, but she would use it to her advantage. She rolled forward on the balls of her feet, while Daenor moved into position across from her.

"Ready?" he asked.

"Always."

Daenor lifted an eyebrow, his lips curling up in a sardonic smile. The arrogant bastard. He bounced lightly on his toes, then lowered into a casual, almost negligent, opening stance.

Rie watched his expression, and his eyes gave him away. He was going to go easy on her. He was going to swing at her face with his right hand, follow up with a jab from his left. She countered, sliding her left arm up to block the face punch while pulling her blade with her right, reverse grip, dodging the slow jab and sliding the knife forward to cross Daenor at the waist without actually touching him. Point: Rie.

"Best two out of three?" She knew she was tempting fate. He'd intentionally taken it easy on her, letting her get the upper hand. Daenor was deadly, she'd seen it in the arena, but she couldn't stop herself.

Daenor's lips lifted in an amused smile. "Pretty good," he said. "You've had some training, but can you really keep up?"

This time there was no tell, no warning of his action.

Faster than human, his arm snapped out in a jab at her face. She reacted without thinking, without knowing what her body was doing. Duck, pull left blade, forward grip, block up, step under, mule kick, spin and crouch. She ended up with one knife poised across Daenor's femoral artery, the other pointed up into his gut. He might have kicked her in the face, but he would bleed out pretty quickly after that.

The grin that spread across Daenor's face felt like the sun breaking through the clouds on a rainy day. Rie couldn't help responding with an equally broad smile.

Daenor tilted his head toward Tharbatiron, but kept his gaze locked on Rie. "I'll do it." He paused, an opportunistic glint in his eye. "But I want the arena free of charge on fight nights, designated warm-up and changing areas, and free food and drinks for the fighters."

Tharbatiron countered. "Half-price, use of a suite as a changing room, and one drink per fighter."

"Done."

Tharbatiron extended his hand. "I'll have everything ready before the next event."

The two men shook, then Daenor turned back to Rie, hand extended, palm flat and open. Nerves jangling, Rie placed her hand in his. With a light touch, he squeezed and released, slowly sliding his hand away and sending a tingling sensation up her arm. His voice was warm. "I'll meet you outside Master Whixle's smithy, day after tomorrow, at fifth bell."

"I'll be there."

"We'll be there." Rie had forgotten about Braegan. Arms crossed, he stood defiant. He glanced at Rie, then back at the prince.

Daenor scowled, his voice hardened. "You're not invited."

"I'm going with her." Braegan's voice never quavered, but the bravado sounded hollow to Rie. He was worried.

The prince stepped forward, his amber eyes threatening violence. "If I see you at the smithy, I'll let the redcaps have you. Don't test me."

"I suppose that means I won't be able to take my friends, either," Rie interrupted before Braegan could incite the prince's fire. The pixies were always good for a distraction. They popped out of their hiding spaces, making everyone but Rie jump.

"Fucking bugs," Braegan whispered, but looked contrite when Rie glared at him.

"Interesting choice of friends," Tharbatiron commented.

"And she's a pixie tamer," Daenor muttered with a shake of his head.

"None of you saw us. No one knew we were here. We get to go." Niinka hovered in front of Daenor, her hands on tiny hips, determination in her tinkling voice. She had been hiding in the vines above Tharbatiron's head, invisible in the dark foliage.

"I don't think anyone could stop you," Daenor answered, voice droll. Niinka smiled, pleased with herself, and the swarm rushed to find their seats on Rie's clothing. "But you'll have to stay quiet and out of sight. I don't want to piss off Whixle any more than I have to."

"Not a problem," Tiik replied.

Rie felt better to have backup with her, but it would be challenging for the pixies to behave. She needed to have a serious talk with the swarm before anyone was allowed to go.

"If everything's settled, I have a job to get back to." At Tharbatiron's nod, Prince Daenor turned and walked away. Rie licked her lips. He was beyond arrogant, but she could appreciate the rear view.

"If you're done ogling his ass, I think we still have a few things to discuss," Braegan interrupted.

Rie closed her eyes before turning her attention back to Braegan and Tharbatiron.

"You're right. Tharbatiron, would you by chance have a room available? I don't need much, and I can pay."

"Of course. I would never turn away Curuthannor's ward. And don't worry about payment, I still owe Curuthannor a small debt or two. You can stay as long as you need."

Rie bowed her head. Whether or not the debt was real, she was grateful for the favor.

"But I would suggest you spend a few coin to change your look before going to see Master Whixle," Tharbatiron added.

"What do you mean?"

"Whixle only deals with warriors." He waved a hand at Rie's outfit. "You look like a noble, not a fighter. Elegant, yes. Deadly, no."

Rie looked down at herself. With the exception of her one-time lover, Nils, no one in the Upper Realm had ever commented on, let alone complimented, her appearance. She'd received more positive feedback in one day in the Shadow Realm than she had in a lifetime in the Upper Realm. It was disconcerting. But Tharbatiron was right. Lhéwen's work was designed for the High Court, not the Shadow Realm.

"I know a guy who can help with that." Braegan grinned, a wicked light glinting in his eyes. "Tomorrow, you're mine."

CHAPTER EIGHT

It felt like the middle of the night, but was technically morning, when Braegan took Rie to meet his best friend, a clothier who specialized in "bad-ass finery". He wasn't what she expected from a blood sidhe and Braegan's friend.

"Look what the ash-cat dragged in," he said, as the door jingled closed. Coming around the back counter, the man sauntered toward them with an exaggerated swing of his hips. He was dressed in low-slung leather pants and a purple vest left open over smooth bare skin, but the rough one-handed hug he gave Braegan left no doubt in Rie's mind that their relationship was platonic.

"Here she is," Braegan extended an arm to Rie, and his expression took on a sly smirk. "Nuriel, I'd like you to meet the greatest fashion designer in all of Nalakadr — if only the city would pay attention — Garran Caralagos."

Garran slapped a hand over his heart. "Welcome to my shop. Any friend of Braegan's is a friend of mine, especially a lady as gorgeous as yourself." He winked, and Rie couldn't help but smile.

Coming closer, Garran ran a finger across the fabric of her gown. "You have to tell me where you found this. The silk is stunning, and I've never seen a gray with such depth of color." He continued walking around Rie, soft hands brushing her shoulders. "But we'll have to do something about your hair. You can't go around wearing a dress like this with your hair a braided mess. Didn't your mother teach you anything?"

Rie laughed. "She tried, but I'm afraid I'm not a very good student. Practical braids are about all I'm capable of."

"Not to worry, we'll get you fixed up." Garran began unwinding her braid, his fingers fast, but gentle on her hair. "But I don't think you've come for a general beauty consultation, so what can I do for you?"

"I need a new outfit, something that says warrior, instead of lady." Done playing with her hair, Garran stood in front of Rie and held both her hands.

"Nuriel has an appointment to see Master Whixle tomorrow," Braegan added, helpfully.

"Ah, deadly sexy. My specialty." With another wink and a snap of his fingers, Garran turned and disappeared into the back room.

Surprised at the abrupt departure, Rie looked at Braegan. "Is he always like that?"

"Yep."

"And you two are friends?" Rie could hardly believe that someone as masculine as Braegan would spend time with an effeminate fashion designer.

"The best. We grew up together." Braegan shrugged. "He's a little eccentric, but he's a great wingman." Garran emerged from the behind the curtain carrying a stack of black leather and stretchy red cotton. "If only he wasn't such a lightweight in the pub."

Garran grinned. "This from a man who, a week ago, passed out under my kitchen table."

Braegan lifted an eyebrow and unsuccessfully suppressed a smile. "*Passing out* is a little strong. Yes, I slept there, but I took a pillow with me."

"You drooled all over one of my best velvet throws." Garran shook his head. "But enough of that. On to business." Still smiling, he handed Rie the pile of clothing and ushered her behind a tall screen. "Here you are, my darling. Wear the vest over the red top. We'll adjust the fit when you come out to the mirror."

The long-sleeved red shirt stretched across her torso like a second skin, the color a near perfect match for the handles of her khukuris. She shimmied into the tight fitting but surprisingly comfortable black leather pants, then buckled on the matching leather vest and stepped out to face the men and the mirror.

Garran clapped his hands in glee the moment she emerged. Braegan's smile was slower. It curled up from his lips in an appreciative smirk that warmed Rie from the inside out. Garran impatiently pushed her in front of the large three-way mirror.

"Almost perfect," Garran grinned at her in the mirror, one hand resting on her waist. His gaze traveled her body, but it wasn't lascivious or uncomfortable. In truth, it felt no different from standing for a fitting with Lhéwen. He came around in front of Rie and yanked on the boatneck collar of the red top, stretching it down over her shoulders and under the scooped neckline of the leather vest, revealing a few inches of bare skin at her collarbone and the top of her arms. He then twisted her hair up into a tight bun on the top of her head, holding it in place with four silver-tipped wooden hair sticks. He stepped back and nodded.

Rie stared at her reflection. It was just a change of clothes, yet she barely recognized herself. The unique black leather fit as if it had been custom made, providing free range of movement comparable to her most comfortable training outfits. It was on the heavy side, but still soft and supple, caressing every curve while only leaving her arms and neck unprotected. The oiled steel buckles of the vest glistened in the lamplight, further highlighting her shape. And the hairstyle was completely foreign. She thought she might actually look like a native.

Her fingers slid across the buttery soft leggings. Braegan's gaze followed her hand across her hip.

"What is this?" she asked Garran, while she pushed back the heat rising to her cheeks.

"Amlug hide. It's my specialty. It's expensive, I'm not gonna lie, but it's worth every coin, especially if you're going to be seeing any real fighting. The pants will need to be hemmed a bit. They're not bad, but they should lie flat against your leg, not bunch at the bottom." Garran bent and began marking the pant leg where he wanted the hem. Straightening, he examined his handy work.

"We're still missing something." Garran tapped his bottom lip with his finger. He smiled, and without a word, once again disappeared into the back room.

"So?" she asked, daring Braegan to meet her gaze.

Braegan coughed, covering his mouth with one closed fist. "You look...dangerous."

"That's it? That's all you can say?" Niinka buzzed around Braegan's head while he ineffectually swatted at her. "Do you have cotton for brains, or marbles for eyes? She looks fantastic! Like a red and black tigress on the prowl."

"Like a barbarian princess," Possn chimed from her perch near the front door, surprising Rie. The shyest of the lot, Possn usually stayed hidden and quiet. She and Niinka had chosen to travel with Rie on her shopping trip, while the men explored the city on their own. Braegan had put up with them, seeming to get used to having them pop up randomly out of nowhere. Of course, it was a lot easier to deal with the girls, one of whom barely spoke, than the more mischievous guys.

"No! Like a demonatrix!" Niinka tinkled a laugh.

"Don't you mean dominatrix?" Braegan asked.

"Nope. A demonatrix. She'll suck out your soul while she sucks you dry, and you'll beg for more!"

"Ew," Rie replied, chuckling. "I'm not sure that's what I'm going for, here."

Braegan's laughter bubbled up from deep within his chest. He paused just long enough to say, "Don't listen to her. You look perfect for Whixle."

"Almost," Garran said, returning from the back room with a twinkle in his eyes. "Here's the finishing touch."

He set a box down on a narrow table next to the mirror, lifting the lid. A matched set of bracers lay nestled in soft cloth, glistening in the golden lamplight of the shop. Made of hardened amlug hide, an intricate rose mandala had been embossed on the black surface.

Rie lifted one of the bracers, examining the workmanship.

"Beautiful," she said, the word flowing out on a breath.

Garran rolled forward on his toes, a proud smile straining to break free of his lips. "The design is a shadow rose, a plant found only here in Nalakadr on the slopes of the volcano. They say that the lava nourishes its roots, and without the strain of fighting through the ash, the flower will never bloom."

"I'm sure I can't afford this level of craftsmanship. They must have taken weeks to make." She looked up, hope warring with resignation.

"They did, but they're yours. I may not have known you, but I made them for you." Garran helped strap them to her forearms, adjusting the buckles to keep them tight without being uncomfortable. They were exquisite.

"You honor me," Rie replied.

"Quite the opposite," Garran said with a smile.

"Besides, any girl strong enough to tame Braegan needs some armored leather." He winked, a teasing light hiding in the depths of his eyes. "Now go shimmy out of those pants, and I'll take them in the back. You can put on your old leggings for now and wear the rest of the outfit, if you want to wander around the city for a bit."

After changing and handing over the pants, Rie reached for her bag. "Before you alter anything, let me pay you. I don't want to find out later I didn't have enough."

"Tsk. You get the friends and family discount. One gold should about cover it."

Rie gaped. "The bracers alone must cost twice that much."

"The bracers are my gift to you, the rest is at cost. One gold, not a silver more." Garran held out a hand, palm up, and wiggled his fingers.

Unable to believe her good fortune, Rie handed over payment. "You are too generous."

"Not at all. Be back in half a bell, and the pants will be ready."

***

Braegan led Rie down the street toward an ancient looking stone building named Hrold's Tower. He insisted it was a sight she couldn't miss. From the ground, the building looked like a tiered cake made out of stone and lit with candles. No one bothered them as they began the climb to the top.

"Before the Great War, Hrold's Tower was a look-out point for the city. Guards stood watch with a 365 degree view of the entire city limits. Since then, the city has grown too much for the tower to be very useful as a look-out, but it's still a great view," Braegan said between breaths as they trudged up the stairs that wound around the exterior of the tower from one landing to the next.

"How many stairs did you say there were?" Rie asked, trying to hide how winded she was. She wasn't out of shape, but her legs were already tiring and she had to watch her feet carefully to make sure she didn't miss a step. Torches burned from sconces in the wall every fifth stair, providing barely enough illumination for her human eyes, and a low railing was the only protection from a deadly fall. The darkness weighed on her mind as she struggled not to look into the abyss on her right.

"Three hundred eight. You're not giving up already, are you?" Braegan teased. "We're only halfway to the top."

"Of course not." If she were going to stay here for an extended period of time, she would have to be sure to use the tower as a training ground. It would be painfully sweet to run the stairs. Focusing on each step, Rie almost didn't notice when they'd finally reached the top. Braegan stood across the open platform, arms crossed over his chest as he stared out at the blue and yellow-lit city.

"It's beautiful," Rie gasped as she came to stand next to him.

"It's home." A note of bitterness crept into Braegan's voice. "And we're stuck here."

"What do you mean?"

Braegan glanced at Rie out of the corner of his eye, as if deciding what to tell her. "When the upperworlds closed off, my family lost most of its business. We were the wealthiest, most profitable importers and exporters in Nalakadr, but the majority of our trade was with the upperworlds. By the time I was born, our business had dwindled to almost nothing."

"You don't look poor to me," Niinka chirped from her perch on Rie's shoulder.

"Yeah, well, luckily the Human Realm finally got its act together and started producing some decent fabrics, and human goods are actually in demand now. In fact, I wouldn't be surprised if the cloth of your shirt was imported by my family."

"Wouldn't you have brought it across?" Rie asked.

Braegan's eyes shifted to the side. "Not that one. Maybe one of my cousins or something, though. We've all had to work hard to bring the family back from the brink of total ruin. Someday, they'll open the portals again, but until then, we have to make do with what we can."

"I don't know. From our side, the treaty is sacrosanct. I doubt King Othin will agree to drop, or even modify, the restrictions."

"Well, something has to change eventually. The fact you're here is a sign that not all is well in King Othin's court." With a shrug, Braegan changed the subject. "What about you? Do you come from a line of warrior women?" His expression was so bland, Rie couldn't tell if he was making fun of her.

"No. I'm a changeling."

Braegan wrapped an arm around Rie's shoulders. Together, they walked the perimeter of the platform. "There are human warriors here," he said.

Rie didn't believe him. "Really?"

"Not many, but it's not totally unheard of. So how did you learn to fight?"

"My warden taught me." Braegan lifted his eyebrows and stopped to face her, asking without words for more details. She sighed. "I was orphaned as a child, taken by the fae to be a changeling, and sold as a servant to a high elf family. My wardens, Curuthannor and Lhéwen, purchased me from the High Court central market. I was lucky. They have treated me as their own child. As much as they're allowed, anyway."

"What do you mean?"

Rie grimaced, shrugging out from under Braegan's

arm. It was an old hurt, and relatively insignificant, but one that stayed with her, regardless. She looked out at the city, avoiding Braegan's searching gaze.

"Humans are allowed two positions in the Upper Realm: servant or paramour. Curuthannor taught me to fight, gave me the ability to protect myself. And Lhéwen tutored me in all of the common subjects. Without that, I would be little better than an illiterate slave, and I would never have made it into the messenger corps. As it was, I needed special dispensation from the king to allow my service with the messengers."

"Then why are you so determined to go back?"

"It's my life. It probably doesn't seem like much, but Curuthannor and Lhéwen are the only family I have, and I've worked hard for my position. Being labeled a traitor casts a shadow on my wardens, so even if I don't go back to face the executioner, they'll be branded by the association."

"Being the target of an assassination shouldn't put your head on a pike."

Rie gave a one-shouldered shrug. "Any unsanctioned contact with the enemy equals treason under King Othin's law."

"Rock and a hard place." She expected to see pity in Braegan's eyes, but instead found support, maybe even a little empathy. It was still hard to swallow.

"I suppose we should be getting back," she said.

"Yeah, probably."

They returned to the shop in silence, Rie's head full of their conversation. She'd never really thought about the consequences of restricting travel between the realms. To be fair, the treaty had been imposed a millennium before her birth, and she'd never been in a position to consider its affects. But if she understood Braegan's story, there were a lot of people, probably on both sides, that had every reason to want the treaty to fall. And it wouldn't be limited to the traders and merchants. Craftsmen, inns, and restaurants would have all lost business. Unlike the Upper Realm — which still had access to the other four upperworlds — the Shadow Realm was limited to open dealing only with the Demon Realm, which had little to offer.

It wasn't long before they were back at Garran's shop, the door chime jingling. When Garran didn't immediately come out from the back, Braegan headed toward the curtain. "I'll see how it's going. Be right back."

Seeing her new leggings hanging over the dressing screen, Rie decided to change. She reassured herself that Garran would probably want to make sure they fit correctly, anyway. Just as she finished tying her boots on, Braegan came rushing out from behind the curtain, as if the demon dogs were biting at his heels.

"We need to leave. Now." Shoving her bag into her hands, Braegan grabbed Rie, forcefully moving her toward the front door. She tried to jerk free. His grip didn't slacken, his nails biting into her flesh.

"What's going on?"

Braegan didn't answer. He dragged her through the front door. Rie twisted, spinning beneath his outstretched arm and breaking his hold. The pixies zipped to her side.

"Where is Garran?" Rie glared at Braegan. Her hands hovered at her sides, itching to draw steel. She wouldn't be going anywhere without some kind of an explanation.

A loud crash reverberated through the building. Rie spun, hands dropping to her blades. A giant of a man hurtled toward them, barreling through display cases and mannequins. At least three hundred-fifty pounds of solid muscle, he topped seven feet, even while bent in his charge.

"Run!" Braegan shoved Rie ahead of him. She stumbled, but found her footing before she fell.

Rie turned and faced the oncoming threat, removing the three black throwing knives from her satchel. The barbarian crashed through the glass of the front window, moving as if he hadn't felt a thing. He was mindless, gone berserk in the heat of a hunt. A woman screamed. Rie took aim.

"Fuck." Braegan took a position beside her, vibrating with energy. Rie set him out of her mind, her concentration focused entirely on the beast before her. Three rapid flicks of her wrist. The knives found their targets, landing center of the beast's chest with an audible thunk. He kept coming.

Rie ran to meet him. Blades cleared their sheaths. She closed in, slicing her khukuris across his midsection. He blocked, golden bracers clanging against steel, keeping her knives from reaching their targets. Niinka darted in, harassing his face. A roundhouse kick drove two of the throwing knives deeper into the beast's pectoral. The man stumbled, gasping. His right arm dangled, loose. Rie struck again. The man blocked, not entirely out of the fight. A claw scraped across Rie's back as she spun away, the new vest proving its worth.

Braegan appeared on the man's back, his arms and legs wrapped around the beast's midsection. His jaw gaped impossibly wide; long white fangs snapped down and into the beast's neck. Blood gushed, sliding out the sides of Braegan's mouth even as his throat spasmed, gulping the red liquid in heaving pulls.

The man lunged and flailed, trying to dislodge Braegan. Inch-long claws erupted from Braegan's hands and hooked into the beast's pectorals. Rie slid in to cut across the monster's hamstrings, sending him to his knees. Braegan rode him down, continuing to feed. His eyes closed, ecstasy softening his face like a baby at the breast.

The pixies took their share of blood and flesh from the man's exposed torso. His good arm barely moved in protest, the fight eventually leaving his body. Had it not been for Braegan holding him upright, the man would have fallen to the ground, unconscious.

Rie backed away, unable to take her eyes off the gruesome scene. She had witnessed the pixies feeding countless times, but this was more intimate, and somehow worse. Lines of red coursed down the beast's chest and the coppery stench permeated the air around them. Rie shuddered, realizing for the first time the danger she courted.

The blood flow slowed. Braegan disengaged, snapping his fangs back into his mouth. Blood coated his chin and stained the white collar of his dress shirt. He extracted a black cloth from a pocket, wiping his face clean.

"What?" Braegan demanded, meeting Rie's gaze across the wide expanse of cobbled street.

Rie lowered her hand, uncovering her mouth and nose. She shook her head. "Nothing."

She swallowed her disgust and approached the fallen giant. Knees bent behind him at an awkward angle, the man was dead. Rie placed a hand on his chest to confirm, but the heart couldn't pump without blood, and Braegan had done a good job of draining his victim.

Blood drunk and exhausted, Niinka and Possn crawled up her arm and into one of the vest pockets. Cuddled together like littermates, the pixies fell asleep in seconds.

Rie clenched her fist, her fingers brushing through a thick pelt of blond fur. The man was only half dressed, wearing a brown leather kilt, boots, and a golden mask that covered his entire head.

"He's a rougarou," Rie said as she stripped away his

mask. The man's face was covered in more of the blond fur, lips protruding from a severe underbite. His nose, black and shining wetly, was smushed flat, deep wrinkles radiating out beneath dull brown eyes.

"Ugly. No wonder he wore a mask." Braegan bent to pick up the discarded metal. "Gold plated iron. Mostly decorative though, considering he wore no other armor."

"I think he's from the Upper Realm." Rie opened his kilt purse, looking for a clue to his identity or his master. "The rougarous are sometimes hired as bodyguards to the nobles of the High Court. This one doesn't have any clan markings, though, so I can't be sure."

They found nothing but a few copper coins and a lock of brown hair in the bag. No further clues. Rie put it all back out of respect for the soul of the fallen warrior.

"Interesting. We should go."

"I'm not going anywhere," Rie said. Braegan still owed her an explanation. With the rougarou dead, there was time to talk. Something had happened in the back room, and she wanted to know what it was.

"Someone may have called the Guard. You can't be here when they arrive," Braegan said.

Dusting off her hands, Rie drew her knives. "What happened in there?" she asked, keeping her voice level and calm, but lacing her words with a thread of command.

"It doesn't matter, we need to go."

"What about Garran?"

"He's a competent fighter, and they're after you, not him. Plus, the guy was badly injured before I left."

"What guy?"

Braegan sighed, running both hands through already mussed hair.

"When I walked into the workroom, I found Garran being interrogated by two men, this...rougarou...and another man. He was wearing a cloak and gloves, so I didn't see him, but he was asking about *you*. He insisted you're a traitor."

"They've already found me, then."

"Guess so. I distracted them long enough for Garran to stab the guy in the cloak with a dagger. He told me to run, to make you safe. Which is why I have to get you back to the Crossroads. Tharbatiron will be able to protect you."

"I don't think so." Rie strode back toward the front door of the shop, but didn't make it three steps before Braegan stood in front of her.

"We can't go back in there," he said, gripping her arm, but more gently this time. "The assassin is either dead or long gone. Garran can handle the clean up here. You don't want to be here with the guard arrives."

"Where's your loyalty? Garran's your best friend," Rie said, pointing at the door with her khukuri. The flickering amber light of a lantern danced across the blade and front bolster, looking as if the Tiwaz rune was lit with its own internal fire.

Braegan hesitated, glancing back at the shop, then shook his head. "He'll have it under control," Braegan insisted, sounding like he was trying to convince himself more than Rie.

She pushed him further. "Then why isn't he out here? We need to find out what happened, make sure Garran isn't injured before we leave." Rie shook off Braegan's loosening grip. "I'm going in." She hoped he followed, but in the end it didn't matter. She couldn't live with herself if she let a near-stranger fight her battles for her.

CHAPTER NINE

"I smell blood," Braegan whispered, his normally laughing eyes serious. He sniffed, letting the door swing closed behind him, the chime jingling without a care for the violence inside. "Sidhe blood."

Rie's right thumb twitched against her thigh. She spun the naked blade in her hand to hide the nervous tic. Like a shark, Braegan could probably identify a single drop of blood in an ocean of water, and be able to tell you who it belonged to, their blood type, and if they should see a physician.

Stepping forward, Rie's foot crunched through broken glass. All but two of the lamps had been extinguished in the rougarou's rampage. The shadows dancing in the corners made it near impossible to see what littered the floor.

"I'll lead," Braegan whispered, moving around her without a sound and wending his way through the shop.

Rie followed, even as she hissed in protest. "Braegan, you have no weapons. No armor. I'll go first."

Without saying a word, Braegan flipped a short, thick knife out of a hidden sheath. He put it back just as quickly, then flicked his nails, drawing attention to the inch-long points that graced each spindly finger. With a quick flash of fang, he dashed through the curtain, a speeding blur to Rie's human eyes. Growling beneath her breath, Rie cursed the sidhe. Before the curtain dropped, she was through the entry and stepping to the side, placing her back to a wall.

The workroom blazed with light. Her eyes adjusted quickly. Garran lay on the floor, soft white bone showing through a wide slit at his throat, dark red blood pooled beneath him. No one else was there.

"No," Braegan moaned, approaching Garran's body one pained step at a time. Rie stayed on guard, watching the exits to ensure they wouldn't be taken by surprise. Braegan knelt, ignoring the blood that soaked into the knees of his tailored black pants.

"Gods, I'm so sorry. I shouldn't have run." He pressed a hand to Garran's chest and his head dropped, hanging between his shoulders.

"Is there no chance for recovery?" Rie asked. She had heard amazing stories of blood sidhe healing powers; men and women who had regrown limbs lost in battle, walked away from a dozen arrows in the back, and even survived gut wounds after pushing their intestines back into their stomach cavity.

"It's too late," Braegan replied, voice trembling. "We're too late."

Giving Braegan a moment to collect himself and grieve for his friend, Rie paced the room. It reminded her of Lhéwen's workshop in Etsiramun, and a pang of homesickness clenched her heart. Six low worktables, each at least eight feet long and surrounded by six short stools, filled the space. Long gas lamps hung from the ceiling and provided the intense light necessary to produce the exquisite craftsmanship Rie had seen in the shop beyond. But now the room lay abandoned, in disarray. Unfinished garments, shoes, and jewelry were left stranded on the open tables, and several of the stools were knocked over. A precision magnifying glass lay broken on the jeweler's table, glass shards reflecting the light above and mixing with the jewels left out on a black velvet cushion.

Her foot slid on the tile floor. Catching herself, she found a thin red smear beneath her boot. She crouched to get a better look. Red drops scattered across the floor, leading through the open back door.

"Braegan," Rie whispered. He didn't look up. She tried again, a little louder. "Braegan, there's blood going out the door."

Braegan's head lifted, his eyes glazed with grief. "What?"

"If we hurry, we might be able to catch him."

Braegan's pupils dilated and his nostrils flared. He cocked his head to the side, sniffing with his mouth open and fangs extended. "Elf."

"It was a high elf, but he's already g-gone," a small voice squeaked from beneath the cabinet. Braegan hissed, and Rie drew her blades. Peering into the shadowed depths, Rie tried to make out the speaker.

"Who are you?" she asked, her tone demanding an immediate response.

"P-Plink," the terrified female voice replied.

"How do you know he was an elf?"

"His m-magic. He forced Master Garran to his knees without a touch. He couldn't move, even when the knife pressed against his throat. The cloaked man sent the big one after you two, then started asking questions."

"What did he want to know?"

"Where you were staying, who you were with, how you got here. Master Garran didn't know much, and didn't say anything. So the cloaked man k-killed him."

Rie gentled her tone, "Can you come out so we can see

you? I won't hurt you, and I prefer not to talk to the shadows."

A small form, slightly bigger than the pixies at about six inches tall, detached itself from the wall and came into the light. With large round eyes set above a wide pink nose, a horn protruding from behind each broad ear, and a body covered in light brown fur, the imp looked like a cross between a large rat and a tiny goat. A goat wearing a blue floral print dress with white ruffles.

"Hello," Rie said, sheathing her blade. Imps could be pranksters and spies, but not particularly violent.

The imp hiccoughed, a tear running down her fuzzy face as she bobbed her head in response.

"You saw everything?" Rie asked.

"Yes." Her voice was soft and high pitched, a slight lisp marring the 's'. "There was no one here for Master Garran to feed from, to heal himself." The little imp clutched her hands to her chest. "Everyone left when the fight started. I could do nothing but watch his soul leave." More tears poured out, and soon the imp's fur was soaked and matted. Rie handed her a small cloth from the counter, which Plink wrapped around her shoulders.

"The other workers didn't help?" Rie asked.

Braegan watched, but stayed near Garran's body and said nothing.

"They have no loyalty. No honor. They work for anyone who will pay them."

"What happened?"

"The leprechauns let a cloaked man and his bodyguard in the back door," Plink began.

"They didn't ask any questions?"

Braegan answered before the imp could speak. "Garran had a side business in sex toys and BDSM costumes. Some of the more sensitive nobles liked to keep their dealings anonymous."

Plink nodded, her ears flopping. "But when Master Garran greeted them, the bodyguard grabbed him and held him up by the throat. The leprechauns ran away. That's when Master Braegan came in."

Rie lifted an eyebrow at Braegan, but his eyes were wet. She didn't press him.

"The bodyguard tried to grab him, but Master Braegan was too quick. While the guard was distracted, Master Garran slipped free and stabbed the cloaked man in the side, but the cloaked man pushed him away. He said *'the woman is an Upper Realm traitor. Give her to me, or die.'* Master Garran told Braegan to run, and he did."

Braegan shook his head. "I should have stayed."

"Why are you still here?" Rie asked Plink.

"Garran was my Master, my friend. I have nowhere else to go. His soul is gone, but his body must be tended."

"I will see to that," Braegan said.

"Thank you, Master Braegan. You are a good friend. Master Garran always said you were one of the few who never failed to see both sides of the deal."

Braegan coughed and looked away.

"What was the service you provided to Garran?" Rie asked.

"I did what he asked, mostly watching his customers to make sure they didn't steal." Her gaze dropped away.

"Did you spy on me?"

The imp nodded, snuggling deeper into the washcloth, as if the soft material would protect her from trouble. "Please don't be offended," she whined. "I watch everyone. I make sure Master Garran is not cheated, make sure he knows what goes on in his shop. I am... was...his eyes and ears."

"That's okay, Plink." Rie pushed aside the imp's armor to see her face. "I have my own set of friendly eyes and ears." Niinka and Possn popped their heads out of Rie's pocket and gave a lazy wave, their eyes still half-closed.

Plink's answering smile appeared hopeful.

"Can you tell me anything else about the cloaked man?" Rie asked.

Plink nodded. "He was careful not to be seen, but he was definitely a High Elf. He talked funny. Like you. And he was very tall. He wore gloves and his face was hidden by his hood, but the cloak material was extremely lightweight and shiny black."

"Spidersilk," Rie said.

"His shoes looked like slippers, and the broach holding his cloak together resembled a falling star."

"What of his wound?" Braegan asked, returning to the conversation. "I saw Garran stick him, and there's a blood trail. What happened?"

"He was wounded, but he walked out of here on his own, after..." Plink hiccoughed again, holding back the tears this time.

"It's okay, Plink," Rie murmured.

"No, no, I must finish," Plink replied, taking a deep breath. "He pulled out the knife after cutting Master Garran. He bled, but he was able to walk."

"Do you know what direction he took from the back door?" Rie asked.

"He turned left, toward the center of the city."

"And no one else came?"

"No." Plink shook her head.

"We'll see that the cloaked man is punished."

"Thank you, Lady. Thank you."

"Now, what do we do with you?" Rie asked with a smile.

"Could you use another set of eyes and ears?" At Rie's hesitation, Plink hopped forward and pressed her hands against Rie's bent knee. "I can also help with household chores, and make a decent stitch, if you have any sewing that needs doing."

"I travel a lot, Plink, and I'm not from here. Are you sure you want to join me?" Rie asked. "Eventually, I will return to the Upper Realm."

"I would follow you," Plink replied, hope surging in her eyes. "I will be your lady in waiting, if you'll allow it."

"In that case, you are most welcome to join me."

"Thank you!" A fresh wave of tears slid down her cheeks.

"But you'll have to stop crying, or I'll be forced to swim everywhere," Rie teased.

Plink nodded and smiled through her wet fur. "I'll do my best."

"What about Garran? What should we do?"

"Nothing. I'll stay here and wait for the guard. I'm sure they're on their way." An edge cut through Braegan's tone. "You need to go back to the Crossroads before they arrive. Plink will be your guide. If you have a way to call your pixie friends, do it, or at least wake up those two before you go. You need to be careful and stay out of sight as much as possible. When you get there, stay there. And send a pixie back here to let me know you're safe. I'll meet you at half past four tomorrow to take you to the smithy."

Rie crossed her arms. It was sort of sweet that he seemed so concerned, but it was unnecessary.

"You don't need to be here when the guard comes, either. It will just raise more questions."

"Trust me, they won't bother me about it." Braegan's humorless smile stretched his lips to thin lines.

Rie narrowed her eyes. Something wasn't adding up. "You should come with me."

"I can't. I have...there are things that must be done. But you need to go. Now. I'll see you tomorrow."

Suddenly suspicious, Rie decided to cut ties with

Braegan. She would ask one of the pixies to monitor him, but she wouldn't involve him further in her investigation. "No, that's all right. I appreciate your help to this point, but I don't need an escort to meet Prince Daenor at the smithy."

Braegan's jaw clenched. "I can't let you go alone."

"You've lost a friend because of me. I won't drag you farther into my troubles."

"It's too late for that." Braegan slammed a hand down on the counter, causing the wood to vibrate and Plink to disappear with a pop of displaced air.

Rie didn't even flinch. "I won't be bullied. Prince Daenor issued a single invitation. Thank you, but you've done enough."

Braegan took a steadying breath. "Nuriel..."

"I prefer Rie. After what we've been through, I think you can use my common name."

"Rie, then. I don't doubt your capabilities, but you need someone to watch your back. I don't trust the prince. He's not a bad guy, but he's the Commander of the Shadow Guard. And with everything that's happened today...well, I don't want to go through it again. I'll be there tomorrow at half past four to be a second set of eyes. That's all."

Rie's stomach fluttered and her resolve melted in the face of Braegan's pain and worry. "You can escort me to the smithy, but I want to arrive early and you must be out of sight before the prince arrives."

Braegan nodded. "I'll see you tomorrow at fourth bell."

CHAPTER TEN

To Rie, a smithy implied a forge, an anvil, and maybe a few apprentices, not a compound surrounded by fifteen foot walls topped with razor wire. The term 'fortress' barely covered it. Two swarthy guards stood on either side of the massive reinforced gate. Viscous dark blood left trails down their battle-scarred faces, splashing down on the cobbled stone beneath their feet.

"What are they?" Rie asked Braegan, as they paced around the stronghold.

"Redcaps."

Her eyes widened. She had heard the stories of redcap blood lust. Though no bigger than humans, redcaps were notorious warriors and sell-swords who cared only for the glory of battle and the thrill of the kill. Their caps were magically drenched in the blood of their victims; the more blood, the more kills. It was also rumored that they ate what they killed. Whatever they killed. That they acted as guards, instead of out on a battlefield somewhere, meant these redcaps were well paid and, most likely, kept entertained with frequent unwelcome visitors.

The guards eyed Rie, watching her every breath as she paced across the street. She couldn't blame them for being suspicious. She and Braegan had walked the perimeter of the smithy, scrutinizing the security and considering her possible escape routes in case there was trouble inside. Unfortunately, it looked like the only way in or out was through the front gate and the redcap guards.

"Watch your back in there," Braegan warned. "It could be a trap."

"I'm only going to talk to the man, and I'll be with the prince."

Braegan sighed. "Daenor isn't all he's cracked up to be. He's prince, yes, and Commander of the Guard, but they're a bunch of misfits with very little standing in court. Glorified bodyguards and policemen, really. He might not be able to protect you as well as he thinks. Be careful." Braegan surprised Rie. He pulled her into a hug, his arms a symbol of solid support, but the hint of bitterness in his voice couldn't be masked.

Rie pulled away. "I will."

"You're sure you don't want me to stick around for awhile? I can wait for you."

"I know how to get back, but I do have a favor to ask."

"Anything."

"Take Hiinto, Niinka, and Tiik with you. Keep them out of trouble." Rie had explained her hesitation about taking all of them into the smithy and leaving Braegan alone. After the scene at Garran's shop, she felt a niggling sense that something strange was going on with him. She wanted to know more. Niinka and Hiinto had been thrilled to have a job that would let them ask as many questions as they wanted. Meanwhile, Tiik thought it would be fun to annoy the blood sidhe. That left Gikl and Possn acting as Rie's invisible bodyguards.

In truth, that had been Rie's plan all along. As the quietest and least mischievous of the bunch, Gikl and

Possn could be trusted to reveal themselves only if absolutely necessary. Until then, Possn had camouflaged herself as an elaborate black lacquer and ruby jeweled hair pin attached to her braided bun, and Gikl clasped the buckle of her black belt in matching splendor. Together, they looked like nothing more than fancy accessories.

"Seriously?"

"You mean you don't like our company?" Niinka hovered in front of Braegan, her hands on her hips and an exaggerated frown on her thin lips.

Tiik sat on Braegan's shoulder, crossing one leg over the other. "Did you have something better to do?"

"Well, no. I mean, yes, I need to meet with my family to plan the next venture to the Human Realm."

Niinka clapped her hands. "Fun! We can meet your parents!"

"Ugh. Boring," Hiinto complained. "Can't we go somewhere interesting, like that bar where we met you?"

"Not a good idea."

"Please, Braegan. Keep them out of trouble. Just for the time I'm gone." Rie wasn't opposed to begging, if it got her what she wanted.

"Fine. But you owe me."

Rie grinned. "I'll see you back at the inn, then?"

"Sure. Try not to take too long." Braegan brushed a thumb across Rie's cheek. "I'll be waiting." He turned and walked away.

Unable to hear anything in her shock at the sensitive gesture, Rie watched until the group turned a corner. When they were out of sight down the cobbled road, Rie unlocked her muscles and sat on a low stone wall to wait for the prince. She didn't wait long.

Clopping toward her on steel gray hooves, Daenor rode a beast that was part war-horse, part dragon. Its face was long and narrow, small slitted nostrils snorting sulphur-scented steam into the already humid air. Three flexible whiskers protruded from each side of the beast's head, as if the trunks of six elephants had been attached to a lizard skull. The monster was covered in silver scales from the tip of its nose to the tip of its serpentine tail, but from withers to hooves it wore fur. Two knobby bumps resembling unformed wings protruded from its back, and half of its serpentine tail was covered in needle-thin spikes. As they approached, Rie stood and craned her neck. The creature's back rose above her head, its face higher still.

Shoulders tense, Rie struggled against her impulse to flee. She clenched her jaw, frozen in position. The dragon-horse snorted at her, and one of the shorter whiskers near its mouth reached out to touch her shoulder. The whisker slid along her arm, curling around her forearm with the softest of squeezes, then drifted away, almost like a handshake for a creature that didn't have hands.

Daenor's deep chuckle startled her out of astonishment. "He likes you." He slid off the dragon-horse's back and landed with a graceful thud. "Rie, may I introduce you to Turant. He is a longma of the line of Lúroch."

"Greetings." Unsure of the appropriate protocol, Rie dipped her chin in the dragon-horse's direction. The creature snorted again, and Daenor chuckled.

"Turant wants to know if you've ever met a longma before."

"No, I can't say I've had the pleasure," Rie replied. "How are you speaking with him? Does he understand my speech?"

"Turant and I have a telepathic bond, but yes, he understands the common tongue."

"Well then, I'm very glad to meet you, Turant."

Turant nodded his head up and down several times before settling. "He says he looks forward to knowing you better. Quite the compliment." Daenor turned to pat Turant's back. "But now, we should probably get going. I'll call you when I'm done." The last was directed at Turant. He flapped his stubby wings a few times and meandered off to lay on a small pile of steaming volcanic rock nearby, wrapping his scaled and spiked tail around his snout.

"Or, you can stay right there and wait, as if you have nothing better to do," Daenor mumbled, shaking his head at his mount. Turant snorted, and closed his eyes, seeming content to take a nap.

"You look different," Daenor said, turning his attention back to Rie.

"Tharbatiron thought my dress wasn't intimidating enough, but after trying on this amlug hide, I can't say I'm upset about spending the coin."

"I'd like to thank the tailor." Daenor's eyes twinkled. "But I liked the dress, too, so maybe it's not the tailor's skill I should be complimenting."

Rie ducked her head, unable to contain her smile even as her heart clenched for Garran.

"And where are your little friends hiding?"

Gikl responded with a flash of yellow and a wave. "Possn is riding on my braid, but the rest are back at the inn." Rie shrugged. "I didn't want them bringing trouble here."

"Good idea." Daenor examined his gear, pulling each blade from its sheath to test the weight and draw. Rie couldn't help but admire the play of muscle under his tight, long-sleeved shirt as his hands found and removed blade after blade. He carried a short sword in a sheath across his back, a dagger on his left thigh, and black bracers on each forearm with knives tucked into the front and back of each, handles pointed toward his elbow. A total of six knives that she could see, and probably more hidden elsewhere.

"You're not carrying guns today?" she asked, still admiring his physique. It couldn't hurt to look, right?

"Good eye. No, I won't carry guns in front of Master Whixle, and if you have any mechanical weapons, I suggest you remove them now." Rie shook her head. She had trained a bit with human weapons, but preferred her blades. "Whixle seems to think guns are weapons for the unskilled, and refuses to see anyone who carries them."

"You disagree?"

"Anything that will kill my enemy and protect my own skin is useful. Why discriminate? But I humor him when I'm here."

Daenor glanced up after sheathing the military knife on his thigh. Hand still on the grip, he faced Rie and lowered his head to look her in the eyes. "Before we go in, I need to know the truth."

Rie took an involuntary step back. "What do you mean?"

"You're not from Nalakadr, that much is obvious. Who are you?"

"I told you, my name is Rie."

"I need more than that." Daenor paced forward, pushing Rie into the wall she had been sitting on.

Rie's heart raced, this time in fear. Her hands dropped to the grips of her blades. He obviously knew something of the truth.

"You have to tell me why you're here, and what it is you want. Otherwise, I will be forced to arrest you."

Truth.

Startled by the ringing in her brain, Rie nearly stumbled over the wall. Thinking Daenor had done something to influence her, her eyes narrowed. "For what?" She hadn't done anything wrong, at least, nothing he could possibly know about.

"I don't want to arrest you, I really don't, but if you draw those blades, I'll have no choice."

Truth. The words rang through her brain again, but this time, she realized they were coming from some part of her psyche. Somehow, she knew that he was being honest with her.

"What are you doing here?" He enunciated the words carefully.

Letting go of her blades, Rie forced her shoulders to relax. "My name is Nuriel Lhethannien, but I prefer to be called Rie. I am a changeling from the Upper Realm."

Daenor clenched his jaw. Before he could say anything else, Rie pushed on with the story. She had no choice but to trust that he would be reasonable.

"It's true, what I told you before. I am investigating an attempted murder. My own, in fact." Rie paused, gauging his reaction. He didn't draw his blade, just tilted his head to the side and lifted an eyebrow.

"Go on."

Rie told the story as quickly as possible, laying out the facts from the first day on the beach, to the fight with the rougarou. "I swear, I am not a spy, and I'm not a traitor. My only chance to avoid execution is to find out who hired the assassins. And that's why I need to see Master Whixle, and soon. They already know I'm here."

"Say I believe you, why shouldn't I arrest you? You *are* a traitor, just for crossing the portals."

"Ask yourself, why would anyone want to kill a low-level messenger in the Human Realm? What purpose could my death possibly serve? The Human Realm is neutral territory; both sides agreed to keep the war from reaching human soil. Had the assassins succeeded, Lord

Garamaen would have discovered my body practically on his doorstep."

Daenor rubbed a hand across his chin. "You think someone from Nalakadr is trying to start a war?"

"Not necessarily, but it's one idea. I need to know who commissioned the blades from Master Whixle. Once I have the assassin's identity, I can try to find out who hired him, and then figure out the reason why. That's my plan, anyway."

"Well, I guess it's as good as any. Let's go." Daenor stepped back and turned toward the gate of the smithy.

"That's it?" After what she had just revealed, he should have more questions, be angry with her for lying, or at least skeptical.

Daenor shrugged. "I knew most of the story before you told, me, but I needed to hear you say it. Of course, my dear half-siblings failed to mention that this could be the opening gambit of a larger game, but I suppose that's to be expected."

"Your half-siblings?"

"Yes. The heirs." Daenor sneered the last and curled a lip in distaste. "Faerleithril and Faernodir. Thirty years younger, and a bit twisted in the head. With luck, you'll never meet them."

"How did they know? How are they involved?"

"I'm not sure, but they ordered me to apprehend you. Since I'm now with you, I'm counting that as mission complete. Whatever scheme they have in motion, I'm not playing. I won't send a refugee back to her home world for execution. But right now we need to focus on figuring this out before they send someone less discriminating after you."

Rie's heart sank and her feet stopped moving. The heirs knew she was here, and the king would soon, if he didn't already. She was doomed.

Some expression of fear, or disbelief must have shown on her face, because Daenor grabbed her shoulders and shook her gently. "The best thing you can do for yourself right now, is solve this puzzle. The heirs might be crazy, but the king is reasonable. Usually. Just keep moving."

Rie nodded, wanting to believe him, but unable to tame the mounting dread that she would soon be facing death. Burying it out of mind was the best she could achieve.

Giving her a rough pat on the back, Daenor urged her toward the solid wood and wrought iron entrance to the smithy. The redcaps crossed their pikes and glared, not a word exchanged.

"I have an appointment," Daenor said.

"Name," the redcap on the left demanded, his voice a gravelly rumble. The stench of raw sewage and maggot infested meat wafted toward her on his exhalation. Rie swallowed the bile that threatened to crawl up her throat and attempted to hide her disgust, not sure she achieved it.

Daenor made a low rumbling noise in the back of his throat and his eyes rolled. "Prince Daenor Shadowsson, Commander of the Guard," he replied. "As if you don't know who I am." The redcap repeated his name into a speaker box at the side of the gate.

"Approved," a nasally voice responded. The redcaps stepped back and the gate swung open, allowing their entry. They stepped through into another world.

Inside the gate, Master Whixle had put together his own tiny city. Gremlins of all shapes and sizes ran back and forth across the courtyard, their green skin sagging on bow-legged frames. Some pushed wheelbarrows full of ore or other materials, others practiced with the freshly made blades, still others loaded coal into the furnace on the left.

Unlike most of the gremlins in the compound, the one running toward them wore a dress shirt and trousers, and carried a thick ledger under one arm. "Prince Daenor. Welcome," he said, his voice the same odd nasally voice from the speaker. Sharp, serrated teeth clacked in his mouth. "But who are you?"

"My guest," Daenor replied before Rie could say anything.

"Guests are not welcome."

"Yes, well, I invited her anyway." Daenor smirked at the much smaller gremlin. If there had been any doubt he was royal, it was eradicated with that one comment.

"Hmm. Well, I suppose Master Whixle will decide her fate. And yours. Come." The gremlin turned, his clawed feet digging furrows into the ground.

"This is quite impressive," Rie shouted as they passed through the courtyard and into the forge proper, where the roar of the flames and banging of hammers made it near impossible to hear anything. The uppermost branches of four giant elm trees had grown together, creating a roof over the area. Three large gremlins worked the massive bellows, blowing air into a furnace the size of a small cottage. Heat waves billowed from the opening and radiated off the external steel. Several smaller gremlins placed rods of iron into the furnace to heat, removing the rods that were already red hot and pounding them flat. "But I thought Master Whixle did all his own work."

"He does," their guide responded. "These are his apprentices. Some people need blades faster or cheaper than Master Whixle is able or willing to provide. The apprentices take up the extra work."

"I see. And they are all gremlins?" Rie asked.

"Yes. With the exception of the guards, Master Whixle only employs gremlins. He is a true paragon of our race, advancing our interests and improving our image amongst the fae." The guide uttered the words with religious adoration. "Gremlins will no longer be scavengers and malcontents, known only for breaking technology in our search for understanding. No, we are finally becoming what we were meant to be, valuable innovators in the field of ironworking. Elvish blades are beautiful, but ours are designed to amplify the abilities of the owner. No one else has that technology."

Rie considered his words. If what he said was true, she was lucky to be alive. The throwing knives now in her possession shouldn't have missed their mark.

Passing beneath the elm trees, the group moved beyond the large forge and into a smaller, separate area where a lone man bent over a short sword. The blade glistened in the flickering red forge light, appearing as if sheathed in fire. The hilt was deep black, so dark it seemed to be absorbing the light around it. The gremlin sat polishing the blade, fully absorbed in his work to the exclusion of all else.

"Ahem," the guide coughed into his hand, attempting to get the master's attention. He tried again after waiting a moment, while the master continued to work on the blade. "Master Whixle, sir, Prince Daenor has arrived. With an uninvited guest."

Finally, Whixle looked up. There was little to distinguish him from the rest of his workforce. He was shorter than Rie by at least a head, but thick with corded muscle from working the forge. His limbs were long and bent, like an ape, but his fingers and toes were capped with pointed talons. Despite his obvious strength, his green skin still sagged off his body. Like most of the gremlins in the forge, he wore a dirty brown cloth wrapped around his waist and legs, with a leather apron that protected him from chest to knees. Burn marks scorched the skin of his arms in several places, and a long thin line etched his face from above his right eyebrow, across his nose, to end beneath his lower left cheekbone.

His voice was a low growl that somehow managed to echo over the roaring forge. "Throw them out. The prince can come back some other day, without her."

CHAPTER ELEVEN

Frantic to stay, Rie blurted out the only thing she could think of. "Four days ago assassins ambushed me. One of them carried knives with your mark."

Slitted eyes narrowed in fury. "How my knives are used is of no concern to me. I'll give you three-seconds to turn and walk away, or the redcaps can have you."

Four guards stepped out of the shadows, pikes lowered. Rie's hands dropped to the grips of her blades. The handles warmed to her touch, and Rie got the odd sense that they wanted to be used.

Rie laced her words with all of the urgency she could muster. "Please. I only have a few questions. It won't take more than a minute."

"Who are you?" Whixle's gaze targeted her hands on her knives. She let go, spreading her fingers wide to show no intent to harm. The harsh lines around Whixle's eyes softened and the anger faded. "Ah! My beauties have returned."

"Excuse me?" Rie asked.

Master Whixle gestured to her knives with a knobby hand. "Have you blooded them, yet?"

"You made my khukuris?" Rie pulled the right knife from its sheath. Sure enough, three little dashes adorned the blade near the hilt.

"My greatest achievement, thus far."

Rie frowned. How could Curuthannor have commissioned the blades? She was sure he would never deal in the Shadow Realm, it would put too much at risk. "I didn't know. They were a gift. But they're magnificent blades, Master Whixle. Thank you for your work." Sometimes a little flattery went a long way.

Master Whixle's mouth split into a vicious smile, revealing long yellow serrated teeth. "The client wouldn't tell me who they were for, but it looks like they fit. I hope you're worthy of them. And I suppose, given the coin spent, I can answer a few questions."

He turned his attention to Daenor. "But first, Prince Daenor, your sword is finally ready." He held out the freshly polished blade on one arm. "I've imbued the blade with as much fire as possible, while still keeping its strength and edge. The hilt has been covered with black dragon skin for improved grip and limited visibility, and the sheath is made of the same. Once blooded by your hand, it will respond only to you."

Daenor grasped the hilt of the dual-edged straight sword and lifted it from Whixle's arms. He swung the blade out to the side, pointing away from Rie and their guide. His hand tightened on the hilt, and fire surged along the length of the blade. Daenor's amber eyes gleamed, filled with their own flames. He flowed through a complex form that started slow and built in speed, until the blade disappeared and Daenor danced within a blazing tornado.

Rie stood transfixed. She had never seen anything so beautiful. Daenor leapt and prowled, slicing high and low, the inferno following his form like a sparkler in the night. Even Curuthannor would be hard pressed to match the speed and precision of Daenor's movements, and Curuthannor was the best swordsman in the Upper Realm. Adding in the fire was almost too beautiful to comprehend.

It could have been hours, but might have been minutes, when Daenor began to slow, his movements changing from a whirlwind into a gentle breeze that caressed bare skin. Rie sighed, her own heart rate slowing.

"He has skill," Master Whixle said from behind her right shoulder.

"Yes." There was nothing else to say on the matter. He was brilliant.

"So, do you have the knife?"

The words jolted Rie back to reality. She had a purpose, and it didn't include admiring men so far out of her reach, she might as well be in another dimension. If only there was a realm in which she belonged. Rie squeezed her eyes shut, erasing that line of thinking.

It took her a moment to understand the question, but eventually she realized he was asking for the assassin's blade. Rie nodded, and Whixle motioned for her to join him at his worktable. They sat on two low wooden stools and Whixle began polishing yet another weapon, this one a small boot dagger, maybe six inches long, including the hilt.

Rie placed the knife on the table within Whixle's line of sight. He glanced at the blade without pausing in his work.

"Yes, I remember this one. He was a new client. These were his first purchases from me, or at least from me directly and not one of my apprentices. He had just received his first off-world contract."

"Who was he?" Rie asked, impatient. She was finally getting somewhere.

"Blood sidhe, I believe, but one of the most human

looking I've ever seen," Whixle continued, as if he hadn't heard her question. "Dark hair, dark eyes. Very average."

"Perfect for an assassin working in the Human Realm."

"I suppose he's dead now, hmm?" Whixle lifted a bony eyebrow without looking up.

"Yes. What was his name? Who was he working for?" She needed more information.

"See, this is why I don't make knives for lesser fighters. It's a waste."

"Master Whixle, I need to know the assassin's name and employer."

"And I need to maintain client confidentiality." Whixle might not have fire in his blood like Daenor, but she felt the heat in his gaze all the same.

"What will it take to earn the information?" Everything and everyone had a price.

"My client list is confidential. No exceptions."

Rie leaned forward, clasping her hands on the table. "Perhaps he mentioned the details of the contract, or the name of his employer? No one could fault you for repeating a simple conversation that wasn't held in confidence."

Whixle smirked, scratching his bald head with a single black claw. "As I was saying, he was very human looking. He was good with a blade, not great, but good, and he wanted simple but effective weapons. I offered him the services of my apprentices, but he insisted that he needed master quality. He had the money, and the blades wouldn't take long, so I agreed. When he returned to pick up his order, he let slip that he had been hired by an elf lord to kill a changeling messenger. He thought it would be an easy kill."

"He was wrong."

"Clearly."

"Do you know which lord?" Finished testing his blade,

Daenor sat next to Rie at the table. She glanced at him out of the corner of her eye, noticing that not a single bead of sweat dotted his forehead. He didn't even have the decency to be out of breath.

"Not a clue. My client didn't say. However, I can tell you that he paid with gold from the Upper Realm."

"How do you know?" Rie asked. She'd asked Braegan about Shadow Realm coinage, afraid she wouldn't be able to use her Upper Realm coin without being discovered. It turned out, both realms still used the same standard metal weights. The chits were flat pieces of copper, silver or gold, stamped with the weight, but nothing else. Most merchants used a scale to confirm the weight, but otherwise it was near impossible to fake currency, particularly since most fae couldn't outright lie.

"People forget that all metal has a signature. A good metalsmith can separate the impurities and determine their identity, thus determining their origin. It's quite simple really. The gold chits that my client used were formed from ore found only in the high mountains of the Upper Realm.

"However, my client also quite proudly told me that his employer was a regular visitor to the Shadow Court. Make of it what you will." Whixle set aside the blade he was working on, and stood, leaning forward onto the table.

"I believe it's time for you to go. My next client will be arriving shortly. Enjoy your trip home. I've informed my guards that the one who strikes a death blow can commission his own weapon. Touch the wood of the main gate, and you're safe." He shooed them away with a wave of his hand.

Rie turned slowly in her seat, gazing out through the large forge and into the courtyard. Redcaps lined up in rows at least three deep. They were waiting.

"All the redcaps?" Rie wondered aloud.

"This is sadistic, even for you," Daenor said.

Master Whixle chuckled, the sound grating down Rie's spine. "Maybe, but this is the price you pay for my work, and my answers."

"And the stacks of gold."

"That too." Whixle smiled, a twinkle in his eye. "I have to get my entertainment somehow. And now I'm going up top to watch. The apprentices will do the same." Every gremlin within range quickly dropped what they were doing and ran toward the nearest elm tree, scrambling up the trunk. They sat on the branches, like a congregation of vultures above their next meal.

Rie and Daenor stared out at the redcaps. They must have been told to avoid damaging the forge, because not one had ventured beneath the elm overhang. Several wore feral grins, others had a neutral but determined look of concentration. All of them carried naked weapons in their hands.

"Shit," Rie said under her breath. She rarely swore, but when she did, she meant it. They were in deep. The redcaps were trained fighters, used to fighting together as an army. Perhaps, since they were after an individual prize, they wouldn't work together as well as usual, but they would at least have some familiarity with each other's skills. Rie and Daenor had barely known each other a day, and with the exception of the brief sparring at the inn, had never fought together.

"This should be fun," Daenor said, with a smile that bared his bright white teeth. "Try not to get lost."

"Don't worry about me," Rie replied through clenched teeth.

"I won't. Let's go."

Rie and Daenor strode through the forge together, stopping at the edge of the elm trees. Rie forced her spine straight, halting the shakes that threatened to overwhelm her. She had never fought against an army of trained opponents like this. Until recently, she hadn't fought much at all outside of Curuthannor's training grounds. She couldn't let them see that. She stood tall, weight balanced on the balls of her feet, her khukuris gripped comfortably in her hands. Her thumb spasmed a few times, but otherwise, she kept herself under tight control.

"Anyone who doesn't want to die, should turn around and walk away," Daenor announced, his voice carrying over the throng. Not a single redcap twitched.

"Apparently, you're not scary enough," Rie quipped, unsheathing her blades.

Daenor cocked one eyebrow. "Maybe you should go first, in your fancy new clothes."

Rie turned her lips down in a mock frown. "And here I thought you were a gentleman. Chivalry must really be dead if a prince lets his lady lead."

"My lady's going to have to be more than a damsel in distress. Think you can keep up?"

Rie grinned. "Watch me."

Daenor angled his body to the side, the sword held in a two-handed grip, the tip pointing down and to the rear. Flames leaked into his eyes and down the blade.

"Well, that's scary enough for me." Rie mentally thanked the gods that she wasn't facing off against the fire lord.

Daenor rushed forward, pulling his sword behind him. As the first of the redcaps approached, his blade swung up and around. A head rolled, the eyes still blinking, lips curled in a snarl. The oddly blood-free kill seemed to motivate the rest of the crowd. They surged forward, surrounding Daenor, who gleefully waded into them, cutting and maiming in every direction. His sword cauterized the wounds as it sliced, and the stench of burning flesh wafted into the air.

The pixies launched themselves to the sky, laughing as they dodged weapons and bit into any exposed skin, confusing the guards who weren't expecting pint-sized opponents. The redcaps swung wildly, clubs and blades too slow to catch Rie's frolicking friends.

Rather than fight her own way through the masses, Rie followed in Daenor's wake, keeping the rear guard and protecting his back, while the pixies distracted the biggest opponents. She deflected a blade aimed at Daenor's kidney, trapping the guard's arm and sending her khukuri into his gut with a rapid downward slice. She ducked, a mace whistling above her head. She cut across the hamstrings, opponent down. Low spin, slice up, across the back of a charging redcap attempting to disembowel Daenor. Knocked back by a kick to the side, recover, spin, slit opponent's wrist, sever the hand. A thrown blade aimed at her head knocked aside by a well-timed fire blast from Daenor. Sword thrust at Daenor parried by Rie's khukuri.

One by one, the redcaps fell. The rhythm of the fight consumed Rie. She let her instincts rule. Her vision simultaneously narrowed and widened, highlighting her next cut while watching for threats from any direction. She moved with speed and finesse, spinning around her adversaries as they slid toward the front gate.

More guards poured down off the wall. Pushed back by an axe-wielding redcap, Rie found herself separated from Daenor. The guard was good, blocking her strikes and using his own heavier weight to push her back into the compound.

"Daenor!" She was surrounded. Ducking beneath an axe aimed at her head, she took a blow to the side and fell to the ground. Gasping for air, Rie rolled to avoid another strike, the club landing next to her in the dirt. Gikl flew in, distracting the club-bearer, but there were too many of them. She lifted her blades to deflect a heavy axe with a sharp clang. Her arms went numb. Her left khukuri slipped out of her fingers. The axe lifted.

A fiery blade sliced through the guard's arm, and the axe fell. His head followed. "Up!" Daenor shouted. "We're almost there!" He threw a knife at the club-wielding guard.

Rie stood, clutching her side. She was pretty sure there were at least two broken ribs, but she couldn't worry about that now. She collected her dropped blade.

Possn buzzed around her head. "Quick, the way is clear."

The door was less than ten yards away. She just needed to touch the wood.

She stumbled away from the headless redcap, Daenor at her back, the pixies leading the way. A guard stepped in her line of sight. Muscles rippled in biceps bigger than her head. Resting the tip of his two-handed long sword on the ground, he wiped at the rivulets of blood that poured from the spongy cap on his head. He licked the red off his hand and then grinned, his grimy teeth dark with old blood.

That was it. Rie had had enough. She would not fall to one of these creatures. Her grip tightened on her khukuris and heat radiated up her arms. She straightened, the pain of her ribs falling away. Her vision turned red. Air sucked into her lungs. A wordless scream tore through her throat, releasing all of her anger and frustration into a single note of defiance.

The redcap rushed forward, swinging his sword up and over his head. Rie met him in a flash of steel. He was strong, but he was slow. Rie harried him, darting in and back, cutting small slices into his arms and looking for a weakness in the plated armor across his chest. Gikl tore a chunk from the guard's face, but the redcap ignored the annoyance with a low growl. He thrust his sword at Rie's stomach. And there it was, a gap where the armor plate above his kidney had come loose.

Ducking under upraised arms, Rie threaded her knife into the hole and twisted. The redcap's arms came down, pulling her into a crushing hug that squeezed the breath from her body. Rie struggled, shoving against the solid strength of the redcap's chest, but his arms didn't budge. Trapped tight, the air was slowly being squeezed out of her body. She had no leverage to pull the blade out. She had no room to move. Rie twisted the blade deeper into the redcap's side, hoping to damage something vital. Warm blood gushed over her hand. She kept digging. Her vision began to blacken around the edges. Where was everyone? Didn't they see she was about to be snuffed out?

A knife whistled past Rie's head and lodged in his throat. The guard staggered back, reaching up to remove the blade. Rie pulled her own knife from his side, then sliced across his neck. Blood spurted, covering her face and hands. She kicked him in the gut. He doubled over and fell.

Daenor gripped her wrist. Together, they ran the last few feet to touch the heavy wooden doors. Rie's vision returned to normal. She gasped for air. She surveyed the damage. Most of the redcaps lay on the ground, many wounded, some dead. A few rested, their weapons sheathed, breathing hard. Others sat in the dirt, cradling injuries. One poor fellow carried his own arm, severed through the bicep, and another wept over the loss of both legs below the knees. Blood saturated the hard-packed clay of the courtyard, highlighting their path from the forge to the gate. A few of the less wounded redcaps stared at her, eyes wide, many removing the bloody caps from their heads.

Daenor stood by her side, finally having the grace to breathe hard. He grinned, wrapping an arm around her shoulders. "We survived." Relieved laughter underscored words.

"Well done! Well done!" Master Whixle shouted from his perch in the elm tree. "It seems I'm going to have to supplement my guards. Perhaps a troll or two. I look forward to our future business."

CHAPTER TWELVE

Rie bent at the waist, struggling to catch her breath and ignore the pain. Whatever power or energy had been sustaining her was spent. Broken ribs throbbed with every breath, and her upper right arm dripped red where a blade had glanced off her shoulder. Had it not been for the amlug vest, she likely would have lost a kidney.

Daenor rubbed her back gently, his touch surprisingly tender. "Are you all right, sweetling?" The laughter was gone, concern taking its place.

"Fine." Rie straightened out from under his hand. He stepped away, his arm dropping to his side. The pixies landed on her shoulders, tucking in against her neck. Possn comforted her with a gentle hand on the curve of her jaw. Rie sighed, accepting the gesture of reassurance.

"You handled yourself well, and your friends were surprisingly helpful." Daenor took a cloth from a small bag attached to Turant's back, tossing a spare to Rie before turning to wipe down his sword, his movements focused and deliberate. Sweat coated his face. Otherwise, he appeared irritatingly unaffected by the battle.

"Without you, I wouldn't have survived. I owe you my life."

"You had my back, I had yours. We make a good team."

Daenor glanced back at Rie, holding her gaze with an appreciative smile. Rie averted her eyes to clean her khukuris.

"Here, let me help you with your shoulder." Warm fingers pulled at the hole in the red fabric above the sliced flesh, his gentle touch raising bumps along her arm and across her neck.

Rie pulled away. "I appreciate the offer, but it's just a surface cut. I'll take care of it later."

"I have a wound kit right here. Please," he said, a warm plea laced with command, "let me help you."

Rie swallowed a thick lump in her throat, then nodded.

Daenor finished cutting away the cloth around the wound with a knife, then carefully slid the detached sleeve down her arm to the top of her bracer, where it stuck. Unbuckling the leather, he pulled it from her arm along with the ruined sleeve and set them on the ground. His hand lingered on the now bare skin of her wrist. Rie's breath hitched. She licked her lips, drawing Daenor's gaze and another heated smile.

Daenor led Rie beneath a tall lamppost, the wisplight inside providing better light to examine her arm. Calloused hands used a clean cloth to wipe away the blood, revealing a shallow cut that wouldn't require anything more than a simple wash, suture strips, and a dry bandage. With a practiced hand, Daenor opened a tube of healing ointment, smeared the oily goop on the wound, then applied the sticky sutures and wrapped Rie's entire upper arm with bright white gauze. He tied the ends off in a knot, his touch seeming to linger against her skin.

Rie met his gaze, his amber eyes intense. She cleared her throat, craving cold water. Anything to cool the sudden warmth that burned through her system. She stepped back and out of reach.

"I appreciate your help tonight, but I should be going. I'll leave you to your evening." She dipped her head in a hint of a bow, then turned and walked away.

Within four steps, hooves clicked on stone. Rie turned, surprised to find Daenor already astride Turant and the two of them only an arm's length away. She lifted a hand to Turant's scaled muzzle and gave it a quick pat. The creature snorted sulphur scented steam in her face. She coughed, covering her mouth with one hand and gripping her ribs with the other.

"Let me take you back." Daenor reached down to offer a hand up.

"I can walk. It's not that far."

"It's at least five miles, and you're tired and injured. Hop on." Daenor patted Turant's shoulder. The longma bent his front legs and kneeled, one of the facial tentacles reaching out to pull Rie closer. Rie resisted. Even kneeling, Turant's shoulder was at Rie's eye level. "Turant insists," Daenor added.

"I don't think I can get up there." An excuse, but a legitimate one. Rie's ribs ached from the few steps she'd taken from the smithy. Any more significant movement, and she would be in serious pain.

Daenor slid from Turant's back. "What else is hurt?"

"My ribs."

"You should have said something earlier." The muscle in Daenor's jaw tensed while he examined her injury. "You're not walking. I'll give you a boost, Turant will help you the rest of the way." Daenor laced his fingers together, creating a step for Rie's foot. Rie still hesitated.

"It's safe. Trust me."

Rie nodded. There was no reason not to trust him, and she really didn't want to walk back alone. She took a deep breath, steeling herself for the jump. She placed her left foot in Daenor's hands, put her left hand on his shoulder and her right on Turant, then grit her teeth and pushed. Pain lanced her side, but Turant wrapped a whisker beneath her butt, taking most of her weight while she struggled to throw a leg over his back. Rie settled herself in front of Turant's wing stubs, panting from the effort, then gasped when he rose from his kneeling position.

"Slide back a bit," Daenor instructed.

Rie watched in awe as Daenor took two quick steps and launched himself into the air. Grabbing a knobby scale that protruded slightly from Turant's neck, Daenor pulled himself up and swung a leg over his back.

He twisted around to face her. "Hold on tight."

Rie leaned into Daenor, letting his broad shoulders carry her weight. Turant leaped forward, and Rie pushed her face into Daenor's back to muffle her pained cry. After a few steps, Turant's movement smoothed into a rolling gait and Rie could once again breathe. The scent of toasted cocoa and woodsmoke — Daenor's scent — filled her lungs as she pressed the side of her face between his shoulders. With each breath, Rie relaxed a little more, until the sharp edges of pain dulled to insignificance. All too soon they were back at the inn.

Daenor eased Rie down to the street level at the gate. "Let me help you to your room, and I'll find you a healer," he said after her feet touched the ground.

It wasn't a question, more an order, shaking Rie back to reality. Daenor was a prince of the Shadow Realm, and she needed to stay focused. He would only get in her way.

"Again, I appreciate the offer, but I can manage."

The right side of Daenor's mouth lifted in an ironic smile as he shook his head. "You haven't been any trouble. The opposite, in fact. Let me help you." His eyes smoldered, and extended his hand, palm up, an invitation.

Braegan emerged from the shadows inside the gate.

Daenor was a brilliant fighter. He'd believed in her when he could have just followed orders and arrested her. She could admit she was tempted, but too much stood at risk. She turned away.

"Where in hell have you been?" Braegan asked. "Your pixie friends have been nothing but trouble."

"What have they done now?"

"First, they attacked Tryg's pet goat..."

"Tryg, the troll bartender? He has a pet goat?"

"Cliché, I know, but true nonetheless. And your pixies thought she was fair game for dinner. Tryg disagreed. I eventually calmed him down, but not before he caught one of the pixies in a jar."

Niinka zoomed out from the crowd and fluttered near Rie, but out of reach of Braegan's swatting hand. Her shrill voice vibrated with anger. "Liar! He ratted on us, to get us out of the way. He's only mad Tryg couldn't catch us all."

Rie frowned, her thoughts scrambling to catch up. "But you were trying to eat Tryg's goat?"

"Well, yes," Niinka admitted. "But we didn't know it was Tryg's goat. It was all a set up. *He*," Niinka thrust a tiny finger in Braegan's direction, "told us to go in back and find something to eat. What were we supposed to think?"

"Maybe that you should get some salami or something. Not eat a live goat, lovingly tended in her own private stall," Braegan said.

"Ew. Cured meat? No, thank you!"

Rie rubbed a hand across her face. "So who's in the jar?"

"How should I know? They all look the same to me."

"Hiinto! The troll is wearing him in a jar strung around his neck, like a necklace."

"I see." Rie smiled apologetically at Daenor. "It's

probably best you leave. Have a good night." She turned and followed Braegan and Niinka into the inn, Gikl and Possn dashing ahead. She refused to look back at the prince.

"What happened to your shoulder?" Braegan asked over the noise of the crowded courtyard as they wove their way toward the back bar and Tryg.

Images of the fight and aftermath flitted through Rie's head. She grimaced. "It's just a flesh wound, nothing to worry about. And Whixle answered a few questions, so it was worth it."

"Do you know who gave the order?"

"No, but whoever it was paid the assassin in Upper Realm chits and is welcome in the Shadow Court."

"That narrows the field some, but finding a dark elf with connections to the upperworlds is going to be near impossible."

"That's why I'm taking Rie to court tomorrow."

Rie nearly jumped out of her skin at the sound of Daenor's voice. She turned and smacked him on his chest. "Don't sneak up on me like that."

Daenor smirked and caught Rie's hand. "You should be more aware of your surroundings."

Braegan glared at their entwined fingers. "I see you've gotten to know each other better," he said.

"A fight to the death will do that," Daenor replied.

"I need to save my pixies from being eaten by a troll. Where's Tryg?" Rie freed her hand.

As if on cue, the troll lumbered out from the kitchen, depositing a tray of food onto the bar. Hiinto, trapped inside the jar strung around Tryg's neck, pounded on the glass. Possn and Gikl joined the other two flying around Tryg's head.

"Oh, Hiinto," Rie murmured. Of all the pixies, he always seemed to be the one to get caught causing trouble. The others caused just as much, but they were better at getting away with it. Rie waved Tryg over to their location.

"Welcome back, this evening," Tryg said. "What can I get ye?"

"Get Hiinto out of there!" Niinka screamed.

Rie winced and held her hand over her ear. The siblings might bicker, but they looked out for each other.

Gikl dashed forward. He avoided Tryg's swatting palm by a hair's breadth, then zipped back to Rie, his black eyes wide. "He didn't put any air holes in the lid."

"Tryg, you have my friend held in a jar. Is there any chance I can convince you to let him out?"

"I caught this one trying to take a bite out of my dear Bessie. I'll not 'ave 'im free to bite her again," the troll rumbled. His eyebrows pulled low over his deep set eyes, hiding most of his face in shadow. "He's a troublemaker. He deserves what he gets." Tryg made a futile attempt to swat Tiik as he buzzed past his nose, then crossed his arms.

"What if I promise he won't do anything like that again?"

Tryg shook his head.

"Buy you another goat?"

Tryg paused, the wheels slowly turning behind his eyes. "Ye'd buy me a friend for Bessie? She's a social creature, and I hate to see her lonely."

"I'll do you one better," Rie said. "I'll buy her a mate. That way, she can have babies, too. A whole little goat family."

"Ah, she'd like that." Tryg leaned forward, placing his hands on the bar and putting his gnarled face in front of Rie. "But the pixie must be punished."

"Agreed. What do you propose?"

"He has to clean Bessie's stall. I want it spotless by the

time my shift ends. The others need to help."

Rie looked meaningfully at Niinka, hovering just out of reach behind the troll's shoulder. "That's the cost of Hiinto's freedom," Rie told her. "You all have to assist, or he stays in the jar. I imagine he must be close to running out of air by now."

Niinka worried her lower lip for half a beat, then began to talk in Pixl to the others. Within moments, all four lined up in front of Rie, facing Tryg.

"We accept the terms," Niinka announced.

Tryg eyed her warily. "No funny business. Ye will clean the stall from top to bottom, clean straw, not a trace of muck. Ye will *not* try to bite Bessie again, ever."

"Agreed." Niinka stuck out her hand. The others followed suit. Tryg carefully placed a finger in each palm to shake on it. He sighed, then lifted the jar to his eye.

"You, too," he told Hiinto. Hiinto nodded vehemently. Tryg sighed again, twisted the lid off the jar and released Hiinto to the air. Hiinto gleefully flew above Tryg's head, then sped over to Rie.

"Thankyouthankyouthankyou," he said. "You arrived just in time. It was getting hot and humid in there!"

"You're welcome, but you all better get to work." The swarm flew off.

"How you stay sane with that lot, I'll never know," Braegan said.

Rie shrugged. "They are a handful, but they're loyal."

"Now about that goat," Tryg began.

"As soon as I've finished my business here, I'll find Bessie a mate."

"Good enough. Now, can I get ye some supper?"

"Please," Rie said.

"And a bottle of A positive, if you have it," Braegan added.

Rie lifted an eyebrow.

"What? I have to order my meal in a bottle. Unless you want to offer your services..." Braegan teased.

Daenor's voice was a low growl. "She will do no such thing."

"Of course, not. We've already dealt with that little misunderstanding," Rie replied.

Braegan snickered. "I would have shown you a good time."

A burst of flame lit Braegan's eyebrows, singeing the hair to a crumbling mess. Braegan clasped his hands over his eyes and leaned back until he almost fell out of his chair. "What the hell was that for?"

Daenor's own eyebrows were angled low over fiery red eyes. "Say that again, and the rest of your head will catch fire, too. In fact, if you *ever* even *think* about treating Rie like a blood slave, you can kiss your pretty little face goodbye."

"Geez, I was just joking." Braegan patted the spots where his eyebrows once resided. With each pat, the hair seemed to materialize from thin air. "It's going to take weeks for these to grow back properly."

"That was uncalled for," Rie added, amused by Braegan's ordeal but unwilling to show it. "Like I said, I made it perfectly clear when we first met that I was not food. I don't need you to fight my battles for me."

Daenor grumbled, but was interrupted by Tryg, who arrived with a steaming platter of white prawns cooked in some kind of red sauce and a loaf of soft white bread.

Rie couldn't hold back. The fight had taken all her energy. She tore into the bread and sopped up the sauce. She peeled the prawns and ate them with gusto. It took a few minutes, but eventually she slowed down enough to speak between bites. "Now, what was that you were saying about taking me to court tomorrow?" she asked Daenor.

"The king sees petitioners for two hours every day, in public audience. It's the daily entertainment for most of the courtiers. Refreshments are even served to the Lords and Ladies in attendance, who laugh behind their hands at the common-folk and make private business deals in the wings. You'll tell him your story. I'll support your claim and give credence to the facts, so he'll take you seriously. Whoever is behind the attack will either be present and scared into action, or will find out about your petition and will try to stop you." Daenor shrugged. "Simple."

Rie struggled to hide her fear. "I can't go to court."

"Why not? I'll admit the king isn't the most pleasant person to be around, but he's fair."

"He might not take my head himself, but he's bound to send me back to the Upper Realm, where I'll be dead as soon as I arrive. Besides, I doubt a petition will be enough to force the culprit into revealing himself. I need a name, first."

Daenor kept his voice low and controlled, but it was clear he didn't like having his plan opposed. "Do you have a better idea?"

Rie ignored his glower, choosing to focus on picking the last of the meat out of a prawn shell. "Actually, I do. Messengers know everything. If you can get me in to see the chief, I'll find out what's going on."

CHAPTER THIRTEEN

After a night spent tossing and turning in the plush confines of the room at the inn, Rie wakened aching and sore, with a niggling worm of dread buried in the depths of her belly. Performing her morning stretches didn't ease her worry, or the aches and pains, even after Plink insisted on drawing a warm bath scented with some kind of flower and brushing her hair until it shone. The darkness of the realm was beginning to wear on her psyche, the few hours of daylight insufficient to chase away the grim reality that she was in unfamiliar territory and way out of her league.

There was no help for it, no choice but to keep going.

Donning grey silk over the amlug hide, Rie left for the messenger headquarters and found the men facing off at the gate. Glancing her direction, Daenor dropped his head and stared into Braegan's narrowed eyes, his expression rigid. His voice was low, nearly inaudible, but Rie thought she heard him say, "Just stay out of the way," before stepping back. Flickering orange and red lit his eyes as he focused his attention on her.

"Ready?" Daenor's voice held no hint of the tension she'd witnessed, but Braegan wouldn't meet her gaze.

Rie lifted an eyebrow. "Of course." She wished she

could be rid of them both, but Daenor would secure an audience with the chief, and Braegan had a cousin in the lower ranks she could interrogate for gossip. She needed them.

Rie rubbed a hand across her injured side. Daenor's gaze caught the movement and a crease formed between his eyebrows. "How are the ribs?"

"Not too bad. A bit sore, but nowhere near what I expected. Unless I healed magically in the night, it must not have been that bad, after all."

He smiled. "Good, that's really good."

Braegan cast an accusatory glance her way. "I didn't know you had broken ribs."

"Apparently, I don't."

Rough gray stone passed beneath their feet. It wasn't long before they approached the twin spires that marked the entrance to castle grounds. The guards stood aside, nodding to Daenor. The group passed beneath the high arch and across the moat bridge without challenge. The less prominent second gate stood open, allowing free passage into the compound. Rie noted the watchful eyes peering out of inconspicuous bolt holes in the walls on either side of the passage. She counted four more soldiers pacing the top of the wall before passing beneath the black iron portcullis.

Daenor led them across the courtyard and up the curving ramp to the castle gates on the second level. Made of obsidian, the edifice gleamed in the low light of day. Rie shuddered, seeing her own ghostly reflection in the stone before entering the keep.

Shadows laced the walls, soft blue uplighting doing little to reveal what lay beneath curved arches and down dark passageways. Just like the city of Nalakadr outside, there were few right angles inside the building. Hallways curved gently instead of going straight, making it difficult to see what lay ahead or draw a mental map of the building. Where stairs would have lead up to the higher floors anywhere else, the shadow castle had smooth stone ramps that wound in circles up a central column. It felt to Rie like they were walking through the innards of a great snake, smooth and sinuous, promising death at every turn.

The walls, decorated with woven tapestries, depicted scenes of life in the Shadow Realm. Some appeared innocent and pastoral, showing groups of both lesser and greater fae gathered at banquets or sitting beneath a rising moon. Some were strange scenes Rie didn't understand, filled with dark elves and vague apparitions. And still others contained horrifying images of battle and sacrifice, the woven red blood somehow glistening in the dim light.

Daenor slowed, approaching closed double doors beneath a heavy stone arch. "This is the courier's wing. Their chief is Ratoska, a lady with an unwarranted high opinion of herself. Let me do the talking, at least until we're sitting down."

Rie nodded her agreement, and Braegan said nothing.

Daenor pushed open both doors at once, striding to the front desk without pause. The massive room was crowded and chaotic, flurries of paper and people everywhere. Everyone was in a rush. Everything was an organized mess. It was just like the messenger hall in the High Court, and Rie felt right at home.

The woman at the front desk, a goblin with three chins and four eyes, greeted them without looking up from her work. "Incoming or outgoing," was all she said, her voice filled with broken glass and sandpaper.

"Neither," Daenor replied, his resonant voice catching her attention.

Her back straightened, at least as far as her hump

would allow. Her gaze drifted up from the paperwork in front of her.

"Is Ratoska in?"

"Prince Daenor. It's good to see you. Unfortunately, Ratoska is out on a delivery at Court. She won't be back for at least a bell."

"That's fine," Daenor replied. "Is there somewhere we can wait?"

The goblin examined Rie and Braegan with a critical eye. "Who're they?"

"Friends," Daenor said.

She squinted at them a second longer, then relented. "I s'pose you can wait outside her office. Let me get you some chairs." She moved quickly for someone with a hump and bow legs, and she was strong, carrying three solid wood chairs without assistance. The crowd of couriers parted before her as she plowed through the room.

As quietly as she could manage, Rie whispered instructions to the pixies. "I need to know if someone has been traveling back and forth from the Upper Realm, and who they are. Go talk with the courier swarm and see if they know anything."

Possn and Tiik responded by darting off into the pixie swarm hovering near an open window to their left. Niinka, Hiinto and Gikl remained in place, maintaining their disguises.

"Sit there," the goblin instructed, pointing at the chairs she set down against the window of the corner office. "Don't move. Don't get in the way."

Taking the right-most seat, Rie followed the goblin's instructions. Daenor sat next to her with Braegan on his other side. The chair was probably the most uncomfortable item of furniture Rie had ever had the misfortune of perching on. Made of thick twined branches left in their natural state, it felt like the back leaned forward, and the seat poked her in the rear end no matter how she shifted. She did her best to hide her discomfort.

Braegan didn't bother hiding anything. He twisted and leaned, crossed first one leg, then the other, pulled both legs up onto the seat of the chair, then dropped them both to the floor and leaned forward. All in all, he looked as miserable as Rie felt.

Daenor, on the other hand, seemed at ease. He stretched his legs out in front of him and clasped his hands across his stomach, for all appearances about to take a nap. Perhaps the goblin had given him the most comfortable chair, or perhaps he was accustomed to the discomfort. Rie envied him his composure.

After awhile, Rie began to make out the patterns of movement in the room. As elsewhere in the realm, the various fae mostly kept to their own kind. Two human changelings, a man and a woman, played a card game in the corner to Rie's right, near the pixie swarm. A troll slept against the left wall, curled up on his side, using his hands as a pillow and taking up half the length of the room. A group of at least six gremlins chattered at a long table in the center of the room, and three goblins tussled toward the front. Several young dark elves acted as internal mail, bringing in messages from court and delivering them to the appropriate courier to take on a run out in the city.

Half a bell of waiting, and Ratoska was still out. Rie leaned forward, grabbing Braegan's attention. "So where's this cousin of yours?"

Braegan shrugged. "He's a court runner. He'll be here eventually."

"I would rather not wait around all day."

"Don't complain to me. It's your plan." Braegan's voice

sounded bitter and angry, uncharacteristic of the normally jocular blood sidhe.

"Why the mood? What has you so twisted up today?" Rie asked.

"Nothing. Never mind. He should be here soon."

They waited another half bell before there was a sudden commotion. The sleeping troll was being shaken awake by the goblin from the front desk. He lumbered up to a standing position, and the woman handed him a thick envelope with what looked like a black wax seal stamped on the front. The goblin gestured wildly as she spoke to the troll. The troll lumbered out of the room at a gallop. "Niinka, Hiinto, find out what's going on," Rie said.

"Finally," Hiinto said, sounding aggrieved. "Something to do."

"Stop complaining. This is a new level of deviousness for Rie. We should be proud," Niinka said, as she and Hiinto crawled down Rie's back. Rie lost the rest of the conversation as they buzzed away to follow the troll.

A few moments later, a blood sidhe approached Braegan with a smirk on his face. "Hey, cuz, I see they've got you sittin' pretty today."

"These chairs are the worst." Braegan stood, stretching his back with a groan. "But at least I'm not running my ass off." He grinned and thrust his hand out to the courier. They grabbed forearms, and the other blood sidhe pulled Braegan in for a hug.

"Long time, no see. What brings you to my stomping grounds?"

"We're waiting for Ratoska. Any idea when she'll be back?"

"It'll be awhile. Who're your friends?"

"This is Rie, and you know Prince Daenor." Rie stood to shake the sidhe's hand, but Daenor didn't move from his lounge, his eyes closed and hands clasped across his stomach.

"Ignore him," Rie said. "He's being grumpy today." A soft snort was the only indication that Daenor heard her. "It's a pleasure."

"The pleasure is all mine." The sidhe bent over her hand, caressing her knuckles with a soft kiss before Braegan yanked him up by the collar.

Braegan's voice was light, but his eyes threatened violence. "You'll stay alive longer if you keep your distance from this one."

"Understood." The sidhe brushed invisible dust off his uniform. "I'm Farrell, by the way."

Rie nodded. "Braegan thought we might see you. Any idea what's going on?"

"It's a mess. The High Court's chief messenger arrived today, which always complicates things, but he's been sequestered with Ratoska and the king all morning. It's thrown off the whole schedule."

Tension radiated down Rie's spine. Rolimdornoron — High Court Chief Messenger and Rie's boss — was in the Shadow Realm, speaking with the king somewhere in the castle. What was he doing here? King Othin must have sent him. Somehow, they knew she was here. Her time was up.

The urge to flee threatened to overwhelm her, but Rie held fast. She needed more information, and needed it fast. Rolimdornoron must know she was here in the city, but not her precise location. Staying close might actually be the best way to avoid detection.

"What are they talking about?"

Farrell grinned as he glanced around the room. He stepped closer. "From what I've heard, King Othin is demanding the return of an Upper Realm defector. The woman is selling court secrets. If she's not given into his custody immediately, he's threatening war."

Rie felt the blood drain from her face. It wasn't true. They were lying, but why? They didn't need a pretext to collect her. Rie froze, her brain stuttering against the realization she was being framed for a crime much worse than just having contact with the Shadow Realm. She would be tortured and chained, destined for a long and painful death, not the swift execution she had imagined.

Chills raced down Rie's arms. King Othin's torturers could break a person's spirit with a thought, their magic dedicated to shattering the individual psyche until nothing but a shell remained. The lucky ones were killed once the torturers finished. The unlucky ones shuffled around, witless and following every order, no matter how base. It was the worst fate imaginable, and Rie knew, if caught, it could be hers.

Daenor seized Farrell by the throat. Much taller and stronger than the immature courier, he easily lifted him up into the air. The elf scrabbled at Daenor's hand and flailed his legs, trying to get a purchase on the ground and relieve the pressure on his trachea.

"What message was sent to the trolls?" he demanded.

Farrell choked, attempting to answer, despite his blocked airway.

Braegan's fangs snapped into place, his claws erupting from the tips of his fingers. "Release him."

Daenor let up slightly, allowing the blood sidhe's toes to touch the ground, but didn't release him. "Tell me."

"I said, let him go." Braegan stepped forward, his lips curled in a snarl and head extended forward, a predator about to launch an attack.

Farrell snarled, his own fangs extended. "They are called to assemble."

"For what purpose?" Daenor asked.

"They're to guard the portals, shut down any traffic in

or out until the spy is found and brought to the king. That won't take long, though." Farrell's eyebrows tilted down and he pursed his lips in an enigmatic smirk.

Some deep instinct rose to the surface. Rie broke free of the stasis. "What does that mean?"

"It means we need to go. Now." Daenor threw the apprentice to the ground.

Braegan's gaze followed his cousin to the ground. Farrell rubbed his throat, but waved away any help.

Blowing out a breath, Daenor took Rie's hand. "Let's go."

"You're not going anywhere," Farrell said. He handed a slip of ivory paper stamped with another black seal to Braegan. "You've been ordered to hold her here until the Guard arrives to arrest her."

Rie's heart raced. "What have you done?"

Braegan's fangs and claws retracted as he read the message. "I'm so sorry, Rie. It's my job."

"Explain."

"He's an Observer," Daenor replied with a sneer. "A spy. I warned you to stay out of this," he said to Braegan.

Breagan's expression drooped. "When you came through the portal, you were my ticket to promotion. But then I got to know you." He paused, took a deep breath, his fangs and claws returning. "I'm just following orders."

"Not anymore." Daenor pulled the pistol from the holster under his left armpit. With calm precision, he shot a round into each leg and shoulder.

The crowded hall fell silent, every courier in the room turning to stare, as Braegan screamed curses.

"Run," Daenor said, pushing Rie in front of him.

Rie didn't hesitate. She dashed forward, shoving everyone and everything out of her way. No one tried to stop her, but she ran with little hope of escape.

Daenor grabbed her arm and spun her around before

she reached the courtyard. Footsteps sounded up ahead.

"This way," he said, leading her back the way they had come.

They didn't make it far. Four guards dressed in black marched forward, shoulder to shoulder across the breadth of the hall. Naked blades glistened sharply in the flickering lamplight. Four more guards approached from the rear. Trapped in a section of the corridor with no doors or windows, they were surrounded. Daenor pushed Rie against the wall behind him.

"By order of His Majesty the King, this woman is under arrest," said a haughty dark elf clad in black scaled armor and carrying a wicked looking long black katana.

"Cendir, this woman is my guest. Stand down." Daenor's voice echoed off the paneled walls.

The elf grinned, obviously relishing his current duty. "My orders come direct from King Aradae. Stand aside or be arrested with her."

"She isn't a threat. On what grounds is she being taken before the king?"

"Treason." White teeth flashed between thin lips.

Daenor didn't budge.

When Cendir didn't get a reaction, he continued. "She's a spy from the Upper Realm, a traitor here in violation of the treaty." The smirk grew wider.

Rie suddenly recognized the man before her. He was the same warrior Daenor had fought in the arena just a few nights earlier. Though fully recovered from the fight, Rie still understood his grudge against Daenor.

With eight guards trapping them in a confined area, there was no escape. Even if Rie attempted to fight through the guards, Daenor couldn't support her. He was their commander, their leader, not their enemy.

Rie placed a hand on Daenor's back, just above his waist. A slight trembling betrayed his fury. He twisted to glance over his shoulder. "I'm not a spy. Everything I've done and said up to this point has been the truth."

His eyes softened, begging for understanding. "I know, but I can't disobey the king." Rie's breath deserted her, and her head dropped. A finger lifted her chin. Rie opened her eyes to stare into the burning depths of Daenor's gaze. "You're not done, yet, Sweetling. You survived trained assassins and a legion of redcaps. You can and will survive this."

Finding strength in his words, Rie nodded. She would fight to the end, even without a chance of survival. She would make Curuthannor proud.

"Isn't that sweet? The Bastard's found a friend. Too bad she'll be dead within the hour. Now, be a good girl and hand over your weapons." Cendir pointed his sword at Rie's blades.

Daenor clenched his jaw, and narrowed his eyes at the dark elf. His hand grew dangerously hot where it rested on Rie's arm. When he finally spoke, his voice was low and barely controlled. "I will escort her to the king. You are no longer needed."

Cendir held his ground, his gray eyes twinkling. "Like I said, my orders are direct from your father. He wants her disarmed and all of her belongings brought to his office before the trial."

The muscles in Daenor's jaw twitched, but he turned to Rie, palm up. She had no choice.

Thank you, he mouthed before turning her weapons over to Cendir.

"And the bag," Cendir said.

Rie sighed, but pulled the strap over her head and handed it over.

Daenor's lips spread to a thin line. "You can follow us, if you must, but I warn you, any threat to this woman will be taken as a threat to me."

"We all gotta do what we gotta do," Cendir replied. "I can't wait for the king to see how you've fallen."

Gritting his teeth, Daenor placed Rie's hand on the back of his wrist and walked through the throng of guards. Marching footsteps took up a cadence behind them. Rie refused to look back.

CHAPTER FOURTEEN

Voices rose and fell in waves of indecipherable noise that pulsed through the open doors of the throne room. Rie took a steadying breath before she stepped across the threshold on Daenor's arm. The guards trailed behind them.

The room was more than a hundred yards long, and crowded with fae. The lesser fae gathered in segregated groups near the door, each race sticking together with only a few exceptions. The goblins were the most eye-catching of the lot, their physical deformities displayed for all to see. One woman in particular was only half-clothed, wearing a floor-length yellow skirt and baring her six breasts to the world. When she caught Rie staring, she wiggled her shoulders from side to side, making her sagging breasts wobble. Rie looked away as quickly as she could, but heard the woman laugh and make some comment to the man who stood beside her.

Daenor pulled her forward. They wound their way around a group of blood sidhe mingling with a few humans. The woman giggled and cupped the back of the sidhe's head with a perfectly manicured hand. As much as the feeding disturbed her, Rie had to assume it was consensual.

Dark elf heads turned as Daenor drew them toward the far end of the room. Men and women, who stood at official looking tables, paused in their dealings to watch the procession. Within moments, the once noisy crowd hushed to gossiping whispers as everyone stared.

The king's throne sat on a raised dais at the far end of the room. As far as thrones went, it was simple and elegant. Black lacquered legs with clawed feet supported a wide cushioned seat and tall peaked back. Carved dragon heads capped the ends of the armrests and silver inlays accented the wood, highlighting the curves of the chair. A silver seal of the royal crest, a dragon wrapped around a globe, graced the top center of the back. Three smaller thrones were carefully placed on the dais behind the king's throne, one to the right and two to the left.

Daenor led her to a spot a short distance from the dais, while Cendir proceeded through a door behind the throne. The rest of the guards formed a semi-circle around them, their weapons held at attention.

Rie clenched her stomach against the trembling nerves that threatened to overtake her, and pushed a hint of a smile into her lips. No matter what she felt on the inside, she wouldn't let her captors see her distress. Next to her, Daenor stood at attention, the twitch of jaw muscle and slight vibration in his arm the only outward indication of his tension.

The talk in the room picked up again, first as whispers, then working up to audible taunting from the crowd.

"She looks human, but she must have bewitched the prince," a dark elf woman with sparkling diamond rings outlining the edge of her highly pointed ears told the man next to her. "Why else would he stand with her?"

"What do you expect from a half-breed?" the man sneered.

Daenor's eyes tightened and his nostrils flared. The

heat emanating off his skin was almost unbearable. Rie rubbed her thumb in gentle circles where it rested on the back of his wrist and the fire subsided. Rie might be the one on trial, but the prince was equally alone. Somehow, that thought made her feel a little better.

After a few minutes of standing with nothing to do, a young-looking goblin approached Daenor. He was the same goblin Rie had seen at the fight in the Crossroads Inn. At least, she thought he was the same. He had three eyes and appeared about the same height, with the same brown skin. Mud-colored hair was tied at the nape of his neck, and elegant tailored clothing accentuated a narrow waist and strong legs, while minimizing his hunch. The conservative attire was nothing at all like the goblins gathered near the doors, marking him out as unusual for his kind.

"Sir, ye should know the guard is behind ye, whatever comes. Cendir has a few followers, but the majority trust yer judgment." Intelligent caramel eyes fringed with straight lashes glanced at Rie, then back at the prince.

Daenor nodded, his jaw relaxing. "I appreciate it." Rie didn't know what was going on, but the goblin was clearly an advisor of some kind.

A bell sounded out across the hall, the lingering tone pure and ethereal. The goblin moved away through the crowd, leaving Rie and Daenor alone before the throne. The crowd hushed. The rear door opened. King Aradae entered the room, followed by a female dark elf wearing a tall crown sparkling with layers of diamonds, another male and female dark elf dressed in slightly less ostentatious splendor, a cloaked and hooded figure, and Cendir, carrying Rie's belongings. The king paused at the throne before sitting down, his gaze raking the room.

King Aradae stood well over seven feet tall, with ebony skin and high pointed ears that poked out of loose hair.

His eyes were a light gray so pale the iris blended with the white. This was made even more prominent by the chin length white hair that framed his face and highlighted high cheekbones and a pointed chin. His only sign of office was a subtle white-gold circlet that kept his hair out of his eyes.

After gathering the crowd's attention, the king sat, casually crossing one ankle over the opposite knee. As soon as he was comfortable, the queen and heirs took their places, but there was no seat for the cloaked man, who stood awkwardly on the floor to the left of the dais.

"Ladies, gentlemen, greater and lesser fae, office hours are now open. I trust you all know the rules, but just in case, let me reiterate. I will hear any and all petitions that are brought forward in the next two hours. I will choose the order of preference for the hearing. In the case of a dispute, all involved parties must be present or the suit will be thrown out. All judgments are final." Rie was certain he saw her standing with Daenor, but if he was disturbed by his son's presence, he didn't show it.

"Today, we begin with a case brought forward by a representative from the Upper Realm," he continued. The crowd didn't gasp or titter, apparently word had already spread through the court. In all likelihood, the entire crowd had gathered just to see the spectacle.

"King Othin, of the High Court of the Upper Realm—" a hiss echoed around the room. King Aradae lifted a hand to quiet the crowd. "King Othin's chief messenger arrived today, demanding the immediate extradition of one of his low-level staff members. However, it is our law to provide fair trial to every individual in the Shadow Realm, regardless of status."

The cloaked man jerked forward, the hood falling back from his face. Gikl hissed from his camouflaged position on the bodice of her gown. He didn't like Rolimdornoron.

No one did. He was pompous and snide, and it was no secret that he thought he should be a member of the High Court Council due to his position as chief messenger. What he didn't realize was that his position only qualified him as a slightly more prosperous servant to the king.

Secretly nicknamed The Squirrel by the messenger service, Rolimdornoron possessed the face of the rodent from which he derived his nickname. In fact, he was one of the few High Elves Rie would categorize as ugly. Or at least funny-looking. Wide set eyes, a short, up-turned nose, and thin lips would be enough, but add to that big ears and prominent front teeth, and you had a face that was comically unforgettable.

What really set him apart was his coloring. The Lords and Ladies of the High Court were pale and perfect, with bright blue or green eyes and blonde hair. Rolimdornoron, on the other hand, had dull brown eyes and a skin tone bordering on taupe. His hair was blonde, but the messenger service had a secret bet that he paid someone to have it done, possibly in the Human Realm. There were also rumors that a nisse or a gnome had a branch on his family tree. People said his impure bloodline was half the reason he had never moved beyond the messenger service. The other half was his irritating personality.

His lips curled in a twisted sneer and his finger lashed out to point at Rie. "Nuriel Lhethannien stands there before you, with your *son*, and you claim ignorance?" His voice rose to a high-pitched squeal. "She will be taken to the High Court and executed for her crimes."

Even knowing it was her boss, the sight of Rolimdornoron's livid white face somehow solidified the reality that Rie's old life was irrevocably gone. Her heart sank.

"Silence!" The king's voice boomed out across the hall.

"The accused has been arrested and is now in our custody. She will be brought forward to face her accusers and make her case, if there is one."

"This is insupportable," Rolimdornoron sputtered. "She is a High Court citizen in violation of the treaty, and a traitor to her king. You do not have the authority —"

King Aradae's voice dropped to a dangerous growl. "This is my court, and *I* am ruler here. I will have my trial."

The look in Rolimdornoron's eyes could have frozen flowing lava, but he shut his mouth without another word. A goblin servant brought a chair for him to sit in, placing it a good distance away from the throne and dais. Rolimdornoron ignored the offered comfort.

"Now," the king continued in a calmer tone, "in as civil a manner as possible, please identify and state the case against the accused."

Rolimdornoron narrowed beady eyes and glowered at Rie. "Nuriel Lhethannien, standing there," he pointed a bony finger, "was a messenger for the High Court. We discovered she was selling information to the Shadow Realm when she killed two blood sidhe in the Human Realm. She escaped our search and has been hiding here in Nalakadr. King Othin demands she be returned to the Upper Realm and executed for her crimes."

Whispers echoed around the throne room. The group of blood sidhe shifted forward to stand closer to the throne, but maintained their distance from the noble dark elves.

"And what have my intelligence gatherers discovered?"

A woman wearing a shimmering gown embroidered with thorny roses stepped forward from the edge of the crowd of dark elves. "One of my Observers, Braegan Sangrresen, has been trailing the girl since she arrived. He can make his own report." She held an open hand out to the back of the room.

Rie spun to see Braegan moving slowly through the crowd of lesser fae behind her. His clothes were bloody and torn where Daenor had shot him, and he grimaced with each step, but he was moving on his own. The blood sidhe rumors must be true; one good feeding and they would be healed. Rie briefly wished Daenor had shot him somewhere harder to fix. Like his head.

Braegan glanced her direction with a sorrowful expression. Rie wouldn't give him the satisfaction of meeting his gaze or forgiving his betrayal. Braegan carefully bent to one knee before the throne.

"Go ahead then, give your report," the king said, a touch impatiently.

"A High Court changeling is here in the Shadow Realm. She claims to be searching for information about a violation of the treaty that took place in the Human Realm."

"How do you know this?"

"I followed her from the portal and arranged to be her escort in the city. She believes someone hired assassins to kill her in the Human Realm, then framed her as a traitor when the assassination was unsuccessful. She has been asking about the maker of a black throwing knife, and visited Master Whixle. The original owner of the knife paid for the blade with Upper Realm chits."

Rie forced the air through her nose with an audible whoosh and ground her teeth to keep from screaming at the subservient blood sidhe who had been spying on her all this time. She felt like a fool, but it didn't lessen the anger that surged through her system. Curuthannor had taught her better than this. She wouldn't make the same mistake again.

The High Court chief messenger rose to his feet, sputtering. "Impossible! Upper Realm citizens are banned from contact with the Shadow Realm, by penalty of death, unless specifically sanctioned by King Othin himself. She was a traitor the moment she met with the blood sidhe."

Rolimdornoron was right. No one was allowed across the portal, with the exception of the chief messenger. Only *Rolimdornoron* was allowed to travel on King Othin's business. Rie watched him, thoughtfully. Could it be that the chief messenger hired the assassins? He would have had access to the Shadow Realm, and he could easily have arranged the timing of her delivery, but what was the motive? Why would he want to kill one of his own messengers? It didn't make sense, and yet, it was too coincidental to overlook.

King Aradae steepled his fingers together in front of him. "Are you done?" When there was no response, he continued, his voice carefully controlled. "Then sit down, and remain seated and silent. You have no authority here, and your next outburst will have you removed."

Rolimdornoron thumped into his chair and swished the ends of his cloak over his lap.

The king waved Cendir forward. He approached the throne, carrying Rie's belongings, including her travel bag. The king rummaged through the items until he found the throwing knife, pulling it from the bag and holding it up to the light for examination.

"This is the knife?" he asked, twisting and turning the blade.

"Yes, Your Majesty," Braegan replied.

The king studied it for a few heartbeats, then set it on a low table next to the throne. "How did she get in to see the smith?"

"I escorted her." Daenor's voice carried over the hall. He let Rie's hand drop and stepped forward, inclining his head slightly, but without bowing in obeisance.

The king sat motionless. "I see. Did you know the woman was from the Upper Realm?"

"Faernodir and Faerleithril made me aware of the situation shortly before the visit to the smith, yes. But I believe Rie's story. She spoke to Master Whixle briefly, and only about the knives. I don't believe she's a threat."

The king pressed his lips together in a thin line before responding. "That wasn't your decision to make."

"As Commander of the Shadow Guard, it is my duty to protect—"

King Aradae interrupted, his voice cold and precise. "As Commander of the Shadow Guard, it is your duty to *uphold* the law, not interpret it."

Daenor took a measured breath, his face rigid. "I can't do one without the other. Rie is a pawn, not a traitor. I won't condemn her for someone else's treason."

Without taking his gaze off his son, the king curled the pointer finger on his right hand and ordered Rie brought forward without saying a word. The guards shoved her toward the dais, then kicked her knees out from under her, causing her to fall before the king. The crowd tittered. Daenor moved to help her up, but Rie quelled him with a glance. She was fine. She could do obeisance with the best of them, and Daenor didn't need to further weaken his position for her sake.

Rie softened her face; lips loose, neither smiling nor frowning, head bent in deference to the king, gaze held at the level of his knees, not challenging but not entirely submissive either. He was the king, and was owed respect, but she was better than a servant. If nothing else, the last few days had taught her that.

He let the silence draw out as the crowd shifted and murmured.

"Well, go on then," he finally spat.

Rie took a breath. "Some of what you have heard is

true. My name is Nuriel Lhethannien, and I am a changeling from the High Court, formerly of the messenger service. However, my only offense was being the target of a failed assassination, and my only goal is to find out who ordered my death, and why."

"King Othin is demanding your extradition for trial in the Upper Realm. So far, I have seen no reason to deny him." The king drummed his fingers on the armrest, watching her with a skeptical eye.

Rie paused, considering. Did the king want a reason to deny the Upper Realm its victim? "I am, or was, a messenger." Rie glanced at Rolimdornoron, but his attention was focused on his hands. "It is a simple enough occupation, but very few humans are allowed into the service. Most changelings are slaves or menial servants, certainly not to be trusted with important messages. It took decades of hard work to earn my place. Even so, had I stayed in the Upper Realm, King Othin would have ordered my execution without even this much of a trial." Rie gestured, arms out and pointed, open handed, at the floor. "My only chance to survive was to seek out the traitor and prove my loyalty."

Rie paused, waiting to see if the king would stop her, but he waved for her to continue, then rested his elbow on the armrest of the throne, chin on his hand. Rie told her story, beginning with the fight on the beach and ending with the visit to the courier office.

"All I ask, your Majesty, is a chance find the individual behind the attack."

"So you believe that someone from my court attempted to have you, a changeling, assassinated. And why would your death matter to anyone?" The king was blunt, she'd give him that.

"No, that's not entirely correct. Master Whixle was confident that the assassin had paid for his blades with chits from the Upper Realm, which leads me to believe that someone from the Upper Realm hired a Shadow Realm assassin. As to why my death matters, I don't know, but someone wanted me dead on Lord Garamaen's beach."

The king leaned forward, resting his elbows on his knees. "He isn't precisely a Lord of the High Court, you know."

She didn't know how to respond, so she didn't.

"Let me clarify. Garamaen is Sanyaro of the nine realms, the only individual granted unlimited access to any realm, despite the treaty. He is the mediator, the truthseeker. Did he order you on this mission? Is he an interested party?"

Rie quickly weighed her options. She didn't understand all the implications, but Lord Garamaen's name had more weight here than she realized. She might be able to use that to her advantage, but she was wary of invoking his name too much, for fear that he didn't want to be involved in such a trifling matter. She could attempt to lie, but she'd never been very good at it.

"She used Sanyaro's portal code to cross into Nalakadr," Braegan interrupted, before Rie could form a response. Rie had almost forgotten he was still kneeling just a few feet away.

"This is ridiculous," the queen interrupted from her seat beside the king. "She just admitted to treason and was caught with a stolen portal code. Let's send her back to the Upper Realm, appease King Othin, and be done with it."

The king shot a piercing glance at the queen, but said nothing. Returning his attention to Rie, he forced her to meet his gaze and defend herself.

"Lord Garamaen gave me his code so that I could avoid the Upper Realm portal Watchers. He didn't order me to do anything, but he advised that it might be prudent. This is my best option to prevent my own execution."

"I fail to see how a trip to a forbidden realm could prevent your execution. If anything, I would think it would be further proof of treason."

Daenor stepped forward, about to say something, but Rie held him back with a quick shake of her head. "Even had I not made this trip, the fact that Shadow Realm assassins attacked would be proof enough of treason for King Othin. I apologize for being blunt, but he hates everything and everyone related to the underworlds, and your court in particular." Rie gave a wry smile, and the king chuckled, but let her continue. "He wouldn't pause for trial, he would simply take my life. This trip buys me some time, and if I can discover the man or woman behind the attempt, and determine their motive, I can prove my innocence."

Rie paused for a breath. "I am nobody, sir. Just a changeling. My wardens might be upset if I'm killed, but otherwise, no one would care about me as a person."

"You must be somebody, or Garamaen wouldn't bother with you. He might be infatuated with the Human Realm, but he doesn't waste time on inconsequential things."

"This trial is a farce." Rolimdornoron rose to his feet. "If you won't abide by the treaty, I demand trial by combat."

The king glanced in the chief messenger's direction and tapped his chin with one long manicured nail. "That's not a bad idea."

Rolimdornoron sputtered, his forehead furrowing in consternation. He sat down hard, as if unable to believe his request was approved.

The king turned back to Rie. "You fought your way out of Master Whixle's smithy, through his redcap guard?"

"Yes, Your Majesty."

He looked at Daenor. "Was she good?"

Daenor gave a tight nod. "Better than most of the guard would have been, in the same situation." He paused, as if carefully choosing his next words. "She's more than human. She's faster and more focused than any changeling I've ever met." King Aradae quirked an eyebrow, but reserved comment.

"The first day I met her, she resisted my compulsion, and then she drained my energy when she realized what was happening," Braegan added, still kneeling before the king. If he had been just a little closer, Rie might have smacked him. Instead, she shook her head.

"I'm only human. I've never expressed an ability to manipulate energy, and my wardens would have told me if there was more to my ancestry." No one seemed to be listening.

"I can't tell what she is. Human, yes, but also something more. I'd bet on her winning a one-on-one fight against almost anyone," Daenor said.

King Aradae stared at Rie, the intensity of his gaze making her feel like an insect under a magnifying lens. "I'd like to see you fight. I'll even let you use your own blades. If you survive, we can talk about your future."

Daenor took another step forward, his eyebrows drawn down low over flickering amber eyes, but Rie lifted her chin and answered before he had the chance to protest. "Name your fighter." If she was going to go down, she'd go down fighting. At least this way, she wouldn't have to face endless torture and a slow death.

King Aradae turned to Rolimdornoron. "Who will it be?"

Rolimdornoron leaned forward in his chair. "Who's the best fighter in this room?"

"Daenor," the king replied without hesitation.

Rolimdornoron scowled. "Unacceptable. He's made his

feelings quite apparent."

"Then you'll have to go with the second best. Cendir, step forward. Think you can handle this one?"

Cendir grinned, white teeth glistening against black skin. "With pleasure."

"First to draw blood wins." King Aradae motioned for Rie to come forward and claim her weapons.

CHAPTER FIFTEEN

A roar echoed around the chamber. "No!" Fire coated Daenor's hands and lit his eyes. The guards surrounded him, their weapons held ready, but they seemed hesitant to engage their commander. Daenor drew the new sword at his back, the blade instantly encased in flame, and stalked forward.

Cendir grinned. "The prince is unstable. Again. Perhaps he should be relieved of his responsibilities."

"He'll kill her. He won't restrain himself to simply drawing blood."

Cendir's eyes narrowed to slits. "I have no need to cheat."

"You'll have no chance." Flicking his wrist toward Cendir, Daenor launched a fireball at the dark elf. Jumping out of the way, Cendir tossed Rie's weapons to the side and drew his own long straight sword. Without thought, Rie slid forward to claim them. As soon as her hands grasped the grips of her khukuris, energy surged through her body, wrapping around her forearms and squeezing her shoulders. She popped up to a standing position, prepared for battle.

"Control yourself," King Aradae boomed.

Daenor gave no indication of hearing the command

and launched into an attack. The two men met with a clash of steel. Braegan scuttled out of the way and the crowd parted, clearing a space for the men to maneuver. For several heartbeats, no one interfered. Even Rie stood immobilized. In the Upper Realm, this kind of violence in an open forum was unheard of. Yet here, people looked on without a hint of concern.

Rie watched the fight with avid interest, concentrating her attention on her future opponent. Where Daenor was all heat and anger, Cendir was cold and unemotional, but vicious. He was fast and precise, his movements sharp and controlled. Every thrust intended to kill. His style was more linear than Daenor's ever shifting circular steps, but he controlled the fight by keeping his center and resisting Daenor's attempts to draw him out into the open.

The king rose from his throne, pacing forward to the edge of the dais with measured steps. "Prince Daenor, Commander of the Shadow Guard, as your king and father, I order you to *stand down.*" Though Daenor stood twenty feet away, the king reached out a hand and yanked, as if grabbing Daenor's collar and physically pulling him away from Cendir. Daenor stumbled back and fell, his sword clattering to the floor. When Cendir made to swing a final, killing blow, the king shoved him back with an open palm and sent him careening into one of the tall marble columns.

"Unsanctioned violence is not tolerated in this room. Cendir, you will fight the changeling. You will fight fairly, and you will not strike a killing blow. If the girl loses, she will be sent to the Upper Realm, where King Othin can have the honor of her execution. Am I understood?"

Cendir's eyes remained defiant, but he nodded his head. "Yes, sire." The king released him from the invisible restraints holding him against the column.

"As for you, *my son*, this behavior is embarrassing. You are the Commander of the Shadow Guard, not some heartsick little princeling. I have made my judgment. If she's as good as you say, she stands a chance, but if you interfere again, I will be forced to send her back with the messenger."

Daenor struggled to stand, but the king spread his fingers and pushed him to the ground with the invisible force he wielded. Daenor lowered his head in a small bow. "Understood." At his acquiescence, King Aradae removed the pressure. Daenor rose from his forced sprawl, his face hard but impassive.

"Wonderful. Let's get started." King Aradae gestured for Daenor to join him on the dais. The prince clenched his teeth but followed the king's instructions, standing with a stiff glower and arms crossed, slightly behind and to the right of the king. The king nodded to Cendir. "Young Nuriel has already acquired her weapons. You may begin."

Rie swallowed and turned to face Cendir as he paced toward her position. Her thumb twitched, nerves rising to the surface. A sneer slid across the dark elf's face and his eyelids dropped to half-cover stormy gray eyes. He was a slim man, wiry, but corded with tight muscle. His ebony skin reflected a soft blue sheen from the wisplights hovering above the dais and surrounding area. His murky white hair was pulled back into a tight knot at the crown of his head — a look that had gone out of fashion in the Upper Realm before Rie had even been born — and hardened black leather covered his body from the top of his neck to the tips of pointed black boots.

Rie stretched and twisted, testing the limits of her injuries. Her ribs, though not broken, ached where they had been bruised, and even though it had been a shallow cut, her shoulder pulled and throbbed beneath the bandage. But the pain was manageable, and she pushed it aside as she spun her blades, preparing for the first strike. "Gikl," she whispered sotto voce, keeping her lips as still as possible, "find the others, and stay out of the fight. Follow Rolimdornoron if he leaves."

"Got it," the pixie replied, zipping off into the crowd. If anyone saw him leave, they said nothing.

Rie let her mind wander free, taking in everything, filtering nothing, until she could place every rustle of fabric, breath of air, and shift of weight in the room. Simultaneously full to bursting and clear as a mountain lake after the snow-melt, Rie's senses expanded even further, splitting to reveal multiple possible actions, all at once. She gasped, but held the Sight. It was as if she was watching dozens of fights in a personal arena in her head. Each decision point divided into a new series of possible outcomes. She let the scenarios waft through her mind, parsing them for information on her options.

"Feel free to begin, any time," the king announced, sounding a bit exasperated. A small part of Rie's brain wondered if he had expected her to launch herself immediately at Cendir, but that wasn't her style. No, Curuthannor had taught patience and control in a fight. She waited, watched, and grew accustomed to the flickering images in her Sight.

In an instant, the view changed. Cendir lunged forward in a lightning fast feint toward Rie's right side, and the arena of fights in her head divided in half. Rie pivoted and blocked the blade with the flat of her knife, avoiding the cut and reducing the possible futures in half again. Cendir stepped back, his cold gray eyes assessing. Rie spun her blades, first one, then the other. She waited.

A hint of a sneering smile was all she saw before Cendir launched himself forward. He attacked in a fury of sweeping blows, pushing Rie back toward the wall as she blocked and parried. If she stayed on the defensive, she Saw she would never recover. If her back hit the wall, the fight was over. She sprang forward, ducked under a slicing strike to her upper chest and pivoted into a tight kick, landing a solid blow across Cendir's ribs. He stumbled back, and Rie dashed toward the center of the room.

Cold anger replaced the sneer as Cendir rushed to follow. His sword sliced toward Rie's legs. She flipped herself out of the way, then pushed off in a forward leg sweep, her foot connecting with and hooking the elf's knee. He fell, rolling backward and avoiding Rie's blade before she could connect. He sprang up into a narrow-eyed defensive stance.

Taking advantage of his momentary pause, Rie attacked, twirling into a series of high kicks and sweeping blades, aimed at the elf's chest and head. Always a fraction of a second ahead of her, the elf dodged every strike, hardly bothering to block or parry. It was almost as if he, too, had the Sight. Rie continued to push the elf back, staying on the offensive even though she failed to See a way to win. There were still too many options, and in most of them, Cendir ended the victor. She couldn't let that happen.

All she had to do was draw blood. To do that, she needed to be unpredictable. Blocking a downward strike with both khukuris, Rie kicked Cendir in the stomach, pushing him back out of range. She took a breath, clearing her mind and letting go of the Sight. If she didn't think, she wouldn't know what she was going to do, and neither would he.

Cendir recovered and returned to attack, spinning his sword in a complicated pattern. Rie backed out of the way, watching the blade without engaging. The pattern never deviated, beginning and ending with the sword pointing at Cendir's right foot. Her knees hit the king's dais. She was out of room. Cendir grinned, anticipation lighting his face. Rie kept her mind quiet. At the end of the revolution, Rie launched herself up, jumping inside Cendir's reach and wrapping her right leg around his head, her body weight pulling him to the ground. When they hit the floor, her elbow smashed into his nose, drawing blood.

Rie had won. She rolled off and away, letting Cendir stand, and putting at least four arm lengths between them. Rivulets of blood gushed from his nose, but he didn't bother to wipe it away. His eyes narrowed to slits and his hand squeezed the grip of his sword. He lunged forward.

Rie wasn't surprised. One of Curuthannor's primary laws of war was to *never believe the fight is over until your enemy is dead*. Knocking an opponent unconscious might end the battle or suspend the fight, but enemies hold grudges. Always be prepared for reprisals.

Cendir took one step before the king lifted a hand and halted his movement. "Bravo! Not quite what I expected, but you certainly proved your skill." King Aradae tapped his lip with a thoughtful frown. "Unfortunately, despite your victory, you are still in violation of the treaty between the upper and lower realms. By rights I should send you back to King Othin, but I find I rather like you. Quite a quandary."

"What would you have of me?"

The king stroked his chin, a gesture that rang with insincerity in Rie's mind. "You seem honest, and your connection to Sanyaro is unique. Perhaps my honorable enemy will accept a compromise. You will stay here, a Conscript to the Shadow Guard, under the watchful supervision of your comrades and commander."

Rolimdornoron rose from his seat behind the throne,

knocking his chair over in his haste to object. "That is unacceptable. She is a proven traitor already. It is my right to take her back to King Othin for judgment. Anything less and you risk war."

"She won. She proved her innocence." Braegan stood at the front of the crowd, his voice hoarse, yet carrying far enough for everyone to hear. "She doesn't deserve Conscription."

Rie was shocked that the betrayer would speak in her defense. She didn't know his angle, but no one flipped sides that easily. She shook her head, knowing that her face showed her disgust, but not caring.

"The Observer is right about one thing. Rolimdornoron, you demanded trial by combat. She won, proving her innocence, so you can tell your king that she lives by your hand. But until I personally feel confident that she can be trusted, she will be kept under lock and key, watched at all times." Braegan scowled, but remained silent while the king continued to speak. "This matter is concluded. Tell Othin that any further attempts to encroach on my authority are not welcome."

Rolimdornoron huffed and left the room in a swirl of cloth and righteous indignation. "You will regret this." He called over his shoulder before disappearing through the door.

The king shook his head. "Perhaps. But not today. So, Rie, what do you say? Will you accept a Conscript position in the guard, or should I call that weasel back and have him return you to your home?"

Braegan stepped forward, pushing into Rie's line of sight but standing out of reach. "Don't do it, Rie. You'll never get out, never be free. Conscript is a life sentence." She didn't want to listen to the backstabbing bastard, but his words rang true. He knew more about what she was getting into than she did.

"Ignore him," Daenor stepped down off the dais. "Yes, there are some Conscripts that die in the service, or that never redeem themselves, but that won't happen to you. It will take time, but you have the capacity to earn your place."

Rie's thoughts spun. She would never be able to return to the Upper Realm, and there was a chance that the sum total of her life would be serving in the guard, but the only alternative involved a giant axe. King Aradae was offering an escape, a way for her to keep her head without running and hiding. What's more, he was offering her a position that would utilize decades of dedicated weapons training, and a chance to redeem herself.

If only she could be sure her wardens wouldn't be harmed as a result of her actions. Letting the rumors of her treason stand uncontested would take decades, if not centuries, for them to overcome. Still, they knew the risks when they wished her a good journey, and they knew that she would make the best decisions she could.

Rie glanced between the men in front of her, weighing their two truths. Braegan stood hunched, still favoring his injuries, his eyes downcast and sad. Daenor stood stoic, but he met her gaze with hope smoldering in his eyes.

"You leave me no choice. I'll join the guard."

Daenor's lips lifted in a soft smile.

CHAPTER SIXTEEN

Daenor led the way through the bowels of the twisting castle, to the rear entrance of the walled palace grounds, not looking back as he hustled Rie and her four armed escorts toward a squat round building nestled against a sheer mountain cliff. Rie followed a few paces behind, struggling to keep up with his long-legged stride without breaking into a jog.

No one spoke, the only sounds were those of footfalls on stone and the guards' breathing chasing behind her.

She might as well admit she was a prisoner. She didn't yet know what the terms of the arrangement would be, but Braegan had warned her away from the guard. But what other choice did she have? She had been moved into position like a player on a board. The king wanted something from her. He had been too interested in her connection to Lord Garamaen and her ancestry. If only she knew why.

But that led to the bigger issue; she wasn't as human as she had been led to believe. Her wardens and the entire Upper Realm had insisted she was a mere changeling, treating her like any other servant in the court. Her freedoms were limited, her opportunities even more so. When she first developed a small skill in precognition,

Curuthannor had advised her not to tell anyone, but still insisted that she had been found orphaned in the Human Realm. Even if that were true, there had to be something else, something more, or she wouldn't be expressing new abilities now. And why now? Why the sudden surge in magical talent? She didn't have the answers, and the uncertainty bothered her more than she liked.

Approaching the curved stone facade of the squat building, Daenor finally broke his silence. "This is the headquarters of the Shadow Guard," he said, gesturing toward the front gate.

Up close, it was bigger than Rie had initially thought, standing at least four stories high, with a crenellated wall at the top. Soft blue wisplights shone through the mostly slit windows in the front facade. A large arched gate was the only visible entrance to the defensive building. Wide enough for six horses to ride abreast, the triple portcullis could be slammed shut with weighted levers. All in all, an impressive building that would act as a rear fortification in the case that the palace was ever overrun.

"For the most part, the Shadow Guard eats, sleeps, and lives here," Daenor continued as they passed into the open-air training yard at the center of the edifice. "Some offices, ready-rooms, and executive living quarters are located in the external building here, but the majority of our operations are built into the cliff. We'll head up to my office first, then get you situated."

Rie tried not to let her curiosity and awe show. Although she had occasionally visited Curuthannor's office at the guard facilities in the Upper Realm, she had never been allowed into the inner sanctum or training areas. She had never seen anything like the Shadow Guard headquarters.

The inner courtyard was larger than it seemed from the exterior of the building, thanks to the apparently natural shape of the cliff face at the rear. The space was egg-shaped, the squat building providing the point in front of a deep round rock wall, and was organized into distinct training areas. Bladed weapons practice was underway to the left of the arched entry, hand-to-hand combat on the right. It was difficult to see from the gate, but it looked like projectile targets were located at the rear against the cliff face, with areas for both archery and human firearms. With plenty of open space in between, the training yard could likely accommodate five hundred warriors in active combat, with room to maneuver.

Not giving Rie an opportunity for more detailed inspection, Daenor led the way past the rack filled with non-bladed weapons to a set of stairs cut into the building wall. Daenor's office was given prime real estate on the top floor, and the stairs led directly to his door. Pressing a hand to the space above the knob, Daenor unlocked the door with a word and ushered Rie ahead of him into the room.

Blue wisplight flickered to life as she entered, illuminating a comfortable, clutter-free space. The office was plush, yet masculine, full of dark leather, dark wood, and the comforting smells of gun oil and leather polish. Large windows overlooked both the exterior courtyard and the interior training yard, providing prime observation of anyone approaching the complex, as well as the efforts of the men and women under Daenor's command. In case of attack, steel shutters could be locked into place from the inside. Narrow tables, designed to fit the gentle curve of the walls, rested under each window.

An oil painting of a phoenix rising from the ashes of a battlefield dominated the wall behind the heavy walnut desk. Rie couldn't help but admire the detail of the piece, the red, yellow, and orange flames licking up the wings of the long-tailed bird, the grimaces of the dying warriors, the glazed eyes of the dead. It was both gruesome and devastatingly beautiful. Closed doors on either side of the painting provided possible exits from the room.

"You're something else, you know that?" Daenor closed the door, releasing the four guards back to their prior duties.

Rie regretfully turned to face her new commander. She had trusted him up to this point, even begun to like him. Now, he was her boss, and worse, the king had set him up as her captor. There was no going back from that, even if she had wanted to.

He prowled forward on quiet footsteps, his gaze thoughtful but intense. Rie leaned back against the desk behind her, her butt on the edge, her arms carrying her weight. Daenor stopped just a foot or two away, close enough to touch without crowding her. He clasped his hands behind his back, the muscles in his shoulders tense.

"Do you realize you just defeated the second best fighter in the guard? I thought you'd be killed, and I doubt anyone bet you would win. How did you do it?"

"What do you mean?"

"Cendir is the only elf I know with the ability to forecast a fight in the middle of the action. He can See every maneuver, plan every attack and counter every strike. He should have been able to draw blood in the matter of a few moves, but you managed to stay ahead of him. How?"

Rie shrugged. "He wasn't the only one forecasting."

Daenor's eyes widened. "You have precognition?"

Rie nodded. "This was the first time it's happened during a fight, though. The number of possibilities was staggering."

"Most precogs can't foresee a one-on-one fight. It's too

chaotic. Battle maneuvers involving massive armies, sure, but not individual choices at the speed of combat. Untrained as you are, I'm amazed you weren't overwhelmed."

Rie pursed her lips, considering. "I was a bit, at first. But I suspected he had a similar ability when he dodged every strike. I figured if I blanked my mind and let go of the Sight, I might be able to surprise him."

"An elbow to the nose in a knife fight would be a surprise."

"I didn't think about what I was going to do before I did it, so I never actually made a decision about my next move. I let instinct and reflex rule. It was sort of like fighting the pixies; they're so fast, you don't have time to think or plan. It probably looked like I'd given up."

"Smart. But Cendir won't let it go. Watch your back around him." Daenor's hand reached up, slowly, so slowly, his thumb tracing a burning line down Rie's cheek. "I thought you would lose. I thought you would be sent back to the Upper Realm, and I'd never see you again."

Rie's breath came fast. She clenched her hands on the desk to keep from leaning into the caress and soaking up all the heat he had to offer. No matter how tempting, she couldn't get involved with him. There were too many questions, too many things she didn't know. And he was dark elf royalty and her new boss, or captor: she still didn't understand her situation. She needed more information, not a quick entanglement in his office. Her body ached to lean forward, to touch him, but she forced herself to lean back, instead.

"Too much?" he asked, the husky murmur tangling with her desire until she wanted nothing more than to reach out and comfort him. It took everything she had not to follow through.

Rie nodded, but her voice betrayed her. "No. It's just that, it's all too complicated. I barely understand what's going on, here. King Aradae could have given me back to Rolimdornoron and saved himself a headache. Why didn't he?"

The amber of Daenor's eyes blazed. "Don't ask me to interpret the king's intentions. At the best of times, he's a sadistic bastard who enjoys manipulating people into doing the one thing they don't want to do. But now you're here, and you'll be safe. At least as safe as anyone in the guard."

"But I'm a Conscript, a prisoner. I don't understand."

"Yes, you're a Conscript. You'll be monitored at all times, and locked in a cell at night. If you fail in any of your duties, you'll be punished. And it won't be pleasant." He cocked his head to the side, his gaze soft, as if gauging her reaction. He placed his hands on her shoulders, thumbs softly caressing the curve of her neck. It was almost as if he couldn't resist touching her. His forehead creased as he stared into her eyes.

"Sweetling, I won't be able to shield you from the lash. For all intents and purposes, you *are* a prisoner. It will be an uphill battle to prove your loyalty to this realm. But you *do* have the chance to redeem yourself and earn a position in the volunteer ranks."

"Why was Braegan so concerned, then? He made it seem like being a Conscript was as good as a death sentence."

"Conscripts are criminals and malcontents, and the past isn't easy to overcome. It's near impossible to earn the king's pardon, but it can be done."

"And if I prove myself, will I be free to leave the guard entirely?"

Daenor's eyes tightened at the edges. "No. It's a lifetime position."

"Or a lifetime sentence."

"Would a lifetime here really be so bad? What do you have to go back to? From what I can tell, the high elves barely tolerated you. Here, you have a chance at a real position, a respected job, with the same rights as any of the fae."

"My wardens are my family. I can't leave them to face my punishment, especially when it's based on a lie. They'll be blamed for my actions. Maybe not executed, but certainly outcast. Curuthannor will lose his position and Lhéwen's business will be shut down. If I clear my name, they'll be safe."

Daenor's gaze burned, and his hands heated on her skin. "But what of your own life? Your own dreams? I'd like to think there are at least a few reasons for you to stay, if you were given the choice." He slid his thumbs across her collarbone, sending tingles down her spine.

Rie didn't respond. She couldn't. Her heartbeat raced. She bit her lip, unsure what she wanted. Daenor's eyes dropped, watching the movement. She might have imagined it, but Rie thought she saw his own breathing hitch. Rie's lips parted, preparing a witty retort about how a pretty face couldn't sway her, but a breath of air was all that escaped. There was no denying she wanted him.

Daenor closed the distance between them in an instant. His lips sealed against hers in a heated line. His tongue darted out, the tip barely touching her own before retreating. Brain startled into insensibility, Rie couldn't help chasing him. Her tongue stroked across his bottom lip, discovering the slight ridge of an old scar. She carefully bit down on the hardened flesh, tugging on the healed wound.

Daenor groaned and wrapped both hands possessively around the back of her head and neck, pulling her impossibly closer. Rie eagerly followed his lead, sliding her right hand up the length of his arm, feeling the corded muscle beneath the soft fabric of his human shirt, while her left wrapped around his waist, pulling him into her body. Her right hand reached his shoulder, then higher, sliding beneath his collar to find heated skin.

***

The body smolders in front of him, charred black flesh interspersed with patches of creamy white skin that ripples like melted candle wax. Pink painted nails stand out from the carnage. She had painted them just this morning, while he played with the metal blocks. They wouldn't give him wood anymore, but there was always something he could burn. Always.

He hadn't meant it. This nurse was nice. But he'd been so angry. She wouldn't let him go outside to see the parade. She'd said the queen wanted him to stay inside, where he couldn't cause trouble. But Father would have wanted to wave goodbye, wouldn't he?

The smell of burnt hair and blackened meat wafts toward him on the breeze from the window where he had struggled to call for Father. He shudders. Her hands had caught fire first when she tried to grab him away. Her screams had brought the guards, but they couldn't put out the fire. The more they tried, the more it spread. Daenor couldn't put it out, even when he tried. He didn't know how to call back the flames.

With Father gone, the queen will be in charge. It won't matter what he says, how much he apologizes or swears he didn't mean to do it. He is in big trouble. He huddles in the corner, hoping to be ignored, but knowing it won't work.

***

With a gasp, Rie broke away from Daenor's passionate warmth. Some of her fear and anxiety must have shown on her face. Daenor's hands lifted away from her, as if afraid he'd hurt her. "What is it?"

She shook her head and closed her eyes, reliving the vision again and again. What she had just glimpsed, it didn't make sense. Was it Daenor's past? Was it a memory? A dream?

"I.." The raspy sound could barely be heard. Rie cleared her throat. "I'm not sure. It's never happened before."

Cold air replaced heat as Daenor stepped back, giving Rie room to think and breathe.

"Look at me." Rie opened her eyes to find Daenor's concerned gaze watching her every movement. "What happened? What did you see?"

"When I touched you, I saw...I'm not sure what I saw. I don't know if it was a dream or a memory, but it was as if I inhabited your body. I knew it was you, and I knew I was separate, but I experienced it all. The fear and despair...you were so young, and had no hope."

"Explain." It wasn't a request, but somehow his voice remained supportive, even in his demands.

"There was a body, burned beyond recognition. Your nurse. You liked her, and you destroyed her in a fit of anger."

Daenor's eyes tightened and a furrow creased his brow. He turned away. "I was four years old. I couldn't control my power." Daenor shook his head, but Rie couldn't see his face. "I figured it out, eventually." He paused, rubbing hands through his hair with a sigh, before turning back to face her. "It's called hindsight, or postcognition, the ability to see the past, usually through touch. You say it's never happened before?"

"No. Never."

"It's a Dark Elf skill, a subset of soul magic. You're sure you're a changeling, and not a halfling?" A smile played around the edges of Daenor's lips, but his eyes were serious.

"All I know is that I was orphaned and taken from the human realm as a baby."

"Mmm."

"High Elves are forbidden from siring children with humans or any of the lesser fae. Entire families have been hunted and killed to preserve the High Elf bloodlines."

"What a tolerant crowd." Sarcasm dripped off his tongue. "But that's not true, here. In fact, I know quite a few Dark Elves who enjoy human company, but halfling children are still rare, and they usually look more elfin than you."

"They wouldn't have sold me as a changeling if I had elvish blood, even dark elf blood. Not if they knew. Halflings are destroyed, and if there was evidence I was an orphaned full-blood elf, I would have been fostered with a willing family. That leaves human."

"It sounds like your wardens treated you very much as a foster child, not the slave you might have been in another home. And you are without question more than human."

Rie crossed her arms over her chest, huddling against herself. There were too many conflicting emotions, too much going on, too soon. She needed time and quiet to think. "I can't deny that anymore, but now I don't know who I am, and never will. The records of my sale are buried in the vaults the Chronicles, in the Great University of the High Court."

Daenor smiled, but the gesture was half-hearted. "We'll test your abilities tomorrow. Find out what else you're hiding away in there."

"I'm not hiding anything," Rie objected.

Daenor lifted a brow. "We already know you're impressive with those blades. What other weapons have you trained with?"

Rie stiffened, shoving her emotions into the mental cage where they belonged. If Daenor could switch from passion to business without hesitation, so could she. In fact, it was probably a good thing. She needed to focus, not let herself get distracted by an unattainable male, no matter how warm and delicious. He was a prince, and her boss. He was too far above her to have an equal relationship, and she had too much self-respect to become a courtesan.

Straightening into an at-ease stance, Rie pretended she was speaking with Curuthannor. "Knives are my primary expertise, but I am nearly equally skilled with a staff. I'm a decent shot with a bow and have been trained in the use of human guns. While I have been introduced to formal swordplay, my trainer felt that my size and situation didn't require a strong emphasis on the discipline."

Daenor nodded briefly, perhaps with approval, perhaps with agreement. Rie couldn't be sure.

"And magic?"

"The only magic I'm aware of is prescience, and now perhaps hindsight."

"And Braegan said you're a drainer."

"I'm still not sure what that means, and I don't know what I did or how I did it."

Daenor paced away to look out the window overseeing the training grounds. "You're untrained, but if Braegan is right, you have both soul and spirit magic. Dark elf and high elf. And human." Daenor paused.

As far as Rie knew, there were no dark elf and high elf half-breeds. The animosity between the courts was too deeply rooted. She had no answers to his unasked questions.

"With your potential background, you can't tell anyone

about your abilities. Not yet. The Queen has been fighting King Aradae for years over his 'progressive' ideas and policies. She used my birth as an example of the 'dangerous implications of the rise of the lesser fae and sidhe'. She's built a small, but powerful group of supporters with the goal of maintaining dark elf power. The heirs are her biggest supporters, and they do most of her dirty work. If your skills are made public, you'll have a huge target painted on your back." Daenor lowered his head to stare into Rie's eyes. "I won't risk you to the out-dated prejudices of the ancient nobility."

Rie swallowed and nodded. If it turned out that she really was some kind of dark-elf-high-elf-hybrid, her life would be as precarious as ever. She had hoped the guard would give her some security, or at least stop the running and hiding, but it looked like the secrets would just keep coming.

Daenor seemed to take her silence as confirmation and began pacing across the burnt orange and red rug, running his hands through his hair in distraction. "We're going to have to run the full contingent of tests at the university, but the testers are duty sworn to keep the results confidential, and I'll make sure you have someone trustworthy. Since Braegan — the idiot — revealed you're a drainer in front of the whole court, we'll have to be extra careful and bury the test results if it's confirmed."

"The king allows humans and Conscripts to attend the university?" Rie interrupted, his words sinking in. King Othin would never allow such a thing, no matter how skilled the student. Only elves were allowed to attend the Great University. There were lesser schools that some of the fae had built to educate their young, but even they wouldn't accept humans.

"Of course," Daenor replied, as if she were daft for asking. "How else would they develop their skills?

Besides, it's not entirely altruistic on the King's part. High performers are quickly drafted to serve the kingdom. And Conscripts need the training as much as anyone else, they're just carefully monitored."

Rie shook her head. Everything she thought she knew of the Shadow Realm was wrong. The books she'd read, the lessons she'd been taught, they all made it seem like the Shadow Court was nothing but a licentious pleasure house filled with selfish beings who sought only to suffocate the light from the Upper Realm. The reality was complex and open, informal and accepting.

The Shadow King's behavior in the throne room proved to Rie that he had an agenda. Monarchs always did. And it seemed he was still at odds with King Othin. But his realm wasn't as black as her teachers had alleged. He seemed to value *all* of his subjects a great deal more than the High King ever did.

"I've always wondered what the university would be like," Rie said.

"You'll have your chance. It won't be easy." He shook his head, blowing out a deep breath. "We'll have to find trustworthy trainers, too."

Watching him worry only increased Rie's anxiety.

CHAPTER SEVENTEEN

A knock on the door interrupted Daenor's frenetic pacing. "Ragnar," Daenor said, after opening the door. "This is Rie, our newest Conscript."

The three-eyed well-dressed goblin darted a quick glance at Daenor, then approached Rie on silent feet, hand extended. "Ah, so ye be the lady with whom Daenor's been romping about the city. Didn't expect to see ye joining us in the guard."

Shaking his hand, Rie couldn't help but smile. "I wouldn't exactly call fighting Redcaps and the second best warrior in Nalakadr 'romping', more surviving, but yes, that's me. Entering the guard wasn't my choice, but it's better than a beheading. I'll try to stay out of your way."

"I don't think that'll be happening. But that's a'right."

Daenor slapped a hand on Ragnar's shoulder. "Ragnar is my steward and second. He's been with me since I was a child."

Directing his words to Daenor, Ragnar continued his examination of Rie. "Am I to take charge of her, then? Find a room, arrange her training schedule, get her situated, and all that?"

"Set her up with a room, yes, but I'll see to her

schedule. She's to be placed in one of the Conscript cells, not the general women's barracks. And she'll need an escort at all times."

"Special interest in this one's training, eh?" Ragnar smiled, revealing a shining gold canine. Daenor elbowed him, sending the smaller goblin off-balance for a step, but he just laughed. "A'right then. But I'll need her schedule to rearrange the duty roster."

Daenor stepped forward, draping his arm over Ragnar's shoulders. "You'll have it tomorrow."

With their five eyes looking her up and down, Rie felt like a bug in a jar. Her thumb twitched, sliding beneath the slick fabric open at her hip.

"And what of her wee friends? Will they need special consideration?"

Rie startled at the mention of the pixies. No one in the Upper Realm would ever consider their needs. They either ignored or condemned them. It was a refreshing change.

Daenor looked at her, expectantly. "Well?" he asked. "This one seems comfortable enough hanging around with me..."

Sure enough, Gikl had camouflaged himself on Daenor's black sword sheath, but at his words he shook his wings and fluttered up, hands on hips.

"How did you know?"

"You may be fast and stealthy, but landing on a warrior's weapon draws attention."

Gikl frowned. "Damn."

"Where are the others?" Rie asked.

"Hiinto and Tiik stayed in the throne room. They'll probably be here soon."

"What about the other two?" Daenor demanded, eyes drilling the little pixie.

"That's for us to know, and you to not find out." Gikl

buzzed to Rie, and stood on her shoulder, one hand gripping her ear. Without turning his head, he whispered, "They're going to sneak through a portal and alert Lord Garamaen. Don't count on rescue or support, but at least he'll know what's happened and tell your wardens." The words were so quiet, Rie was sure the others couldn't hear. An internal pressure valve released, and she suddenly felt more confident. She might not get help, but they would know she was alive and well enough. It was the best she could ask for.

"As Commander of the Shadow Guard, I need to know where they are," Daenor said.

"Rie may have pledged her service to the guard, but we pixies have made no oaths to you or anyone in this dark place. No, we are still free to do as we please."

"Shall I get the spray?" Ragnar asked, an evil twinkle in his eyes.

Daenor looked thoughtful, his eyes narrowing in contemplation. After a tense pause, a grin spread across his face. "That's unnecessary. He's right, after all." He cocked his head to the side, addressing Gikl directly. "I can't order you to reveal your secrets, and considering it's unlikely I could catch you speedy little buggers, I guess I'll have to let it go. For now."

Ragnar turned to look at his friend, wide eyes shocked. "Ye can't be serious. Ye're going to let it go?"

Daenor grinned. "Yes. I can respect his loyalty to his companions. In time, I hope to earn your trust, though, little one. I think we can be mutually beneficial."

"I like him," Gikl whispered to Rie, before responding to Daenor out loud. "We'll see." Rie couldn't help the smile that spread across her face. The impertinent little pixie.

"Now to your question," Gikl continued, "we'll be happy staying with Rie and will build our own hive."

Ragnar snorted. "Fine. With yer leave, I'll get her settled."

"Yes, you're dismissed. Rie, I'll see you here tomorrow morning, third bell. Someone will come for you after second bell to take you to the morning meal."

***

The Shadow Guard headquarters were a warren of tunnels and caves beneath the great mountain of Nalakadr. Riding on her shoulder, Gikl stayed quiet and hidden, allowing Rie to focus her attention on the hunched back in front of her and the twists and turns they took through the curving hallways of the mountain fortress. Despite her best efforts, Rie quickly lost her bearings.

Ragnar took her first to the requisitions room, where the supply master provided Rie with some basic necessities, including two sets of comfortable, if less than fashionable, training uniforms. Like the rest of the Conscripts, Rie would be expected to wear the uniform at all times. When she asked why most of the other guards she'd seen were allowed to wear their own clothing and armor, the response had been a terse, "ye'll have to earn the privilege to dress yerself and wear the badge of office."

After requisitions, Ragnar took her to the mess hall, where they stopped just long enough to gather a sandwich, some white-skinned fruit that Rie didn't recognize, and two flasks of water. Ragnar wouldn't break to eat, so she put the meal in the requisitions sack alongside her new uniforms and spare boots.

The conscript living quarters were buried deep within the facility. Closed black doors lined the smooth carved rock walls on both sides of the hall, with soft glowing lamps lighting the space between each white numbered door. There were no decorations, nothing to soften the austere surroundings. Apparently, the Shadow Guard didn't believe in signs to direct people where to go. You had to know your way, or be lost forever in the tunnels. She was glad she would have an escort, at least until she figured out where everything was.

Without a word, Ragnar stopped in front of a door marked 2114, pulled a key from his pocket, and ushered Rie inside the room. She stood at the threshold, admiring her sparse surroundings. Though small, the room was decently appointed, with a narrow, but comfortable-looking bed, tall armoire, and a bedside table with an oil lamp resting on its smooth surface. A door led into an attached bathroom. From her position, it looked like a basic toilet, sink, and overhead faucet for showering. It might not be luxurious, but it was as much as she needed, and more than she expected.

"Will it do?" Ragnar asked, sounding surprisingly concerned. "Daenor would want ye comfortable, and this is the best of the Conscript cells. I won't have ye telling 'im I've been less than hospitable."

The knowing look in Ragnar's eye made Rie pause. Had Daenor said something? He couldn't have possibly mentioned the kiss, not while Rie was there listening. So what could he know? She shook her head, clearing her thoughts and answering the question. "No, this is fine. I can't complain."

"Well, ye probably will. But that can't be helped. I'm to lock ye in for the night. Conscripts aren't allowed to roam. Did ye have any other belongings at the inn that need to be brought over?" Ragnar asked, remaining by the door, one hand on the metal knob.

"No, I have everything with me." Rie didn't want anyone to know about Plink, at least not yet. If word got out, her usefulness as a spy would be ruined. Rie could only hope Braegan hadn't thought to include Plink in his report. The pixies could retrieve her in the morning, after everyone was gone for the day.

"Wonderful," Ragnar replied. "I won't have to play fetch for ye. Now, I suggest ye get to sleep right away. Ye'll be up early and have a long day tomorrow. I'm sure Daenor will want ye tested as soon as possible."

"What is the testing like? Can you tell me?" Rie asked, anxious to understand what would be expected of her. The Upper Realm never even considered testing her abilities. It had never been an option, and she hadn't concerned herself with the details. Now she was left clueless, and worried about what they would discover.

"It's different fer everyone. I can't say more than that. They'll run ye through yer paces though, so ye'll need all the energy ye can muster. Matches are in the drawer for yer lamp. I'll wait 'til ye get it lit, then I'm off. I've other duties to attend."

Rie nodded, and lit the lamp. Before she blew out the match, the door clicked shut, the lock engaged, and Ragnar was gone.

With a soft snort, Rie set to work arranging her room. She opened the flat-fronted doors of the armoire and was assaulted by the smell of unwashed male underclothes. Gagging, she waved the doors back and forth a few times, hoping to air out the offensive odor. When that didn't work, she took one of her two requisitioned towels and, after dampening the cloth in the bathroom, carefully wiped every inch of the inside. It helped, but the scent was still noticeable. She would have to find some lavender or another herb to make a sachet. Until then, she would leave the doors and drawers open.

Gikl didn't seem to mind the stench, quickly claiming the top shelf on the left side for himself.

"May I use some of the stuffing from your pillow for the hive?" he asked politely. It had taken years for any of the pixies to remember to ask before sneaking off with whatever bits and bobs they wanted.

"Yes, but only a clump or two. I need my rest, too." Rie glanced back to make sure he didn't take the whole thing. Gikl gleefully tore a hole in the corner and, shoving both arms and his entire upper body into the pillow, pulled out a great wad of feathers. Trailing brown and white down, he flew up to his shelf and began weaving the feathers into a complicated basket.

Amused, Rie watched him work while she ate her packaged meal. It was surprisingly decent, a soft cheese spread on thick bread, with slices of a green acidic fruit, similar to a tomato. The white fruit was sweet and crisp, popping into her mouth with each bite. She bounced a few times on the springy mattress while she ate, leaning back into the pillow propped against the wall. Not as comfortable as her room in Curuthannor's hall, but at least as good, maybe better than her quarters at the messenger barracks. It would do fine.

Her thoughts traveled back to Ragnar's cryptic remark. He couldn't know about the kiss, not yet, so did he simply assume that Daenor had made a pass at her? If so, why? She hoped this wasn't a habit, where the Commander got involved with new recruits, or worse, newly Conscripted guards. That would be an unconscionable abuse of power, and she wanted to believe that Daenor was above those kinds of tactics. But the reality was, she had no idea, and he *had* come on to her moments after closing the door. She'd only known him a few days, and while there had been an almost instant attraction — at least on her side — she didn't really know him. He could very easily be a womanizer.

Disgusted with her own thoughts, Rie mentally slapped herself and resettled on the bed. Daenor was a prince. The one crush on a high elf she'd allowed herself as a youngling had ended in disaster, and he hadn't even been a royal. The prick had made it clear that humans weren't worth a relationship, just a romp in bed, and he'd done it in front of Curuthannor's entire advanced class. Not one of them had disagreed. She wouldn't make that mistake again.

A rustling at the door alerted Rie to the arrival of the remainder of the pixie swarm. Squeezing beneath the edge, Hiinto and Tiik squirmed into the room. Before they'd even pulled their wings free of the heavy wood, Gikl was flitting to their sides, and a fast stream of Pixl clicks and hisses flew between the three creatures. Speeding around the room, Rie couldn't keep track of their movements, but she assumed they were inspecting their new surroundings.

"It'll have to do, I suppose," Tiik finally moaned in the common tongue. "A pain to get in and out, what with the door locked and all, but we looked on our way in and didn't see a better option, at least not one that's indoors."

"We can't leave you alone, Rie. The Queen wants you executed as a spy, and is trying to convince the King to rescind the conscription order," Hiinto said.

"What happened?"

"The queen was raging at the king when they left the throne room. She said he risks too much, and will bring war to the kingdom by denying King Othin's demands. She demanded he give you over to Rolimdornoron. When Aradae still refused, she threw her hands in the air and stomped out. I followed her to the heirs suite, where I met up with Tiik."

Tiik picked up the story. "The heirs didn't say a word until they got to their rooms, just stalked through the halls, pulling every lost soul out of the castle walls and sending every living thing running. Did you know they can literally pull the soul from a body? One of the servant girls, a young goblin, didn't get out of the way fast enough. Her body died on the spot, as her soul got ripped out and trapped in the maelstrom. It was impressive. I stayed way back."

"Glad to hear it," Rie said sincerely, urging Tiik to continue.

"I was afraid to go into their rooms, what with all the spirits whirling about and guarding the doors, but I waited out of sight down the hall. I was there for maybe a half bell before the Queen arrived. Guess who else visited?"

"The Squirrel."

"You betcha."

"So after the Queen and Rolimdornoron were denied by King Aradae, they all met up with the heirs. Why?"

"All we heard before the guards closed the doors, was that Daenor was supposed to arrest you when you met with the smith, but he disobeyed the heirs. Rolimdornoron and the Queen were there for awhile. We followed when they left, but they just went back to their rooms. Then we came here."

"So what you're telling me, is that everyone except the king wants me dead."

"And Daenor," Gikl said. "He just wants you in his bed."

The pixies laughed as Rie blushed and half-heartedly tried to swat them away.

"Get out of here," she said, smiling. "He's my boss now, so there's not going to be any of that."

"Right, just like there wasn't any of that in his office."

"Ooooh," Hiinto and Tiik said in a sing-song voice usually reserved for use by children.

Ignoring the twerps, Rie stood and made her way to the bathroom. The pixies laughed again and then swarmed over to the armoire to finish building their hive, clicking and chirping the whole time. Gikl was probably describing the kiss and events in Daenor's office in vivid detail. Loving nothing better than to gossip, they would be occupied for awhile.

Throwing the wrapper and napkin from her meal into the bin, she leaned on the sink and stared at her own reflection. She looked tired, she decided, the skin beneath her eyes puffy and dark. She should get some sleep, let her brain process the new information over night. Ragnar was right, she would need all the energy she could muster for testing the next day.

CHAPTER EIGHTEEN

Rie awoke to a gong reverberating through the mountain. Her eyes snapped open and she was on her feet, blades in hand, before the vibrations faded into the rock around her. When she realized that she was still alone, except for the pixies, she relaxed and turned up the bedside lamp. Without windows, there was no way to tell what time it was or how long she'd been asleep, but she assumed that the gong was the wake-up call to the soldiers living in the guard headquarters. Someone would probably be along soon to fetch her to the morning meal.

Rie quickly dressed in one of the training uniforms, braiding her long black hair into a tight bun on the back of her head, pinning it with two of the plain black hairsticks from Garran. She hoped he would have been proud to see them in her hair.

After performing her morning necessaries, Rie began moving through a series of warm-up stretches and blade forms. Her sore muscles and ribs ached, but eased incrementally as she loosened and relaxed. Moving smoothly and slowly through the positions, the exercise focused her mind and body. It was the best she could do to prepare for the day to come, and the only familiar thing about this place.

The click of the lock was the only warning before the door opened. Finishing the last of her slow routine, Rie completed a series of high kicks, ending with her foot poised inches from the face of the intruder.

"Well, if this is the welcome I receive, I'll be sure to hand off escort duty to someone else from now on," Daenor said, smiling around the sole of Rie's boot. His grin brightened his face, and Rie couldn't help but respond. Her heartbeat sped, and not just from the exertion.

"Sorry about that," Rie replied, lowering her leg. "I was just finishing my morning routine." She stood tall, hiding her attraction.

"Not a problem. I approve, and enjoyed the demonstration of your flexibility." Daenor's eyes crinkled at the corners, and his grin got impossibly wider.

Rie ignored the innuendo. She'd made a decision, and she was going to stick with it. Daenor was off-limits. "I'm sure you'll get to see the full routine in the course of training," she replied, coolly.

"I certainly hope so." Daenor chuckled, the sound sending spikes of desire throughout Rie's body. She needed to ice this line of conversation. Now.

"It's nothing fancy, but my warden customized the forms specifically for my fighting style. He was convinced that I could be as good as nearly any fae, if I could learn to move beneath and within the reach of the taller fighters." Daenor's grin faded, but his gaze remained intense. Rie kept up the technical babble, using it to block her feelings. "I build the speed over the course of several iterations. It makes for better muscle memory, or so my warden taught."

"Makes sense. Can I see it at full speed?"

"I need more space, but sure. Actually, with your permission, I'd like to reserve time in my schedule each morning to keep up the practice."

"Your escort would have to arrive early each day."

"Yes," Rie replied. There was no help for it. If they were going to insist on an escort, then the escort would have to come with her, but she needed to keep practicing. "But I think it's good for my training, and only takes a quarter bell."

"I'll think on it. For now, let's go get some breakfast. I set up your testing with my old University mentor, a woman named Triwen. We can trust her. I don't want any other witnesses to whatever we discover. Not yet."

Rie startled at the casual use of the word 'we'. It was almost as if Daenor was in this mess with her. As if he *wanted* to share her problems and help solve them. She blinked away the disbelief, pulling her attention back to the conversation.

"I trust your judgment," she said. Not that she had much choice.

"Can I tag along with you again, today?" Gikl asked, his voice the sound of purest innocence.

Rie snorted quietly.

Daenor narrowed his eyes, suspicion a poor cover for the amusement in his expression. "If I say no, you'll follow along anyway, won't you?"

Gikl shrugged. "Probably."

"Okay, you can come with me, but if I ask you to leave the room, you must do so immediately. If I find you spying anyway, I'll be forced to do something about it. Maybe send you back to Tryg."

"You wouldn't dare," Gikl said, crossing his arms over his diminutive chest and leaning forward.

"Test me, and you'll find out."

A few seconds of staring and Gikl broke away. "Fine," he huffed. "I will leave if you ask, and I won't spy."

"As for the rest of you, I don't want to know what

you're doing, or where you're going. However, if you get into trouble, you're on your own. As far as the rest of the kingdom knows, you aren't here. And make sure to tell the others when they get back from wherever it is they are."

A quick burst of Pixl chatter, and then Hiinto replied, "That suits us fine."

***

The room was large, white, and empty, but for a long table in the center of the room. Reflective glass lined the far wall, floor to ceiling. The floor was padded with a bouncy, gel-like material, that glowed softly in the absence of overhead lighting. When the lights came on, the floor muted to a dull gray color.

Rie walked steadily forward, head held high. She managed to keep her nervous twitch under control... mostly. Her thumb spasmed occasionally, but she didn't think it was obvious. She hoped not, anyway.

Daenor and the test proctor, Triwen, stood on the other side of the glass. Both had refused to give her any information before shoving Rie through the door to the practically sterile room.

"Approach the table," Triwen said, her voice chiming through a projection box on the wall. Four bowls and two cages rested on the scarred surface of the table, each holding a symbol of one of the magical elements: water, wood chips, dirt, feathers, a dead bird, and a live brerhopper.

"Since we don't know your heritage, we're starting from the absolute baseline," Triwen said. "This first test will determine your affinity for the elements. In whatever way feels comfortable, try to reach out to each of the vessels and control it in some way. For example, you might try to magically sculpt the dirt into a shape, or lift the feather from the bowl. The table — and the entire room, for that matter — is made of an inert material that can't be damaged or affected by magic, so don't worry about breaking anything."

Rie nodded, and looked at the table. Knowing she at least had some level of soul magic, and perhaps a touch of spirit magic, she approached the cages first. Mildly revolted by the bird carcass in the cage, she focused on the brerhopper, representing spirit magic. Energy. It was better to face the truth early than fight it later. She took a breath, centering herself for the test.

If she was a 'drainer', she should be able to make the bouncing little creature slow down, perhaps lie still. She concentrated on the twitching nose.

Calm, she thought. *Slow, still.* The brerhopper stopped bouncing and looked at Rie. Repeating the mantra a second and then a third time, the brerhopper sat, then lay down. Still, Rie chanted in her head, the energy from the brerhopper boosting her own resources. She felt great, the leftover fatigue blowing away on the wind. The brerhopper closed its eyes and fell asleep. Its breathing slowed. Rie couldn't stop, the vitality of the small creature seeming to leave a taste like the sweetest fruit in her mouth.

"That's enough," Triwen called.

Rie snapped out of her trance, glancing at the mirrored wall. Eyes wide, she stared at her reflection. She hadn't expected it to be quite so easy. In fact, she had hoped it wouldn't work at all. Instead, she'd very nearly killed the small creature. And what's worse, she'd enjoyed it.

"Next element, please," Triwen said.

Daenor had promised that Triwen could be trusted, and Rie hoped he was right. The woman didn't sound upset or disturbed by the revelation that there was a spirit wielder in Nalakadr, or that said spirit wielder was an enervator strong enough to kill, but the mirror prevented Rie from seeing her expression. Her life depended on the woman's discretion. Her thumb spasmed, and her body fought to flee.

"You can continue," Triwen called through the box a second time. "There's nothing to fear here in this room." Her voice was calm and rational, her tone soothing. Rie took a deep breath, and another. She nodded, letting go of her apprehension and dropping her gaze back to the table.

The bird was next, the representative of soul magic, a dark elf skill. Rie shuddered slightly at its glassy eyes and wide open beak. She didn't quite know what to do with this one. As far as she knew, she didn't have any abilities with raising the dead. What little soul magic she carried touched the weavings of the fates, not the dead or dying. She reached out anyway, gently touching the black wing.

***

She soars through the updrafts near the man nest. Food is easy to find near the hot room, good things to take back to the chicks. She circles above the stone. A whistling sound, pain, panic, falling. Who will feed the chicks?

***

Rie snapped out of the vision, her composure shaken. "The bird was killed by an arrow to the shoulder, falling to the ground near the castle walls," she said, bowing her head. "The poor thing didn't die until she hit the ground. She had chicks in a nest on the castle wall. Someone needs to find them." She mumbled the last, her voice barely loud enough to hear. It was ridiculous to worry about baby birds. They were probably already dead, killed and eaten by some scavenger. But for a moment, Rie had lived inside the mama, feeling her pain and heartache as she realized she wouldn't make it back to her babies.

It was confirmed, then. Rie had abilities in both soul and spirit magic. She would forever have to live in secret, or risk a blade in the back or an axe through the neck. Less than twenty-four hours ago she had thought she could stop running and hiding. Now the secrets would never end.

"That's fine. Please continue on to the next element."

Not wanting to think about the bird, or the results of the last two tests, at least for a few minutes, Rie skipped the feather, and moved on to the bowl of water. As far as she knew, she didn't have any water abilities. She didn't think she had skill with any of the physical elements, for that matter. Certainly she'd never seen or felt anything that would indicate more than mundane control.

Shaking her head, feeling ridiculous, Rie reached out toward the water with her right hand. She first willed it to move, just a little ripple across the surface would be enough. Nothing.

Then she tried to force it into vapor, then freeze it into ice. Nothing.

She reached out with both hands, cupping them as if to drink the water from the bowl. She thought of bringing the water from the bowl to her hands. Nothing.

She asked it to spin in a tiny whirlpool. Nothing.

Rie didn't know how long she attempted to manipulate the water before Triwen finally spoke. "That's enough," she said. "Next element please."

Taking a deep breath, Rie shook out her arms, lifting them above her had and letting them swing behind her. Though she had barely moved during the water test, and hadn't accomplished anything, she felt like she had run several miles. Her heartbeat raced, and her muscles were tense with strain.

"Um, may I have a glass of water?" she asked, a half smile pulling her lips to the right. The irony of needing a glass of water after trying to manipulate the element was not lost on her.

"Of course," Triwen replied. "Why don't we take a quick quarter bell break."

Rie nodded, happy for the respite. Within a few moments, the back door opened and Daenor entered the room. Seeing a friendly face, Rie felt lighter, less nervous. She moved toward him, meeting near the door instead of the table where the testing materials waited.

"Well, at least we know you're not good at everything," Daenor said, light dancing in his eyes even as he kept the smile off his face. He held out the full glass of water.

Rie laughed, breathing in the delectable scent of toasted cocoa and woodsmoke that was Daenor's natural scent. Her fingertips brushed Daenor's hand as she took the glass, and his heat warmed her inside and out. Pulling her hands away, Rie quickly drank the entire contents down.

"Three down, three to go," she replied. "I don't expect to have any better luck with the other physical elements. Of course, until a couple of days ago, I would have sworn I had no real magic at all."

"You were oppressed by a culture that devalues you, and told that you are no better than a servant to the High Elves that bought you like livestock. You haven't had the opportunity to truly discover yourself. It's no wonder it took so long for your abilities to express themselves."

Rie shook her head, about to argue, but Triwen interrupted from the observation room.

"This isn't yet the time to discuss this. You need to finish all of the tests before we can start to make guesses about your heritage. And it's time to get back to it."

Daenor reluctantly agreed. "Just remember, I'm right behind the mirror," he whispered. Rie gave back the empty glass, and once again Daenor's fingers trailed across her skin. He winked and left the room.

Rie watched the door close, her thoughts filled with the promise in Daenor's eyes. She could still feel the heat from calloused fingertips, where they had caressed the back of her hand. Her stomach fluttered. Was he teasing her, or was he sincerely interested in her? She couldn't let herself hope. Even wishing was dangerous. It was safer to stick to her own kind, the humans and changelings who lived and worked in the faerie realms.

Clenching her jaw, Rie buried the attraction and forced her body to turn and face the mirror. Daenor would be standing in that room, watching her. She couldn't let him see her insecurity. She pasted a calm expression on her face, and walked back toward the testing table. She would finish this trial, and think about the rest later.

The three remaining elements were earth, air, and fire. Still hesitant to consider the feather, afraid it came from the poor mama bird lying in the cage next door, Rie walked around the table to face the fire bowl, a soot-blackened metal canister filled with dry wood-chips.

"You may begin," Triwen said through the voice box. Rie took a deep breath and closed her eyes. No longer facing the mirrored glass, she was able to forget she was being watched. With a second, and then a third deep cleansing breath, she centered herself and prepared to face the fire.

Opening her eyes, she reached out, letting her finger brush the wood as she had touched the bird. With a startling crackle, flames burst to life, burning high and fast. Rie jumped back. She fell, shocked by the intensity of the flame that had almost burned off her eyebrows. She looked at the hand that had just started a fire with a touch. Turning it over, she looked at her palm, then back at her knuckles and nails. Nothing appeared to have changed, and yet everything had changed. Rie was a firestarter. She had at least three different magical affinities. Her humanity burned to ash in her mind.

"Very good," Triwen said, her voice betraying zero emotion, good or bad. She was all business. The flames died down almost as quickly as they caught, but Triwen didn't pause. "Next element please," she said, pushing Rie to finish the trials.

Rie stood and dusted off her spotless uniform. Trying to calm her racing heart, Rie took several more breaths, but she couldn't get her mind off of the blazing fire she'd created. How was it possible? She had never expressed any affinity for fire, ever, in her entire hundred and nine years in the Upper Realm.

Shaking her head and wringing her hands, she yanked her attention back to the task at hand. The bowl filled with dirt sat next to the pile of soot that had been the wood chips. Like water, nothing she did affected the element. The same went for air.

By the end, Rie was mentally exhausted, wanting nothing more than to take a nap in the middle of the bare floor.

"It's now time for the physical trials," Triwen announced from the booth. "We'll break for a bell to eat while the apparatus are removed, then we'll be back to finish the day's testing."

Rie groaned inwardly, turning her back on the mirrors to make sure they couldn't see her expression. She wasn't sure she could face another round, especially one that included physical challenges. Her ribs were still black and blue and her shoulder twinged when the skin pulled across the scabbed-over wound. Under other circumstances, she would have given herself at least a few days off to heal. But she couldn't afford to appear weak or incompetent in this place. If she wanted respect, she needed to step up and stick it out.

Straightening her spine and her uniform, Rie walked to the door, where she hoped someone would be waiting to take her to food. She wouldn't admit it out loud, but she hoped that person was Daenor.

CHAPTER NINETEEN

Daenor opened the door and ushered Rie into the hall, while Gikl buzzed away.

"Nice to see you, too," she called to the pixie's rapidly retreating back. He waved a hand without turning around. "Congratulations on finishing the trials," she continued in a high-pitched mockery of Gikl's voice. "Thanks Gikl, I appreciate your support, anything interesting happen in the observation room?" she mumbled in her own tone.

Daenor chuckled. "They're a bit independent, aren't they?" he said.

"I don't expect them to obey," Rie replied, defensive. Everyone in the Upper Realm had always treated them as pests or eccentric pets, but they were more than that. And less. Rie sighed. "But it would be nice if they clued me in on what they're doing once in awhile. I guess he was hungry. So am I."

"Of course, follow me," Daenor led the way to the University cafe. "My treat today. Once you get settled, we'll get you an advance on your first Guard payment, that way you'll be able to afford to eat away from headquarters when necessary."

"I'll be paid? As a Conscript?" Rie asked, astonished.

"Not much, but yeah. When you're on duty, you won't be able to eat at headquarters. But I'll pay today."

"That's not necessary. I have my own funds." The money from her wardens wouldn't last forever, but it should be enough to buy her meals for a few weeks, or months, if she were careful.

"Consider it a small celebration for finishing your first day of magical trials, and for discovering something in common. You're a fire mage. Like me."

Rie flinched and clenched her right hand. The hand that lit the fire. The smile that had spread across Daenor's face at his proclamation faded on seeing her reaction, but she couldn't contain it. She was scared of what she was, unsure of her role and situation. Not only was she some kind of unknown dark-elf-high-elf hybrid, she had at least a little fire sidhe in her ancestry as well. She wasn't human, and she wasn't like anyone else she'd ever heard of.

Daenor pulled off to the side of the hall, bringing Rie along with a gentle pull to her arm. He glanced around, before leaning in to speak just above a whisper.

"It's all right. Triwen can be trusted, and so can I. We'll figure this out. The good news, I can be your fire trainer, so we don't have to let anyone else in on the secret. No one has to know." Daenor slid his hand down the rough fabric of her black training uniform to grip her hand. He flipped it over, pressing it open and holding it firmly between his two open palms. "You are still the same as you were this morning. There's nothing to fear from your own abilities."

Rie pulled her hand away. His fingers trailed after.

"I'm not afraid," she said. Daenor pursed his lips in a skeptical frown. "I'm not. Not really. It's just...everything I thought I knew has changed. The safety I thought I might have here is gone. The High Court might not have a chance to execute me, but if anyone finds out what I am, I'll be just as dead, which means more secrets and more lies. I'm tired of it."

The words rushed out in a torrent, unstoppable. Rie couldn't believe she was sharing her true feelings with a man who held the power to destroy her if he chose. A man she'd barely known a week. It wasn't like her to relax her guard, but she had no one else to talk to. The pixies lived for secrets. They wouldn't understand.

"I have powers that shouldn't be possible, and I'm the idiot who believed the stories her wardens told her, who believed they might actually care for her."

"I'm sure they do — " Daenor began, his tone too sugary sweet for Rie to handle.

"No, don't patronize me. Let's just go eat. Please."

"Sure." Daenor's face fell. He shut his mouth and started back down the long hall, footsteps tapping softly on the hardwood floor. Rie felt bad for shutting him down, but she needed time to think, time to process. The test results complicated everything. She looked human, but wasn't, and had powers in an impossible combination. Her entire identity had been shredded in one morning. Even if his feelings for her were honest, she couldn't deal with a romantic entanglement right now. And with him, a noble and an elf, maybe not ever, no matter how much she liked him.

Daenor glanced back every few steps, but kept up the pace and didn't speak. Rie trailed behind, taking in the warm browns of natural polished wood and admiring the carved details in the mouldings. She paused on a broad breezeway that connected one building to another, looking out on the city and pedestrians in the street below.

"It's daylight," she murmured. She tilted her face up to the sun, letting it absorb every available ray, then pulled up the sleeves of her training uniform to absorb even more. Ripples of warmth spread outward from every inch of bared skin.

"Do you miss it?" Daenor asked, standing slightly behind her left shoulder. His voice was subdued, almost sad.

"Yes," Rie replied, without hesitation. "It's not that there aren't nice things here, it's just that the light...if you could just experience the light in the Upper Realm once, you'd understand. It's hard to explain, but living without it has been a challenge." Taking a risk, Rie let her instincts take control of her head and forgot that she was trying to keep Daenor at a distance. She reached for his hand and held it out the sun, letting their fingers twine in the already fading light. "Just let it soak in awhile."

They stood like that for several breaths, enjoying the silence and the sunlight, until Daenor finally spoke. "Come on, let's get some food in you. There's a patio outside the cafe where we can watch the crowd and the sunset."

Although the cafe was filled nearly to capacity and a line of people wound out the door, Rie and Daenor were seated almost immediately. Within moments, they were being served a delicate, savory soup filled with long noodles, meat sliced so thin it was nearly translucent, tiny onions that popped with each bite, and a bright citrusy tang of lime. A basket of warm bread with honey butter rounded out the meal.

"I guess it pays to be a prince and the Commander of the Guard," Rie quipped after the server left.

"Nah, I used to be a student here like anyone else. But I ate here every day and made friends in 'low' places. The cooks and staff love me."

"Sure. Whatever you say," Rie teased between bites, smiling to take the edge off her words.

"Seriously. There's enough nobility in this room to gag a royal historian. I'm nothing special."

Rie lifted her eyebrows, surprised at his total lack of ego. The words were spoken without a hint of bitterness or false humility.

"If that's the case, then you're the most progressive noble I've ever met."

Daenor's lips stretched in a shy smile. "I'll take that as a compliment."

They ate the rest of their meal in silence, watching the boisterous students around them and letting the warm soup and hearty bread do its work. Rie's shoulders slowly relaxed, until she put her spoon down and leaned back in her chair. Daenor followed suit, signaling the server to take their bowls and bring the bill.

"I think I need to apologize for my behavior earlier. You're being kind, and I pushed you away. I'm sorry," Rie said, picking up the last piece of bread from the basket and avoiding Daenor's gaze.

"It's overwhelming, isn't it?" Daenor checked the bill and set down the necessary coin.

"A bit," Rie admitted after a moment. Crumbs rained down on the tablecloth as she shredded the crust.

"Not to worry. I think the next set of tests will be more to your liking." Rie didn't look up, just kept pulling at the brown crust, still a little embarrassed by her earlier outburst. "I'll be running the physical trials," he continued, "and all I want to see is the warm-up routine you were doing this morning, at full speed."

Rie glanced up from under her lashes. "Who else will be there?"

"Just Triwen. We need to have an official proctor at all of the tests. She's one of the best."

"Oh."

"She'll stay in the booth, while I'll be in the room with

you. That way I can observe your figure from any angle."

Rie felt her cheeks heat and kept her gaze trained on her hand. Thinking about Daenor watching as she performed her routine sent shivers to all the right places. "Of course." She wiped away the mess on the table, avoiding Daenor's gaze. It was getting harder and harder to resist her attraction to this man.

Daenor pushed his chair back and stood. "They should have everything cleared out by now. We'd better go."

Rie nodded and pushed away from the table, winding her way through the crowded patio and retracing their steps to the testing room. Daenor's footsteps trailed along behind. He stopped her with a gentle hand on her arm before she opened the door.

"How are your injuries?" he asked. "Are you feeling up to this?"

"They're healing. I'm fine."

"Good," he said, "but if you start to hurt, if your shoulder pulls or tears, or your ribs give you any pain, slow it back down and stop. You and I will work on your physical training later."

Rie glowered, but she nodded. It was what she would have done in her own private training, so she could hardly argue. Weakness was a luxury she couldn't enjoy in public. An injury could be exploited, a fear brought to light at the most damaging moment. Curuthannor had trained her to ignore pain and accept fear, to face the challenge without flinching. She decided on a compromise. She wouldn't push herself to injury, but she wouldn't let a little pain stop her, either.

They entered the room, Daenor making his way to the corner. Rie stood in the center, facing the mirrored wall and bouncing lightly on the cushioned floor. As instructed, everything had been moved out of the room, leaving Rie free to move through the entire space.

"Daenor, for the record, please instruct the Conscript on the format of the physical trials," Triwen said through the speaker.

Daenor leaned back against the wall and crossed his arms over his chest, watching Rie with a sly smile. "For your physical trial, perform the custom routine developed by your trainer from the Upper Realm. Start slow, progressively getting faster, as you would under your trainer's guidance."

Daenor nodded to the mirror and Triwen spoke again through the voice box. "You may begin."

Rie bowed to the mirror, then turned and bowed to Daenor before dropping into a loose ready position facing the observation room. Her gaze connected with Daenor's. His lips lifted at the corners in a quiet smile, and Rie tore her gaze away. To do this right, she couldn't let her focus wander.

As instructed, she began to move slowly, but with concentration and purpose. Her right arm swept out in front, palm up. She inhaled, drew her left blade, and smoothly brought it up to point directly in front of her. Imagining the assassin from the beach, she drew the figure eight that would gut him. Exhale and kick, blade back, hilt touching her sternum. Left arm sweep up, pull the right blade. Gut and kick.

Rie turned, pivoting on the ball of her left foot, and extended the blades out to either side at shoulder height. Curuthannor had forced her to hold this position for over an hour without trembling. Tired now, she focused on his lessons, forgetting the ache in her shoulder and the man watching her from the corner. Blades crossed in front of her chest, then returned to point at opposite walls. She drew them back down and in, elbows bent, hilts touching her waist, then spun into a slow back kick, ending facing away from Daenor.

No longer able to see the prince, either in the mirror or directly, Rie was able to sink deeper into the movements of the routine. Inhale. First her right arm, then her left circled out in front of her body. Exhale, side kick to the right. When she turned to face Daenor again, she closed her eyes and focused on her body, the feel of her muscles beneath her skin and the connection to the ground through the soles of her boots. Inhale, blade circles, exhale, side kick to the left. She ended the slow form facing the rear of the room, her blades crossing and dancing in the white light, finally turning with a roundhouse kick to bring her back into the starting position.

Without hesitating, even for a second, she began the form again, moving slightly faster than the first revolution. Breath steady, her mind cleared. By the third revolution she moved without thought. By the fifth, her consciousness drifted on the waves of her breath. She performed the routine seven times, each revolution faster than the last, until muscle memory alone drove her actions. Her blades seemed to cut through the light in the room, reflecting and refracting it into its component rainbow of colors. She ended the final revolution with the same three high kicks aimed inches from Daenor's head.

Slowly retracting her leg, Rie returned to a ready stance, her chest heaving as she struggled to catch her breath. Her legs trembled. Her shoulder ached. She'd pushed herself as hard and as far as her body would allow.

Daenor's mouth gaped, his eyes wide. Without taking her eyes off his face, Rie bowed, first to the prince, then to the mirror, formally ending the session.

CHAPTER TWENTY

Rie dragged her feet down the long winding hall into the mountain and her room in the conscription barracks. Willpower alone carried her forward. Exhaustion pulled at her, mind and body. She ached everywhere. Her head, her arm, her ribs, her hands, her feet, her brain. Everything. Hurt.

Eyes trained on her boots, Rie put one foot in front of the other, trailing the fingers of her right hand along the wall to avoid stumbling drunkenly every which way as she followed the scuffed black boots of the guard in front of her. She was a mess.

Shoes appeared in her line of sight. Different shoes. Nice shoes. Mens boots, polished to a high gloss, with a round toe and soft soles. It took her a moment to process that she was at her room, and someone was standing in front of her, waiting at her door.

Rie pulled up her head, slowly trailing her gaze over muscled legs encased in tailored black pants made of a heavy canvas material. A black belt with a black buckle wrapped a narrow waist covered by a fitted black cotton short-sleeved shirt. Golden arms that seemed out of place in the sunless corridor, crossed over a broad chest. Left shoulder rested on the wall next to the black door.

"Hello? Rie? Are you in there?" Movement as he leaned forward from the waist, cocking his head to the side. Warm brown eyes. Dark chestnut hair.

"Braegan." Rie couldn't think of anything else to say. Her brain was entirely blank. He pushed away from the wall and crouched, bringing his height down to match her own shorter stature so that their eyes were on the same level.

"Are you okay?" he asked, eyes pinched in concern.

"Fine. Just need to get into my room," Rie replied. She pushed past him, reaching for the doorknob. It was locked. She tried again.

"What did you do to her?" he asked, staring at the guard next to her. Daenor had told the heavyset man to take her to her room before disappearing up the stairs to his office. The guard had grumbled for a bit during the walk, but gave it up when she never responded. It had taken all of her strength to keep her back straight and chin up. Conversation was beyond her current capabilities.

"The Commander had her tested today."

"So soon? But she's still injured."

"I'm fine." Rie turned to face the guard with a glare. She wanted to be in her room, alone, behind the closed door where no one could see her collapse in a heap. "Open the door. Please." Her voice sounded normal. That was good.

"She made it here on her own two feet. She can't be too badly injured." The guard shrugged, and unlocked the door.

"Can you give me a minute with her?" Braegan ushered Rie inside the room. "I won't be long."

Rie didn't see or hear the guard's response. She focused on the bed. Four steps. At most, it would take her four steps to get there, a fifth to turn and sit down. She could do it. She'd made it this far. She wouldn't embarrass herself.

One. Two. Three.

A hand pressed the small of her back, guiding her forward and supporting her. She pushed it away, spinning to confront the rat who had betrayed her.

"What are you doing here?" she demanded, pushing him back toward the door.

"Sit down, and let me help you with your boots."

"Not a chance."

Braegan lifted his hands in surrender. "How's your arm?"

"It's fine. What. Are. You. Doing. Here." She carefully enunciated each word, making sure there was no chance of misinterpretation.

"Can I take a look? I'll change the bandage for you." He wouldn't meet her gaze, couldn't even bring his eyes above her neck.

"No. Braegan, look at me." As her anger rose, so did her energy. She didn't need, didn't want to be coddled. Certainly not by a backstabbing rodent. "Whatever you're here for, whatever you have to say, I don't want to hear it. You're not welcome here."

"I came to apologize." Braegan ran a hand through his shaggy hair, the ends immediately falling back into his eyes. "I had to report your presence in the realm to my boss, it was my job. But she said nothing would happen unless you proved to be a threat. You weren't a threat... aren't a threat. I was as surprised as you when you were arrested, and I was called in front of the king."

"Apology not accepted. Now, leave."

"I quit the Observers."

"Really?" she asked, lacing her tone with as much skeptical venom as she could. "And I suppose you're going to tell me you're tired of telling lies, of leading people to trust you and then betraying them at the first opportunity."

"It wasn't right. I knew from the start you were a refugee, not a traitor, but you were my opportunity to prove I could manage an operation on my own. I let ambition cloud my common sense. And now you've been Conscripted, and it's my fault. So I joined up, too. I figured if I stayed close, I could be there if you ever needed help. Don't you like my new look?" That explained the all black ensemble. He glanced up at her from beneath his lashes, eyes wide and hopeful, like a pet hound asking for a treat.

"And you thought that would make it up to me? Make me overlook the fact that I trusted you with my *life* and you threw it in my face? I don't think so."

"Please, Rie, let me make it up to you. Somehow. You can trust me."

"I don't know what your game is, but I'm not playing. I don't trust you. I nearly *died* because of you. I hope the Shadow Guard chews you up and spits you out, but I want nothing more to do with you. Ever."

Braegan's face fell, his shoulders slumped.

"You need to go." Rie pushed him out the door with a hand on his chest. "The guard is waiting to lock up behind you."

"Okay," Braegan replied, but he grabbed her hand before she could snatch it away. "But I *will* make it up to you. You'll see."

Rie yanked her hand out of his grasp and stepped out of reach. "Great. Bye."

Braegan gave a quirky little wave with the tips of his fingers as he closed the door behind him. As soon as the lock clicked home, Rie flopped back on the bed, throwing her hands above her head, flinching as the skin of her shoulder stretched across the wound. Between one breath and the next, she fell asleep.

***

A pinch on her ear and a tug on her hair woke Rie from a deep dreamless sleep. She groaned, rolling over to her side, then groaned again at the throbbing in her wounded shoulder and ribs. Rie felt sure that the previous day's activities had destroyed whatever healing progress had been made.

"Rie, get up! Get up now!" Hiinto hissed into her ear, the high-pitched whine driving nails through her brain. She swatted lightly at her buzzing friend.

"You have to get up! They're coming!"

"Who's coming?" she croaked.

"Cendir and some guards. They're coming for you."

Rie's eyes popped open and she was on her feet before her brain could catch up.

"Why are they coming for me? What's happened? Who sent them?" Rie demanded. She dashed to the closet, pulling open the doors. Plink was already inside, gathering her arsenal. Some remote part of Rie's brain wondered when she'd arrived, but it didn't matter. Plink popped to a shelf and shoved the amlug leggings into Rie's empty hands.

"Don't know. I was on watch. They came through the gate talking about taking the spy to the heirs. I'm pretty sure that means you." Hiinto hovered in front of Rie's face, giving his report, while the other pixies flitted about the room. Niinka and Possn were still missing, but the remaining three each had a mad look of violent glee plastered on their tiny faces. They were hungry for blood.

"How many are there?" Rie asked, continuing to dress. When Plink handed her the red stretchy shirt, she put it on without thinking, and was shocked to discover that it had been fully mended. The tear where Rie had been sliced and Daenor had cut away the fabric was hardly noticeable. Plink was fast and good. Even Lhéwen would be impressed. She swallowed, homesick, then set aside the emotion. She couldn't get distracted now. She buckled on the amlug vest.

"Five. Cendir and four others dressed in black. One of them is a troll. They seem pretty confident."

"They should. They have me at a disadvantage. It's not like I can go anywhere." Rie tied the khukuri sheaths to her upper thighs, strapping them tightly and checking to make sure the draw would be smooth and easy.

"And I suppose we don't count for anything?" Hiinto huffed.

"You wound us, deeply," Tiik said, pausing in midair to grip his hands above his heart and fall back as if dead. It would have been an award-winning, dramatic performance, except that he was now flying upside down.

Rie couldn't help chuckling. The pixies were fearless, and could lighten the mood in even the most dire situations. She wondered whether they had any sense of their own mortality.

"You're right. I certainly wouldn't have survived this long without your help."

The pixies grinned.

"You know it!" Tiik chimed in.

"But now we need a plan. I doubt I'll be able to get past five trained guards without suffering a fatal wound. I'm not ready to die yet. So, I'll have to go without a fight." Rie finished lacing her boots and began to strap on the shadow rose bracers.

"Gikl, you have to find Daenor as quickly as possible. I don't think he keeps rooms here in the mountain, but he may be in his office, or you might be able to find something there that will lead you to his rooms. Come to think of it, I don't even know what time it is now."

"About two bells before daybreak," Hiinto replied. "My

shift was almost over."

"Okay, so Gikl, you let Daenor know what's going on, and that I'm being taken to the heirs. I'm not sure what he can do about it, but at least he'll know. Hiinto and Tiik, you're going to ride with me. You'll have to do what you can to help me get free once I'm taken. If they bind my hands, you can loosen the knots or break the bands. But don't do anything unless you can do it unnoticed by anyone or anything, including any of those swirling spirits you were talking about, Tiik."

"Right. Stay hidden. Got it."

"We'll have to play it by ear, but I need as many hidden weapons as possible," Rie continued, even as she tucked four throwing knives into the slots on each bracer, and a slim boot knife against her right ankle.

"Don't forget the hair sticks. Garran was convinced they could be the saving grace of a warrior in trouble. He had a hard time convincing anyone else of it, though," Plink said, sadness coloring her downturned expression.

Rie raised an eyebrow. "Well, I'll take all the help I can get." She braided her hair in one long cord, then wound it into a knot low on the nape of her neck, securing it with the silver-tipped sticks.

"What should I do, mistress?" Plink asked, eyes wide and hopeful.

Rie blew out a breath, resigning herself to the next command. As much as she hated the idea, she needed the blood sidhe's help. "You're going to go find Braegan."

The pixies hissed, zooming back to hover in front of Rie's face. Hiinto's eyes narrowed dangerously. "You can't trust him. He betrayed you to the Observers. He's the one that got you into this mess!"

"I don't trust him, but the more people that know the heirs have me the better. And if he wants to prove he's sincere, this is his chance."

"I don't like it," Hiinto insisted.

"It doesn't matter whether you like it or not. It doesn't even matter if I like it. The worst that can happen, is nothing. If he does nothing, reports it to no one, then I'm no worse off than I am now. But I need backup. You guys are superb spies, and you can provide fantastic distractions, but when it comes down to it, you can't take down a troll on your own. Even an entire swarm would have a tough time with a troll."

"Only because troll meat is tough and chewy," Tiik said with a grimace of disgust. "Mostly gristle."

Rie smiled and continued on as if he hadn't interrupted. "If you can't find Daenor, Braegan might be able to. And even if he doesn't, he knows this city, and he knows how to move undetected."

"We can move undetected, too."

"Hiinto, stop arguing," Rie said, exasperated. "Braegan knows how to use a knife, and I'm hoping a sword, as well. I need his help, if he's willing to give it."

"Fine. Send the imp," Hiinto huffed, crossing his arms and flitting away to listen at the door.

"I will find him, Mistress."

"If he'll help, take Braegan to Daenor. Together, they might be able to come up with something."

"Yes, Mistress. Thank you." Plink seemed inordinately pleased to have a job.

Heavy footsteps thundered down the hall, stopping outside the door. A key clicked into the lock and the tumblers turned.

"Time's up," Rie whispered, unsheathing her blades. "Plink and Gikl, hide until we leave, then hurry to get the men as fast as possible. I may not have much time."

Rie stepped back from the door, putting the bed between herself and the oncoming guards. It would be hard for her to get out, but it would be harder for all of them to get in and cause harm. She took a deep cleansing breath, bouncing lightly on the balls of her toes. Hiinto and Tiik hid above the doorframe, waiting to catch a ride with the guards or Rie, while Gikl and Plink scrambled behind the armoire.

The door slammed open.

"Cendir," Rie said, tipping her head and plastering an amused expression on her face. "It's wonderful to see you again. To what do I owe the pleasure?"

The dark elf tilted his chin down and narrowed his eyes. The look was marred by the white plaster that covered his nose, but the unsheathed sword in his hand made up the difference. "You're supposed to be asleep."

"I imagine, so are you."

Cendir's blade lifted, the point held steady just a few inches from her chest. "The heirs have requested your presence. You'll be coming with me."

"I see. And do they have the king's blessing for this little meeting?"

"Come quickly, without protest, and maybe we'll be nice."

"In other words, no."

"Make a scene, and we'll be forced to get nasty." He grinned, clearly hoping she chose the second option. She wasn't that stupid. "I owe you for my nose, anyway."

"Lead the way," she said.

"You're no fun. Krick, confiscate her weapons." The troll, small compared to Tryg, but still as thick as a boulder, shoved his way into the room after Cendir stepped out. His mass blocked the door, leaving Rie no exit and very little room to move. It was a solid strategy.

He took Rie's khukuri blades, then checked for other weapons. He found all eight throwing knives plus the boot knife. He didn't take her hair sticks, but bound her hands behind her back with a quick twist of leather cord.

Rie inwardly grinned. She still had six weapons that her enemies didn't know about, plus hidden friends who would take care of the cord in seconds. She had hope.

CHAPTER TWENTY-ONE

Cendir and the guards marched her out of the mountain and back to the palace, quickly navigating the maze to the heirs' suite. As they approached the heavy double doors to the room, Rie felt a brush of cold across the nape of her neck and down her left arm.

"Help me," a voice whispered in her left ear. Rie's head snapped to the side, but no one was there. The pixies had attached themselves to her belt, and the guards were too far ahead or behind to have spoken the words.

"Release me," another voice said, above and to the right. Rie looked, but no one was there. What was going on?

"Don't go in there," a third voice said. "You'll never come out."

Rie tripped, nearly stumbling into Cendir's back. She got her feet underneath her before she face planted into the floor, but it was a close thing.

"Watch it," he said, sending a chilling glance over his shoulder.

It seemed she was the only one that heard the voices, or at least, she was the only one that reacted.

Another cold chill swept across her shoulders, sending goosebumps down her spine. The dark wood doors loomed ominously ahead. A guard stood on either side of the wide entrance. Standing at attention, the dark elves looked like twins, wearing perfectly matched silver armor with a red-feathered helm, their long white-blonde hair left loose to hang down their backs. With ostentatious uniforms like that, they couldn't possibly be Shadow Guards. They must be personal soldiers working for the heirs.

Rie's escort paused before the doors.

"I've brought the changeling," Cendir announced.

"You're expected. Go on in," the guard on the right replied. "But your cohort has to stay out here."

Cendir nodded, waving off his company. He grabbed Rie's bindings, pulling her around beside him before entering the suite.

Decorated in black, gray, and silver, with splashes of red here and there, the twins liked deep cushions and open spaces. Two wide chairs sat directly in front of the entrance, about twenty feet back, positioned to give the impression of mismatched thrones. Two closed doors with another matched set of guards stood sentinel, one behind each chair. Notably, the heirs were not present.

"Kneel," Cendir said, kicking Rie's legs out from underneath her. She landed hard on her knees, and with her hands still tied behind her back, she nearly fell on her face. Again. She straightened up and squared her shoulders.

Time ticked by. Not a word was spoken. Even the spirits were silent. Rie's knees began to throb where they pressed painfully into the thin weave of the pale gray rug.

A twitch at her waist let Rie know that the pixies were on the move. Refusing to look down and chance revealing their presence, Rie kept her eyes trained forward but focused her attention on feeling the slight shifts in their movements. They were going slow, gripping hands and feet and sliding forward toward her bound hands, each traveling in the opposite direction on her belt. A pinch at her wrist and Rie twisted her hands so that the pixies could sit on her fingers between her palms and back, staying hidden while they worked on the binding.

"Where the hell are they?" Cendir grumbled. He shifted his weight from side to side, and he kept glancing at the rear doors. "We're running out of time."

"Time for what?"

"None of your damn business." Cendir turned away, going to speak with the guards in quiet voices. As the leather cord loosened from her wrists, Rie began to believe that she would make it out of this predicament alive. She'd been stuck on that rug for long enough that Gikl and Plink should have had plenty of time to find the men. She hoped. Surely they must be close by now?

A cold, dry mist crept through the room, flowing in from beneath the right-hand door. The mist whispered warnings and threats, caressing Rie's legs and swirling up her body to flow out and around the room. The pixies went motionless in her hands. These must be the "swirling spirits" that Tiik had been talking about.

"It's too late for you now," a malevolent voice whispered in her ear.

"They have you trapped," another wailed from across the room.

"We would help if we could, but we are bound," a third soul stated, as if resigned to his fate and that of anyone else trapped by the heirs.

"She doesn't deserve help. She made her choices," the first voice spoke from in front of her face. Rie couldn't see her tormentor, but the frigid air of the soul's passing pierced deep. It was all she could do to keep her face from reacting and her teeth from chattering.

"She is innocent. She doesn't deserve this fate," the

third voice replied.

"You heard the mistress. She is an oathbreaker, or if not, she is a spy. King Othin wants her head, and we're going to give it to him."

Rie shuddered.

The right-hand door opened, and the heirs entered the room. Rie had seen them in the throne room, of course, but she hadn't been able to get a good look. Studying them now cast malevolent chills down her spine. Both had dark black skin that glistened in the wisplights that floated over their heads. Like their father, their eyes were a gray so pale it was difficult to differentiate the iris from the white; the dilated pupils stark in contrast. White hair was piled in an intricate bun on the top of Faerlethril's head, small curled tendrils drifting down around her high pointed ears to gently caress her long neck. Faernodir left his hair loose and long, but swept it all back, showcasing the twisting silver spiral that wound up the outer earlobes.

Faerleithril's graceful steps brought her closer to Rie, until she stood a few scant feet away, one hip cocked to the side, highlighting a long stretch of leg through a slit in the red silk fabric of her dress. Faernodir dropped immediately into his chair, propping his chin on his hand and staring out the window longingly.

"Such a fuss for such a little girl," Faerleithril said, drawing Rie's attention back to herself. "And human, too. You'd think your kind would know better."

Rie remained silent, holding her face impassive. She'd heard worse slurs in the Upper Realm, had put up with more degrading treatment. It was nothing new and, though it stung, she had long ago learned to ignore such comments.

"Thank you, Uncle, for bringing her," Faerleithril continued when she didn't get a reaction. "She hardly seems worth the trouble."

"It would have been my pleasure, but she came without a fight," Cendir replied.

"How disappointing for you, I'm sure," Faernodir said, still gazing at the garden outside. "Can we hurry this up? The moon blossoms will open for the first time today."

Faerleithril's eyes flashed bright silver, and the souls spun faster around the room. "Brother, please pay attention. We're trying to prevent the collapse of our entire society here. I think that's a bit more important than any silly flowers."

Faernodir sighed. "If you say so. She seems like a ridiculous reason for the realms to go to war."

Faerleithril rolled her eyes while she paced a slow circle around Rie. Rie didn't bother trying to keep her in sight. "Do you know who I am?"

"Of course," Rie bowed, lowering her head in a habitual submissive gesture that was beginning to grate. "You are Faerleithril, one of the twin heirs to the Shadow Court throne. You and your brother," Rie nodded at the man, "Faernodir, are to jointly inherit on your father's death or abdication."

"Neither of which seem likely at this point," she sighed, settling into her chair, one leg crossed over the other and resting both arms on the cushioned armrests. "But I have to agree with my brother. What makes you so special that King Othin wants your head so badly?"

"I don't know. Whatever Rolimdornoron has told you, it isn't true. I don't have any secrets to sell."

"Are you accusing the king's messenger of lying?"

"All I know is that I am not a spy. Whether the Chief is working under a misunderstanding or outright lying, I can't say." Rie was tired of defending herself. It was a waste of time and breath.

"Well, he should be here any minute, and we can ask

him directly. Though, I don't think it will matter." A malicious grin lit Faerleithril's cold face. "King Othin wants you dead, and it's easy enough for us to grant his wish."

"So you'll toady to the monarch of another realm? At least King Aradae protects his sovereignty." Rie could respect that. If she were royalty, she would protect her crown as fiercely as her life. She certainly wouldn't let some foreign monarch dictate her actions.

Faerleithril's hands spasmed on the armrests of her throne. "You should show a little more respect to your betters," she grit out. "It's really quite rude. But perhaps you need a little demonstration. Uncle, there's a servant cleaning my room. Bring her to me."

"Of course." Cendir grinned and left the room, returning with a young goblin not yet in her majority. Rie's heart sank and the anger faded away. She felt sick, her stomach lurching with every tug as Cendir brought her forward. This girl was going to be punished for Rie's insubordination.

"Please," the girl pleaded. "I've done nothin'. Please, don' hurt me." Tears tracked down brown skin.

Rie couldn't let Faerleithril hurt the girl. It wasn't her fault. "I apologize for the disrespect. You can let her go. Please." If she had to beg, she would. She wasn't royalty, after all, and she could afford to negotiate. No one deserved to have their soul stolen, least of all as a petty show of power.

"That's better," Faerleithril's eyes crinkled at the corners as she grinned down at Rie, "but I'm afraid it's too late. A demonstration is still in order."

"Whatever I've done, I won' do it again," the girl pleaded.

Faerleithril flicked her fingers.

"No!" Rie cried. The girl slumped to the floor.

"Too late. Her soul is now mine, to do with as I please. But don't worry, she can't feel any pain." The moaning of the souls floating around the room belied that assurance, but Rie couldn't say anything for fear of infuriating the princess. "It currently floats free, but Faernodir can bind it wherever I ask."

Rie's shoulders slumped. "She was innocent. You didn't have to do that." The woman's pettiness and cruelty proved that the Upper Realm stories weren't all lies. At least some of the things she'd been taught were true.

"Perhaps, but now you understand. You can't fight me. Faernodir, bind her to my ring with the others."

Faernodir sighed, and shook his head. "You've had your fun, but I liked her. She knew the best way to press my shirts and hang them without any wrinkles. Besides, she didn't do anything wrong. I'd like her back."

"You're getting soft. But fine, do what you want with her." The heirs' indifference infuriated Rie, but until she had a way to fight, she couldn't do anything about it. The anger smoldered in her heart, waiting for the opportunity to flame.

Faernodir spun a finger and the body on the floor began to breathe. Her eyes fluttered, and she groaned, rolling over and retching onto the floor. Relieved that the girl would at least live, Rie strengthened her resolve. She would find a way to bring the heirs to justice and stop their attacks on the innocent.

"Ugh." Faerleithril stuck out her tongue in disgust and looked away. "That's revolting. Uncle, take her away, and find someone to clean that up."

Cendir nodded and left, carrying the girl over one shoulder. When they were out of sight, Faerleithril turned back to address Rie, an evil glint in her eye. "Now, back to the subject at hand. I understand that King Othin has charged you with treason in absentia, for espionage and consorting with citizens of the Shadow Realm. Your wardens were held accountable for your actions in your stead, their assets seized. They are being held in the dungeon until you are returned to the Upper Realm."

Rie squeezed her eyes shut, unwilling to respond, but unable to completely hide her emotions. Yet another person would be unjustly punished for her actions. It was hard to believe King Othin could be so angry and vindictive that he punished his best warrior over an unimportant human. How could she ever fix this? Maybe it was better that she go back to the Upper Realm with The Squirrel. At least then the punishment would be applied where it was deserved. Except, she didn't deserve it, either. She was as innocent as anyone. And if he was willing to punish her wardens for her unproven crimes, then it wouldn't be a stretch for him to continue that punishment regardless of her return. Which was precisely why she had started on this journey in the first place. No, she needed to see it through, find out who was truly behind the attempt on her life and why. Only then could she save herself and her wardens.

Rie opened her eyes with a deep cleansing breath. Riling the princess would only make her more volatile, but there had to be a way to implicate The Squirrel in all of this mess. "I don't understand your motives, Your Highness. Why work with the Upper Realm? Why listen to the messenger at all?"

"Rolimdornoron speaks for the king. If he says the king will go to war over you, who are we to argue?" Faerleithril replied. "Besides, who cares about you, a low-level human? It's easy enough to send you back and avoid this whole mess, and King Othin might look favorably on the unattached heir who helped him."

Faernodir turned, suddenly interested in the

conversation. "What I don't understand, is why you came here in the first place. You knew it would only convince King Othin of your guilt."

"What other choice did I have? It was be killed at home, or try to find out why I was targeted. My only leads were the throwing knives, and they led me here. Before they attacked, I'd never seen a blood sidhe, let alone contacted one."

"So you're entirely innocent, framed for a crime you didn't commit," Faerleithril sneered, the sarcasm dripping thick as honey.

"I don't know, sis, she seems to be telling the truth. Maybe mother was wrong."

Faerleithril dismissed her brother's hesitation with a snarl. "We've heard it all before. People pleading for their lives, claiming their innocence before execution. Last minute regrets and repentance. It doesn't change anything."

Rie heard the door click behind her, felt the brush of air as it swung open, then closed. Footsteps approached, muffled by the rug. Rie didn't turn. She didn't have to.

"Here we are, just in time. Rolimdornoron will take you off our hands." Faerleithril sent a wicked grin Rie's direction before standing to greet the new arrival. The prince waved from his chair, but didn't bother to move.

"You're in for it now," the malevolent voice whispered, sending shivers down her spine. Rie grit her teeth.

Rolimdornoron met the princess at her throne, reaching out with both hands to grace her cheek with a kiss. Rie couldn't help rolling her eyes. The man was an insufferable sycophant, as far as Rie was concerned.

"Greetings, Rolimdornoron," Rie said, still kneeling. Her kneecaps were going to be bruised, but she smiled as if her situation was commonplace and comfortable.

The Squirrel turned and looked down his stubby little

nose at her, stepping forward into her personal space. "Here you are, at last," he said, his voice a thin whine. "You've put the whole Upper Realm in an uproar, you know."

"That was unintentional, I assure you," Rie replied, turning on the deferential charm. She had learned, years ago, that the only way to deal with The Squirrel was to make him believe in his own importance.

"Indeed. Well, let's be off then. Trial by combat doesn't hold for traitors in the Upper Realm. Luckily, the Queen and the heirs have some common sense." The Squirrel sneered, his thin lips pressing together and nose wrinkling.

With Rolimdornoron's arrival, Rie began to panic. Daenor still hadn't arrived, and she was running out of time. She had been depending on his backup. Now she needed to stall, keep them talking and find an opportunity to attempt an escape.

"About that, how are you planning on explaining this little kidnapping to King Aradae? I would think the heirs' disobedience would be a problem."

"Oh, that's easy. Faernodir and I decided to meet with our newest citizen to learn more about the Upper Realm, when Rolimdornoron burst in demanding your return. We couldn't harm a messenger from the Upper Realm traveling on official business, nor do *we* have the authority to stop him from taking you."

"Convenient. I suppose that's why the queen isn't here?"

"Of course. If she were, she would have to uphold the king's edict. But really, there's no need to risk war over a human. Father has been pushing his equality agenda for too long. You shouldn't have even been granted that farce of a trial. There was a time in this realm, when the lesser fae and mundane humans knew their place. And it wasn't as part of the guard."

A commotion outside caused everyone in the room to face the doors. It sounded like an argument between the guards and one or more people in the hall. Quickly, while the distraction lasted, Rie dropped the pixies and pulled her hands from the loosened bonds.

"I'm afraid my departure won't be possible," Rie said, shifting to stand. The doors blasted open, flames riding in to the rescue. The boys were here.

Daenor strode confidently through the smoldering entry, drawing back the fire he had unleashed. Within the span of a few heartbeats, every ember was extinguished, leaving only a small singe area around the door frame and on the doors themselves.

He was magnificent, standing tall and proud in black leather armor, the seal of the Shadow Guard stamped above his heart. Braegan followed a few steps behind, his fangs and claws bared for battle. Daenor approached Rie, a question in his eyes.

"I'm fine," Rie replied.

A cold metal blade pressed to her jugular. The prince stopped moving, eyes wide with fear.

It had been a mistake to turn her back on the twins. She shouldn't have let herself get distracted. She should have been paying more attention to her enemies, not her friends.

"You won't get away from me this time," The Squirrel whispered, his breath hot on her ear. His hand wrapped around her throat, skin to skin.

***

"I want her dead. Everything falls apart if she doesn't die. Lord Garamaen won't play his hand, the kings will hold their thrones, and nothing will change. Do you understand?" The man is cloaked, his hood hiding his face in shadow. A gold ring with a ruby the size of a

child's throwing stone flashes in the sunlight.

"Yes, of course. It shouldn't be difficult to arrange. She is only human, after all," Rolimdornoron replies.

"Don't underestimate her. She is more than that, even if no one knows it, yet. Her abilities will awaken soon. Some already have."

Rolimdornoron scoffs, confident in his assessment of the servant who is one of his lowest ranking messengers.

"I don't care how it's done, but the Shadow Realm must be implicated."

"And what of my reward?" Rolimdornoron asks.

"When the kings fall, and Lord Garamaen is reduced to ashes, you will have a place on the council of the unified nine realms."

***

"Your Majesty, I understand your time is extremely limited, so I won't waste a moment," Rolimdornoron says, bowing low to the ground before the queen of the Shadow Realm. "It has come to my attention that your husband, the king, has been negotiating with Lord Garamaen to open legal trade with the Human Realm, and through the Human Realm to the upperworlds."

The queen's eyes narrow. "That scheming little bastard. This time, he's gone too far. Eliminating the underground markets only benefits the lesser fae with existing contacts in the human realm. It won't take long before they think they're as worthy to lead this realm as the dark elves. They will rise up and rebel against our authority, demanding rights they haven't earned. This cannot be allowed."

"Your view is shared with the High King. If you let me, I might be able to help convince Lord Garamaen that the time is not yet right."

***

Rie gasped, her brain scrambling to understand her

surroundings. The back to back visions scrambled her composure. She was back in the room, Rolimdornoron's knife at her throat. Daenor stood a few feet away. He watched her carefully with a gun in each hand. Braegan was just a step or two behind him, hissing through two-inch fangs and holding a naked sword in hand.

"Drop your weapons," Rolimdornoron said. "She is my prisoner. You can't stop me, nor should you want to."

"Don't do it," Rie wheezed around the hand at her throat. "He's the traitor. He's helping someone overthrow both courts."

The Squirrel's face bleached white.

"How could you possibly...?" he whispered, then tightened his hand. "Never mind. Soon, it won't matter."

Rie nodded. "He wants me dead, no matter what happens. He's working with someone —"

"Bitch!" Rolimdornoron screamed, pushing the blade into the flesh beneath Rie's chin, forcing her head back until she was staring at the coffered ceiling. Blood trickled down her throat while his nails dug into the flesh of her shoulder. His teeth snapped in her face. "You don't know anything. You can't know anything."

The possibilities flashed before her eyes as premonition kicked in. Her arm flashed up, pulling a hairstick from her bun and slamming it into The Squirrel's kidney. Rolimdornoron screamed and the knife pulled away from her skin, giving her a little more room to maneuver. She brought her knee up, connecting with his scrotum. The knife dropped as he clutched himself. Holding the back of his head, she brought her knee up again, breaking his nose. She dodged to the side, Seeing Faerleithril's kick coming. Her foot missed its mark, connecting with Rolimdornoron instead. He went down, breathing, but not moving.

Cendir chose that moment to return, opening the door

from Faerleithril's rooms. Daenor shot him twice through the chest. Cendir fell, surprise written over his face as he clutched at the thin armor that was no protection against a bullet. He trained his other gun on Faerleithril, pinning her in place before she could make another move against Rie. "Move, and you're next. You too, Faernodir."

The prince had barely moved through the entire event. He blinked as if coming out of a daze, then lifted his hands. "This whole plan was cooked up by the messenger, Mother, and Faerleithril. I'm just along for the ride."

"Let's keep it that way."

Braegan dropped onto Rolimdornoron, pressing his knee into the unconscious man's back, binding his hands and feet.

"Rolimdornoron is under arrest for violating the king's judgment, and will be brought before the throne," Daenor said.

"You would side with a *human*? A woman you barely know, who has violated the law?" Faerleithril spat.

"She is a Conscripted member of the Shadow Guard. Her presence in the Shadow Realm has been approved by the king. His word is still law, I presume?"

"I am glad you are only my half-brother. I would be ashamed to claim you as anything more than the bastard of my father." The hate and anger burned cold in her eyes. "But I am heir, and I won't be denied."

With a flick of her finger, Faerleithril tore the soul from Rie's body.

CHAPTER TWENTY-TWO

The pain was severe, but lasted a fraction of a heartbeat before there was nothing. Rie screamed, the sound echoing around her own head, but no one in the room seemed to notice. She looked down, watched as her body dropped to the floor, hitting the carpet in a heap. She couldn't hear it, but the thud must have been impressive. Rie sobbed, understanding. Her soul had been cut from her body, the only attachment a braided rope that exited the top of her body's head and looped around her soul's ankle, like a prisoner's chain. Otherwise, she floated free in the void of the room, all of her senses, except sight, gone.

Daenor's expression contorted into an anguished grimace, pain etched in every line, anger breathing behind his eyes. Keeping his guns trained on the heirs, Daenor knelt beside Rie's body. He motioned for Faerleithril to stand next to her brother, then set one gun down, while he checked Rie's body. It was odd, existing without touch, or taste, or smell. For the first time, Rie realized how much she relied on those senses. Even just sitting, there might be a tacky dry taste in her mouth, or an itch on her neck. There was never nothing. But now...

Rie watched as a gentle hand swept the hair away from

her face, the fingers coming to rest on her pulse. She wished she could feel that touch, the warmth of his skin on her own. She wanted him to know she was still present, still alive, even if her body didn't know it.

A loud twang resounded through the room, originating from the rope on Rie's ankle. One of the strings had snapped, leaving just two wrapped threads tying Rie to her body. Somehow, she knew that if those threads broke, there would be no going back. Rie's thoughts fractured. She needed to fix this, but how?

Daenor stood again, saying something to Braegan, while keeping his eyes on his siblings. He picked up his discarded gun and once again targeted the twins. Braegan approached her other side, leaving Rolimdornoron tied and gagged on the floor. He squatted next to Rie's body, eyes riveted on the blood that dripped from the shallow cut on her neck. The viscous red liquid moved slowly toward the floor. Reaching out to touch a small droplet, Braegan brought it up to his nose, breathing deeply. His tongue flicked out so fast, Rie almost missed the motion. Sitting back on his heels, Braegan closed his eyes in pleasure. Rie wanted to slap him.

Which made her wonder; she had no body, so how was she supposed to move? How had the souls done it when she first entered the room?

"It's better if ye don' think 'bout it," a sad voice said, startling Rie.

Rie had been so focused on her own body and the actions of Daenor and Braegan, she hadn't noticed the loose shape of a woman floating behind Faerleithril. A thin gossamer thread tied her form to a clear blue topaz ring on Faerleithril's finger. The woman wore a servant's dress, tied at the waist with a wide apron.

"Don't help her," the malicious voice spat. Also tied to

the ring, his image wound around Faerleithril like a snake in a tree. A translucent hand caressed her hair, his face pressed cheek-to-cheek, but otherwise his image was amorphous and incomplete.

"What's wrong with him?" Rie asked.

"He is being absorbed, strengthening our captor," another voice said. Of the three, he retained his shape the best. He was a nisse, his thin angular limbs gesturing as he spoke. "We will all perish this way, eventually."

"I am honored to serve," the snake hissed. Rie shuddered.

"How did you become bound?" Rie asked, directing her question at the nisse, the most helpful of the three.

The man shrugged. "Faerleithril frees the soul, Faernodir binds it. That is all I know about the how. As to the why, Faerleithril seeks power. She uses souls as spies throughout the kingdom, but it's a constant drain on her energy. So she absorbs the less cooperative of us to increase her magical reserves. She started eating that one shortly before we arrived, but she's used him up faster than any of the others I've seen."

"He doesn't seem less cooperative," Rie said, indicating the snake man. She noticed her own hand was clearly defined, but translucent, more like the nisse than the others.

"Once she starts actively draining a soul, the soul begins to take on aspects of her character, and eventually loses its own. He's nearly done. She'll be next."

"I don' want to lose myself," the servant woman sobbed. "I want to see my ancestors, to go to the summerlands. I don' deserve this."

"None of us do," Rie replied.

Faerleithril turned to face Faernodir. She said something, but Faernodir ignored her. Daenor stepped forward, shouting at his siblings and swinging the gun from Faerleithril to Faernodir and back. Faerleithril held out the ring on her finger, now yelling at her brother, but he simply shook his head and turned his back on his twin.

"Well, that's interesting," the nisse said.

"You can hear them?"

"Of course. You can't?"

Rie shook her head.

"Odd. I wonder if it's because you haven't been bound. You still retain two links to your old body."

"What are they saying?"

"Faernodir is refusing to bind you to her ring. Daenor is shouting now, demanding that the twins return you to your body. He's threatened to kill Faerleithril several times, and he's still pointing that gun at her head. She won't forget that anytime soon."

"Can she hear us? Or you?" Rie asked.

"Not unless she activates the ring. Then it's more of a one-way signal. She only hears what we tell her directly."

"Which is why she needs cooperative souls for spies."

The nisse nodded. "I suppose the benefit of being cooperative is not being absorbed, but I would rather cease to exist than assist her schemes." Rie understood that sentiment.

"Not that I'm complaining, but why isn't Faernodir binding me to the ring?" There was something going on here, some dynamic she was missing.

"He says he doesn't believe Rolimdornoron. He's siding with his father," the nisse said in complete disbelief. "I don't think that's ever happened before."

"Lucky for me. I have a chance to survive this, if I can just figure out how to get back into my body."

"That's not going to happen. Unless Faernodir takes pity on you, like he did the girl, and binds you back into your body, you're stuck. If he binds you to the ring, you'll be absorbed, but if not, you'll have to find your way to the summerlands."

Another twang echoed through the room. Rie clenched her jaw and shook her head. She was running out of time. "That can't be true. There has to be a way. How do I move? How were you all flying around the room earlier?"

"You could feel us?"

"And hear you. You are all quite noisy, and distracting."

"Impressive. There aren't many who have innate soul-speech. But as Althea said, don't think about the mechanics. Just think about where you want to go, and you'll go."

Rie did as instructed, and found herself at Daenor's side. She pasted a light kiss to his cheek, and watched as goosebumps lifted the hair on the nape of his neck. "I'm coming back to you," she whispered. "I'm going to figure this out."

Rie floated over her body. The single thread that tied her together was thin, but still present. She reached for the string, gave it a tug to test its strength. Holding the end by her feet, she tapped it lightly. The thin strand held tight as dulcimer wire, vibrating with a soft hum with each touch. Tugging on the string, her soul floated closer to her body.

Using the string as leverage, Rie slowly pulled herself together. She wrapped any excess around her legs, keeping the thread as tight as possible. Her soul's bare feet touched the top of her body's head, and began to sink into the flesh. She pulled harder and her calves squeezed into the gap. She kept pulling and winding, wrapping her soul tighter and tighter, until all that remained was a thin sliver of her essence outside her body. When the last bit of herself joined, a pop resounded in her ears.

**

Rie opened her eyes, then quickly closed them again. A headache pounded behind her eyeballs, and her vision swam. Her body throbbed with pins and needles, the small pricks of pain a welcome reassurance that she was, in fact, alive, but she didn't want to move for fear of increasing the agony.

"Bind her, now," Faerleithril screamed at her twin, her voice like metal scraping on stone. The woman wasn't paying any attention at all to what was going on in the room.

Rie slowly opened her eyes again, letting her pupils adjust to the light. Glancing her way, Daenor saw her blink. He blew out a breath, relief evident. Braegan shifted forward, wrapping her hand with both of his own. She shook her head in a tiny movement that no one would see unless they were staring right at her. Daenor's eyes narrowed, but he turned back to face the three arguing dark elves.

"I won't bind another innocent against their will," Faernodir said, his voice low and determined. "I'm tired of these schemes and games. Your plans to win the High Throne are doomed to fail."

"But she's *human,* and King Othin will go to *war* over this."

"Says who, the trussed up Squirrel over there? He's been taking this whole thing far too personally. How do we know he doesn't just have some vendetta against the girl?"

"You can't be serious." Faerleithril pointed her finger in her twin's face. "Of all the rotten times to have an opinion, you choose now?"

"You and Mother are wrong in this. For once, I'm choosing to believe that the King is doing what's best, or at least what he believes is best. For once, I'm following my *own* conscience."

Daenor crouched next to Rie's head. Keeping his eyes on the argument, he touched Rie's shoulder. "You're back," he whispered. "You did it."

Rie nodded. "How did you know?" She kept her voice low to avoid alerting the twins, at least for a few more moments.

"The one and only dark elf skill I have is to sense soul magic and identify the user. Not much use. But no one has ever come back without Faernodir's binding."

"The other souls helped, but I never entirely lost the connection to my body. I just had to figure out how to put myself back together."

"Told you so," Braegan interrupted.

"Here," a voice chimed. "We brought your blades. Figured the dead troll outside wouldn't miss them," Hiinto said with a smile. He and Tiik dropped one khukuri at Rie's side, while Gikl dragged the second across the rug toward her. Rie's fingers touched the blade and she instantly felt better. It wasn't just the reassurance of being armed, she physically felt better, as if the blades were redirecting her pain and helping her heal.

"Do we get a prize for helping?" Tiik asked hopefully.

"We'll see," Rie said. She turned so she could meet Daenor's eyes.

"There are three souls bound to Faerleithril's ring. She's feeding on them to power her magic. They're being absorbed against their will, unable to reach the summerlands."

"Gods, even I wouldn't feed on someone's soul, and I drink blood," Braegan said.

"I'm aware. Apparently I taste pretty good, too," Rie said, her tone stinging. Braegan flinched.

"I asked him to," Daenor admitted.

"We couldn't find a pulse. I had to taste your blood to

tell if you had moved on."

"Well, I was still here. Which brings me back to my point. We have to get that ring away from her, destroy it to free the souls."

"Harming a soul, preventing it from reaching the summerlands, is a fierce punishment reserved only for the most vile of criminals," Daenor said. "She's twisted her magic."

"Faerleithril, there's nothing I can do," Faernodir said, flinging a hand in Rie's direction. "She's returned to her body, bound tightly and protected."

"What?" Faerleithril spun, eyes skating over the group on the floor. Anger painted her face an ugly shade of puce. "Did you do this, Faernodir?"

"No, but I wish I had. I wish I had the guts to stand up to you decades ago."

"Daenor, is there something you'd like to share with your little sister? Some ability that you've kept hidden until now?" Faerleithril trembled, her rage barely contained.

"As thrilled as I am to have her back, I wasn't the one that bound her. I don't have the talent, and you know it. But you're lucky she returned. Of the two of you, Faernodir is the only one with any sense. Binding an innocent, especially a member of the Shadow Guard, would have brought you both to trial. Now it's just you who will face our father's wrath."

"Don't you dare threaten me," Faerleithril hissed. "However it happened, it isn't permanent."

"Don't!" Daenor shouted. He hugged Rie tight to his chest, as if he could shield her soul. He was too late.

Faerleithril's fingers flicked. Pain lanced her heart, threatening to tear her into two pieces. Mentally gripping the line that attached her soul to body, she struggled against the force that scrabbled and scraped, trying to find a grip in her psyche. She screamed a war-cry from the depths of her soul; the tug-of-war a torture, but a battle she could not, would not, lose.

Faerleitrhil took a deep breath, her eyes narrowing. The pain intensified, but Rie wouldn't let go. She thought of the binding, winding it tighter around herself, as if wrapping her entire body in chains.

"Stop it!" Braegan screamed, but there was nothing he could do. Only Rie could fight this battle. Only she could win.

"You...can't...take me...again," Rie gasped. She struggled to stand, her body curled around her stomach in the effort of holding herself together. Daenor rose with her, supporting her with a hand on her elbow. Rie straightened, bit by bit, until she stood strong against the power of the dark elf bitch before her.

Faerleithril growled, strain evident in the deepening lines of her face. Rie winced, clenching her jaw against the pull on her soul. She held her ground. Faerleithril wasn't a fighter. She was too used to relying on her power and the fear that it engendered.

Rie stepped forward, holding Faerleithril's gaze. The woman's eyes widened, then tightened in concentration. A sourceless wind picked up around Rie, the vortex blowing loose tendrils of hair into her eyes, then out and away from her face. The pull on her soul increased, the pain throbbing with every beat of her heart. Rie could feel the souls spinning around the room, hear them wailing in agony. Even the nisse, so calm and collected when Rie was adrift, screamed like a banshee. To her right, Braegan fell to the floor, clutching his chest. Daenor stood on her left, fire lighting his gaze.

"Give me the ring, Faerleithril," Rie said, imbuing her tone with as much command as she could muster. "The innocent souls you've bound deserve a chance to reach the summerlands. Release them."

"And if I don't? How will you, a wretched human changeling, make me?" Faerleithril's lips lifted to bare her teeth in a feral snarl, the gruesome expression oddly amplified by her meticulous beauty.

"It turns out, I'm not exactly human. I bound my own soul back to my body. And now you can't touch it." Rie took another step forward and cocked her head to the side. "Did you know I'm a drainer?"

Faerleithril lifted her chin, refusing to give ground, but her expression lost some of its ferocity as uncertainty took hold. The wind slowed, the souls calming down enough to listen to Rie's words.

"Braegan discovered my ability when he tried to enthrall me on my first day in Nalakadr," Rie continued, forcing as much bravado into her voice as she could muster. "I took a pretty good dose of his energy, preventing him from following me. Unfortunately, I'm not very good at it yet. Braegan was lucky I didn't drain him dry. But in this case, I think it will be considered self-defense. Don't you?"

"I'll just use up the souls you want to save."

"Perhaps. But it turns out I have some soul magic in my heritage as well. What did you call it, Daenor? Hindsight? I pulled two memories from Rolimdornoron's psyche the moment he touched my skin, one of which, I think you'll be very interested in. You see, he set you and your mother up. He wants you to foment rebellion in the Shadow Realm, attempt to wrest control from your father. With enough chaos, he and his boss will step into the gap, taking what is rightfully yours."

The wind in the room died and the souls went silent. Even the excruciating pull on Rie's soul stopped. She took another step forward.

"Even if that's true, none of that information gets you

the ring," Faerleithril replied.

"What do you think I would discover in your past? I don't imagine it would be pretty. Do you think the king would be interested in some of your memories? All it would take is a touch. If you're lying on the floor, unable to move, you won't be able to stop me from seeing everything."

"It would be your word against mine. I don't think he would trust *you* over his own daughter and heir." Faerleithril's words were defiant, but her tone was uncertain. She didn't know who her father would side with.

"A few days ago, no. But now you've tried to kidnap and kill me, defying your father, the king. You haven't exactly set yourself up as the most trustworthy individual in this room."

Faerleithril's eyes flashed, but she was listening. She moved to sit in her chair, regally crossing her legs at the ankles and resting both arms on the low cushioned armrests.

"What do you want?" She held herself stiff, in control, but Rie could see the seething maelstrom beneath the surface.

"Free the souls and let them move on."

"Done." *False!* Rie's head ached from the warning that screamed through her brain. As if she couldn't tell when the souls left without the help of her own personal lie detector.

"Don't lie to me," Rie ground out. "I can tell truth from lie, and sincerity from deceit. Don't test me."

Faerleithril's upper lip curled. "Fine." She flicked her fingers. The souls wept in relief, hovering near Rie's head.

"Thank ye," the wailing woman whispered.

"You've done us a great service, one we may never be

able to repay. If there's ever an opportunity to help you from the summerlands, we will come," the nisse added.

Rie nodded, both to the souls and to Faerleithril. "Now the ring. Just in case you try anything else."

Faerleithril grimaced, but handed it over.

"We're leaving now, and we're taking Rolimdornoron with us. I hope you weren't too attached to him," Daenor said.

"I probably would have killed him myself, eventually," Faerleithril replied with a wave of her hand reminiscent of the king.

"I would also expect a summons from our father. I'm sure he'll have something to say about all this."

Faerleithril didn't respond, her eyes set in narrow slits as the trio left the heirs' suite. Daenor led the way while Braegan carried the now conscious and groaning Rolimdornoron over his shoulders like a haunch of venison ready for the fire, the slow trail of blood adding to the image.

CHAPTER TWENTY-THREE

By the time they reached the throne room, Braegan was sweating and Rie felt nauseous. The stress of the last few hours had taken its toll. And now she had to face the king, try to convince him that Rolimdornoron was the real enemy, and somehow get him back to the Upper Realm to prove her innocence to King Othin before he started a war or sent someone else out to kill her.

Right. That was as likely as bonding with Daenor or inheriting a title. But she still had to try. She owed it to Curuthannor, if not herself.

Entering the long hall for the second time, Rie was glad to see it stood empty, except for the Shadow King and a guest. They might have a chance for a private meeting without the gossip-mongers knowing about it.

Keeping a respectful distance from the throne and the private conversation going on at the end of the hall, Rie knelt, resting her elbows on one raised knee. She could wait until his meeting was over to speak to the king.

Daenor apparently had other ideas. He tore Rolimdornoron from Braegan's shoulders, dragging him forward by the bindings on his wrists. The Squirrel pulled against his bonds, eyes pinched, yelling against the gag in muted anger. Daenor ignored it all, fury radiating off his frame.

Braegan knelt next to Rie, out of breath and wincing in pain.

"Are you okay?" Rie whispered while she watched Daenor stalk to the throne.

"Took a little beating fighting off the guards outside the heirs' suite, but I'll be fine. Just need a quick bite." He didn't look good, but Rie wasn't going to offer her wrist, no matter how grateful she was.

"I suppose I'll have to forgive you now, since you came to my rescue and all."

Braegan grinned. "I was hoping you'd say that. Friends?"

"Friends."

"Please excuse the interruption," Daenor said, bowing his head slightly to the king. "This is urgent."

The king raised a brow and glanced behind Daenor at Rie and Braegan. He turned to his guest, a man with shoulder length dirty blonde hair, wearing a t-shirt with the Quicksilver logo emblazoned across the front, and cargo shorts. Recognition dawned as Niinka and Possn zipped to her shoulders, chattering in Pixl to the rest of the swarm who had ridden in on her clothes.

"Oh goody. My son arrives, uninvited, and brings guests. On the bright side, at least one of them was wanted," King Aradae said, sarcasm thick. "Nuriel, someone is here to see you."

Lord Garamaen turned in his seat. "Awesome!" He turned back to Aradae. "I'm glad we had this little chat, but I suppose it's time we're out of your hair."

Startled, Rie opened her mouth to ask what he meant, but Daenor beat her to it.

"What's going on?" His hands clenched, the muscles of his back tensing for a fight.

"This doesn't concern you," the Shadow King replied,

dismissing Daenor with a glance.

"Rie is a soldier under my command. It concerns me plenty."

"And you think you can question *my* authority?"

"Everyone else in this family does. Your *heirs* were going to send her back to the High Court with this piece of trash." He threw The Squirrel unceremoniously at the feet of his father. "*He's* the real traitor."

"Hold on a sec," Lord Garamaen interrupted, approaching Daenor and Rolimdornoron on the floor. "You think Rolimdornoron was behind the attack on Rie outside my hall?"

"Yes. At least, he hired the assassins." Rolimdornoron rolled around on the floor, trying to sit up and talk through the gag in his mouth. Daenor kicked him in the side.

Garamaen turned his gaze to Rie, still kneeling. "Good work," he said, grinning. If Rie didn't know better, she would have said there was pride and approval in his expression, but that couldn't be possible. She barely knew the man.

"How did you figure it out?" Lord Garamaen waved her forward, inviting her to join the conversation with Daenor and the king.

"Yes, please enlighten us. I'm particularly interested in how the twins became involved in all this," the king added.

Rie squared her shoulders, quickly glancing at Daenor before addressing Lord Garamaen and the king directly.

"I became suspicious during my trial. Rolimdornoron is the only Upper Realm citizen who can freely travel the portals, at least that I'm aware of, and Master Whixle said he was paid in Upper Realm gold. But really, it came down to the fact that I Saw him speaking with someone in a vision who ordered my execution."

"What do you mean, you Saw him in a vision?" King Aradae asked.

"She has hindsight. We tested her yesterday," Daenor interrupted.

"And you didn't think to tell me this?"

"What other skills did she test for?" Lord Garamaen asked, ignoring the tension between the Shadow Guard Commander and the Shadow King.

"The tests are still preliminary," Daenor hedged.

"That's all right. The information won't leave this room, I swear," Lord Garamaen said.

Rie watched the unconventional elf, his placid expression revealing little.

"I tested true for Soul, Spirit, and Fire," she said.

"We were supposed to test her sub-skills this morning, but she was kidnapped before first bell. By Cendir. For Faerleithril and Faernodir." Daenor addressed King Aradae, but Lord Garamaen continued the conversation as if none of that mattered.

"What about Warrior specialties?"

"She's faster and stronger than a human should be, if that's what you're asking," Daenor replied.

"Interesting," Lord Garamaen said. His look was thoughtful, but simultaneously knowing.

"How do we know her Sight was true?" King Aradae asked.

"Would you like me to double check for you?" Lord Garamaen asked the Shadow King, nonchalantly. "I can do a reading on him. It might be interesting to see what else he knows."

"If you wouldn't mind." King Aradae waved a gracious hand.

"Not at all." Lord Garamaen rose from his chair. "Let's get this party started." He placed his hand on Rolimdornoron's forehead, pressing the man's head solidly into the floor. The Squirrel's eyes rolled back, and he went still.

"Let's see...we've got murder of the tailor..."

"His name was Garran." Braegan's eyes were trained on Rolimdornoron and burned with hate. "You'll pay for his death, you sniveling coward."

"That's what I'm here for. He's a proven murderer now. But that's the least of his crimes. He's been actively working with someone to dethrone both the High King and Shadow King by seeding unrest and trying bring down the treaty. I can't get a read on the other man, he's been careful to keep his identity concealed. But Roli, here, convinced your wife and heirs to undermine your efforts to open trade."

"Yes, I am aware they're unhappy about our negotiations."

"Faerleithril might be a little too eager to take your place. She met with Roli several times, alone, to feed information to the High Court. She seems to think King Othin will help her claim the throne if she can give him enough to tear you down, and hopes for a political alliance in the process."

"I'll deal with Faerleithril," King Aradae assured.

"It may be time to remind her that she's not queen, yet," Daenor said. The king sent a searing glance his son's direction, but said nothing.

"Good luck with that," Rie mumbled. Braegan chuckled, luckily the only one that heard. It would take a lot more than a lecture to put Faerleithril in her place.

"And let's see, ah yes, well that explains things a bit," Lord Garamaen said, cryptically. He lifted his hand, finished with the reading, and stood. He wiped his hands on his jeans, as if to scrub off the clinging remnants of Rolimdornoron's psyche.

"Rolimdornoron is a fool." Lord Garamaen

straightened to his full height, dropping the laid-back human persona. His face grew reserved and distant, losing the smile and easy charm. His voice rang with authority, resonating with binding magics. "I, Garamaen Sanyaro, vouch under binding oath that Rolimdornoron Rhosg is a traitor, an oathbreaker, and a murderer. Rolimdornoron's crimes are of the highest order, violating the treaty of the Great War and transcending the laws of both clan and realm. Since he is a citizen of the Upper Realm, I will return him to King Othin for trial. I have four witnesses to this truthsaying; Shadow King Aradae, Nuriel Lhethannien, Daenor Kingsson, and Braegan Sangrrsen. The witnesses are now bound to hear and present this truth to any who ask. Let it be so."

The smell of burnt silk wafted through the air, and Rie felt a constricting band tighten around her throat, then sink into her skin. It wasn't painful, just mildly uncomfortable, but the point had been made. There would be no lying or twisting the truth of this event, even if she had wanted to.

"We might as well head out now. I don't see any reason to impose on you any longer. Rie, of course, will be coming with me."

"Lord Garamaen, I appreciate that you've come at the request of Niinka and Possn, but I hope you haven't bargained with the Shadow King for my release. While I would like to return to the Upper Realm to see my wardens, I would prefer not to be in your debt."

"Oh, right. There's no debt. You're free to make your own decisions, of course, but I know something about your heritage that you'll want to consider."

Rie paused, startled. "Why the interest? I'm just the messenger that delivers your mail from the Upper Realm."

Lord Garamaen shrugged. "Personal reasons. If you

come with me, I promise, I won't do anything to hurt you or put you in a position to be hurt. You are free to leave my company whenever you choose."

"Will I be allowed to return to Nalakadr? I mean, if I want to?"

Lord Garamaen lifted his eyebrows, but looked at the Shadow King for a response.

"Yes," he said. "You can come and go as you please. You've proven yourself."

"You will always have a place in the Shadow Guard," Daenor added.

"Wait, you can't just leave." Braegan stalked forward to grab her shoulders. "I joined the Shadow Guard for you. I risked my life to rescue you. You have to stay."

Rie shook her head. "The whole point was to find a way for me to go home. I can't waste this opportunity. And I need to hear what Lord Garamaen knows. I'm not human, but I won't have a place until I know who I am."

Braegan dropped his hands. "So you're just going to go. You trust a man you admit you barely know."

"He's sworn I won't be hurt." Rie looked past Braegan to Daenor. His posture was stiff, not the casual pose she was used to seeing with him. He kept his face expressionless, but his eyes couldn't conceal his concern.

"I'll be okay," she repeated. He nodded once, but his expression never changed.

"So, you're coming then?" Lord Garamaen asked, hauling Rolimdornoron to his feet. He cut the bonds at the man's ankles so he could walk, but left his hands bound and mouth gagged.

"Yes, I'll come."

"Let's go, then. We've got a bit of a hike to the nearest portal."

"I'll escort you," Daenor said, stepping forward to take control of the prisoner.

"Sure, that would be great," Lord Garamaen replied. Rie smiled up at Daenor, but could see the sorrow and worry in his eyes.

"I'll come too," Braegan said.

"No, you need to report for duty. You're a Shadow Guard in training, remember?" Daenor replied.

Braegan scowled, but nodded. "I'm not going to say goodbye. I'll see you again, Rie."

Rie smiled, but made no promises.

***

They stood at the mouth of the portal, a natural arch located within a cave that had once been an active lava tube. Four armed guards in full battle armor stood at attention near the magically modified stone.

"What's with the security?" Rie whispered to Daenor as they approached the gate.

"This is the only remaining portal in Nalakadr that connects directly with the Upper Realm. Only five people can use it; the kings, their chief messengers, and Sanyaro. If anyone else comes through, they'll be killed on sight."

"Oh." Rie fell silent, watching Lord Garamaen as he nodded a familiar greeting to the guards. If only she'd realized how powerful he was before she'd entered Nalakadr.

After a moment, Daenor squeezed Rie's elbow and led her out of hearing range. She followed, realizing it might be the last time she would ever see the prince. No matter what he had to tell her, no matter how stupid she was acting by letting her heart get involved with an elf and a prince, she wanted every moment she could get with him. When they stopped, he took her hands, tracing patterns over her knuckles.

"I can't let you leave without telling you...I mean, I want you to know that I..." Daenor grimaced and shut his eyes momentarily.

"It's okay." Rie squeezed his hands, forcing him to look at her. "You don't have to say anything."

"I do, too." He blew out a forced breath. "I'm not good at explaining my emotions, but I have to try. You're an amazing woman, Rie. One of the strongest people I know, physically, mentally, and emotionally. You've held yourself together through events that would shatter a lesser person, and you've done it with grace and compassion."

Rie ducked her head, unable to meet his eyes as he continued his speech.

"You are special. And beautiful. And worth more than all of the lords and ladies of the Shadow Court put together. I want you to come back here, but not as my apprentice and certainly not as a Conscript."

Rie's head snapped up. "You won't teach me? I thought..." Her heart sank. It was just as she'd feared. He didn't want her. After all the kind words, everything they'd been through, he was backing out. "Apologies, I understand. Someone of your strength and position must not have time to teach a novice like myself." She stepped away, toward Lord Garamaen and the nearly open portal.

"You don't get it." He grabbed her shoulder, gently pulling her back to face him. "That's not it at all. I can't be your mentor because I want more than a professional relationship. I want you, Rie, all of you, like I've never wanted anyone before."

Truth.

Rie searched his face, looking for any reservation, any hidden deception, but there was nothing there but hope. Her sixth sense was accurate. Her chest rose and fell, her heartbeat sped, but she didn't say anything. She couldn't. She had yearned for this moment, but never believed it possible. She hadn't allowed herself to think honestly about her feelings, for fear Daenor couldn't, or wouldn't, return them. She had pushed it all aside, but with his words, every buried emotion rose to the surface in a rush.

"I know you have a lot to think about," Daenor continued, before the pause got awkward, "so don't make a decision now. Just think about it. I've waited nearly eight hundred years to find someone worth pursuing. I can wait awhile longer."

"Daenor, I..."

"No, please don't say anything right now. You've kept me at a distance, probably for good reason, but I had to tell you the truth. I'm in love with you, but if you don't feel the same I don't want to hear it. Not right now."

Rie yanked his head forward and down, molding her lips to his. She didn't need words. She put every emotion into the kiss, her hope, her fear, her confusion, and her love...all of it passed between them. His arms wrapped around her waist, pulling her into his body, until they were pressed together in one long line. Her mouth opened, inviting him in with a flick of her tongue. He complied, tasting her, teasing her with teeth and lips and tongue while one hand slid up her back and into her hair, the loose knot becoming more disheveled as he played with the strands.

She lost track of time, but eventually Daenor relaxed and drew away holding her loosely.

Rie leaned her face into his hand as he gently cupped her cheek. "You're the best thing that's happened to me. But I couldn't let myself hope, until now. You were so far out of reach, so unattainable. A prince, a warrior, a dark elf with a sense of honor. I couldn't believe you would ever want me." Rie stroked his face. "I think I can finally let all that go. I can't make any guarantees about my future, but if there's any way to return, I will."

"Ahem," a deep voice crackled from a few yards behind

Rie. "The portal is open. We can go now."

Taking Daenor's hand, Rie held it for a few brief moments before gently letting go. She turned and walked toward Lord Garamaen and the portal that would take her out of the Shadow Realm, back to the world of the High Court.

"I'll go through first with Rolimdornoron to clear the way with the soldiers on the other side. You can follow after a slow count to fifteen."

Rie agreed, watching him enter the shimmering void. When he disappeared, she looked back at Daenor, still standing at a distance. "Goodbye," she said, her heart heavy with the knowledge she might never see him again. Then she turned, and with one confident step, merged with the portal into another world.

CHAPTER TWENTY-FOUR

They entered the long hall of the High Court, its white and gold marble floors reflecting their movements back at them. King Othin didn't believe in soft comforts. He didn't want anything to obscure the perfection of his surroundings. As a result, there were no rugs to mute the sound of their footsteps, nor wall hangings to quiet the reverberating echoes of voices.

Lord Garamaen led the way, hauling Rolimdornoron by the wrists. Rolimdornoron dragged his feet, but not in protest. It almost seemed like he was falling asleep on his feet.

"I hate to ask, because I don't really care, but is Rolimdornoron okay? He looks drugged."

"I've drained him of most of his energy. He can barely feel his feet."

"You're an enervator, too?"

"Are you?"

"So I've been told."

"Nice. I'm glad your powers are manifesting."

Rie felt herself stiffen at Lord Garamaen's words. "What do you mean, my powers? What do you know?" Her voice came out angrier than she intended. She reined herself back in before she said or did anything worse. She had to remember she was back in the High Court. Insolence wouldn't be tolerated, and every emotion would be used against her.

"We'll talk about all that later. Let's get our friend Roli to his justice."

Rie nodded, dissatisfied with his response, but unable to push for more information. King Othin was in hearing range.

The king sat on his ornate gold throne, placed five feet above the rest of the room on a stepped pyramid. On either side, standing on each step, was a guard of the High Court. Out of habit, Rie looked for Curuthannor at the king's right hand, forgetting that he had been imprisoned until Rie's return. In his place stood Feaquildo, the brooding guard with the lake blue eyes that had seconded Curuthannor before Rie's alleged treason. Rie had never particularly liked the man, but she couldn't say she really knew him. Even when he came to visit Curuthannor at home, he barely spoke.

Glancing around the room, Rie's eyes scanned the gathered courtiers. They lined the hall on either side of the central path to the throne, arranged by rank and hierarchy. The closer you stood to the king, the more power you wielded in the Upper Realm. The closest courtiers were the king's advisers, a small group of five powerful high elves, each with their own areas of responsibility on the council. Curuthannor, prior to his demotion, had been in charge of all military actions and realm defense. Feaquildo probably held that seat now.

Then came the landed nobles, the Lords and Ladies that held estates in the country and managed the production of Upper Realm resources. After that, representatives from the various guilds and the wealthiest of the merchants who could afford to pay someone else to oversee their business interests. Finally, the kings and queens of the lesser fae gathered near the doors, barely able to hear what was being said near the throne.

It was there, near the entrance to the room, that Rie finally spotted her wardens standing chained against the wall at the rear of the crowd. Relief and worry fought for dominance in Rie's heart, but they appeared unharmed. There were no marks on their skin, at least. But their hair hung limp and greasy, and their clothes looked like they hadn't been changed in a month. Which would make sense. The Shadow Realm moved at a one to three ratio; for every one day in Nalakadr, three days passed in the Upper Realm. If her wardens had been chained shortly after her departure, they would have been caught there for nearly a month.

Lhéwen held unshed tears in her eyes, but sent Rie a watery smile. When she met his gaze, Curuthannor's lip twitched, the closest she'd had to a smile in years.

Facing the throne, Rie focused on the trial before her. King Othin wasn't one to forgive and forget, and he didn't like to be proven wrong in anything. He had imprisoned his greatest warrior because of her actions, and he wouldn't reverse his decision easily.

"Lord Garamaen," the king bellowed. "Welcome to the High Court. It has been too long." The king was thin and angular, looking like a shimmering white spider in his golden web. He wore a traditional high-necked robe of silver silk trimmed with gold and purple embroidery.

"Perhaps, Your Majesty." It almost sounded like Lord Garamaen disliked the king.

Standing several feet from the bottom stair, as dictated by court etiquette, Rie moved to kneel. Lord Garamaen put a hand on her elbow, holding her up. He shook his head slightly.

"Stand, and be proud," he whispered. "You have

earned the right to stand before any king, in any realm."

Thinking back on everything she'd been through, she had to agree. King Othin didn't deserve her respect; he had unjustly punished her family for crimes she didn't commit. What's more, she didn't need to give him fealty. She had a place waiting for her in the Shadow Realm, and a prince who had declared his love. She was no mere human to bow and scrape before the throne. She stood tall and faced her tormentor.

"I see you've caught the traitor. Send her forward. Our executioner stands ready." A woman stepped out from the crowd at the base of the dais, her single remaining eye cold and impassive. She wore a gray patch over her missing eye, a long scar curling beneath the leather from her temple through her upper lip. She carried a double-headed axe over her right shoulder.

An involuntary shudder traveled down Rie's spine. The woman was renowned for her frozen brutality, following her orders without hesitation or remorse. Some said she had lost most of her soul in the Great War, a dark elf siphoning it from her body like a child with a straw, leaving just enough to send her home alive.

"I have no doubt," Lord Garamaen replied. "But Nuriel Lhethannien is not the traitor. I have performed a truth ceremony, witnessed by the Shadow King, the commander of the Shadow Guard, and Braegan Sangrrsen, a former Observer for the Shadow Realm."

"Indeed. You will excuse us if we don't recognize the authority of Shadow Realm witnesses. Nuriel has been tried in absentia for crimes against the throne. She will see our justice, as her wardens have done. Step forward, servant, and face your crimes."

"I am no longer your servant," Rie replied, "and I was not the one to plot against the throne."

Lord Garamaen threw The Squirrel on the bottom

stair. "Rolimdornoron Rhosg, Chief Messenger of the High Court, has plotted against this kingdom. He hired the assassins sent to kill Rie on her route to my hall. He planned to overthrow you and the Shadow King and destroy the treaty of the Great War, to assist another in the creation of a unified kingdom under a single banner. We both know that his actions would have eventually led to another Great War. Nuriel was a target, nothing more."

"And yet she traveled to the Shadow Realm rather than face trial here in our court."

"Yes, Your Majesty, I did. Understanding your intolerance of oathbreakers and traitors, I needed to prove my innocence before facing your justice. I can now stand here before you, confident that my actions will be seen in the light that they were intended."

"I see. Unfortunately, you have said nothing to persuade us that you are not a traitor, given that you broke the treaty and traveled to the Shadow Realm without authorization. A lowly human servant should never have been allowed free access to the portals, but you were selected for an honorable duty, against all objections, because one of our esteemed guards vouched for you. Alas, we find ourselves proven correct, yet again."

"Nuriel was given authorization for her quest. I gave it to her."

"Why would you have done that? You are Sanyaro, truthseeker and watcher of the treaty."

"Before this court and crown, I declare that Nuriel Lhethannien is my heir, apprentice Sanyare, and the last remaining descendent of my line."

The gathered nobles gasped. Rie turned, unable to believe she had heard Lord Garamaen correctly. He dropped her elbow, meeting her gaze with a calm expression of his own.

"Surely, you jest," King Othin laughed. "She is *human*," he managed to make the word a derogatory expletive.

"She is human, but she is also sidhe." Lord Garamaen maintained eye contact, speaking his words to Rie, even as he answered the king. "I have been watching over her since she was a babe, waiting for her to reach her majority and manifest her fae powers. When she survived the attempt on her life using a skill she had not trained, I knew she was ready. I sent her to the Shadow Realm to seek the truth. She found it. This is, perhaps, the last piece of the puzzle."

"But I —"

Garamaen shook his head, telling Rie with his eyes to put her questions on hold, to wait until they no longer had an audience. She glanced back at the king, understanding Garamaen's concern when she saw the wrath etched into the lines of King Othin's proud face.

"She cannot be Sanyare. We will not allow it." King Othin stood, pacing down the steps of his pyramid. "She is a traitor. We will have our justice." He waved the executioner forward, holding his hand out for the axe. "Anyone with dealings in the Shadow Realm is to be executed immediately. Such is the law." He grasped the handle, the executioner bowing out of the way. It seemed King Othin would be getting his hands dirty, this time.

Rie felt her energy drain, her will to resist fading away with each intake of breath. Her head bowed as the strength of King Othin's will hit her. She struggled to remain upright against the flood of negative energy that emanated from the king's aura. With the exception of Lord Garamaen, now standing behind her, every individual in the hall knelt in obeisance.

If what Lord Garamaen said was true, then Rie was stronger than she had ever realized. She could fight this, change her thread in the tapestry of life, garner respect and power amongst the fae courts. She could bring justice to the oppressed and denigrated, watch over the balance in the realms.

But what if it wasn't enough? What if being Garamaen's heir changed nothing? She was still the same person she had always been.

The human who had worked her way into the messenger service against all odds.

The woman who had survived an assassination attempt, fought her way through a redcap horde, thwarted a dark elf's attempts to steal her soul and bind her in servitude.

The woman who discovered a plot against the high kings of the Upper and Shadow Realms.

She was strong.

She was *merely* nothing.

King Othin swung the axe behind his back, gripping the wood handle with both hands, preparing to take her head. Garamaen stood behind her, waiting, doing nothing to stop the blade from meeting its target even as he defied the king's power.

Rie lifted her head, slowly forcing her chin into the air, bringing her eyes up to face the king. Daenor had promised to wait for her, to pursue her, not knowing her true heritage. He trusted her with his life and his heart. He believed in her. She would believe in herself.

"Stop," she said, the word fighting its way out of her mouth, like a fish swimming upstream. King Othin glared down at her, his eyes narrowing in angry concentration. The wiry muscles in his arms bunched, lifting the heavy axe above his head.

"I said, stop." The wood of the handle crackled to life, flames bursting out of the grain like popping corn. King Othin cursed, dropping the axe before it crested the arch.

The steel head snapped off the still burning grip, spinning across the room to crash into the dais with a resounding clang. Thick black smoke wafted from the handle, the smell of burning resin traveling with it.

Lord Garamaen laughed. "You wanted proof of her powers, now you have it. You have no authority over me or my apprentice. We are independent of the courts. If you ever attempt to take her life again, you will be destroyed, the treaty nullified, and the courts absolved. Do you understand?"

"Yes." It was unwillingly said through clenched teeth, the king cradling his burnt hands in front of him. It wouldn't take him long to heal, but the damage to his pride would last much longer. The pressure of his forced will on the room abated instantly, sending Rie reeling. A few brave people stood up, mouths agape.

"If the court needs justice, apply it where it's due. I, Garamaen Sanyaro, vouch under binding oath that Rolimdornoron Rhosg is a traitor, an oathbreaker, and a murderer. Rolimdornoron's crimes are of the highest order, violating the treaty of the Great War and transcending the laws of both clan and realm. As a citizen of this realm, it is the king's duty to recognize the crimes of the guilty party and apply the law. In this case, the law demands death."

"Let it be so," King Othin ground out. "Unfortunately, the Executioner no longer has a functional weapon."

"Let one of your guards lend a sword."

"Fine." King Othin's polite veneer was shredding away along with his pride and power. He handed Feaquildo's sword to the Executioner. She held it out, taking the weight and measure.

"Get the convicted traitor ready."

Feaquildo grabbed Rolimdornoron by the back of his tunic, hauling him up to a cross-legged position. The

Squirrel barely moved, his eyes closed as if sleeping, the gag still binding his mouth. He slumped, neck bared for the blade.

The Executioner stepped forward. She paused, looking to the king for a final signal. He nodded. The sword lifted, reaching the peak of the arc above her head and hesitating. With a flash, the blade dropped, a clean slice removing his head from his body.

The head rolled a few feet, ending wrapped in its hair, face-down in an oozing puddle of thick red liquid. The stump pulsed four, five times, each spurt growing weaker, until at last the heart stopped completely.

"Justice has been served," Lord Garamaen intoned.

"Justice has been served," the hall echoed, the voices of the gathered crowd mingling into a single resonant chord.

"Call for a servant to clean this mess," King Othin commanded. "Make sure it's a nisse. I don't want to see another *human* for a very long time."

"Before you go," Lord Garamaen called as the King turned his back on the hall. "Release Rie's wardens from their chains and return them to their former positions. As Rie has been acquitted, so have they."

King Othin's gaze crackled with defiance, but he gave a single terse nod to the back of the room. A guard standing near Curuthannor and Lhéwen unlocked their chains, freeing them from the wall. "Is there anything else you demand, *Sanyaro*," King Othin ground out.

"That should do for now," Lord Garamaen replied with a smile.

"Then I suggest you leave my realm. I have no further need of your services." The king growled, and stomped out of the room, his guard following at a distance.

"Of course." Lord Garamaen nodded his head in a brief bow.

Curuthannor and Lhéwen approached. "We are indebted to you, Lord Garamaen. I understand you need to leave, and must take Rie with you, but I would ask to visit your hall. We all have much to discuss." Curuthannor dropped his gaze to Rie, his gaze boring into hers.

"Of course. Come as soon as you can get the portal clearance. We'll have dinner."

CHAPTER TWENTY-FIVE

Rie followed Lord Garamaen down the beach to his house, the tiny joys of her usual walk, gone. She neither heard nor saw the waves, the sand, the sun, the wading tourists in their too-small bathing attire. Her thoughts were in turmoil. Of all the things she had ever dreamed about, having the power to stand up to the High King and becoming heir to a powerful Lord had never crossed her mind. Finding out her real parents were still alive, or that she had a real family somewhere, sure, but this? This was too much.

She was related to Lord Garamaen, a man she barely knew, but who wielded an immense amount of power across all the nine realms. She was his heir, apprentice Sanyare, and the last descendent of his line. What did that mean? What had happened to the rest of her family tree? She was left with too many questions, and only one person could answer them.

"Follow me." Lord Garamaen walked through the open living room, past the kitchen, and out French doors with billowing white curtains. They proceeded down a gravel path lined with small, beautifully trimmed rosemary bushes and tall lacy sage in full purple bloom. At the end of the path, a driftwood gate opened into a circle with twelve plinths, each standing at least six feet tall, the top carved with the face of a man or woman.

Rie walked the circle, examining each totem. The faces were all unique, but somehow resembled Lord Garamaen. Sometimes it was the eyes, sometimes the chin, but without a doubt they were related.

"What is this place?" she asked, running a hand over the smooth stone warmed by the afternoon sun. A list of names in Elvish were carved the length of each plinth.

"This is your history," Lord Garamaen said, stroking the cheek of a young man carved in black stone. "These are your ancestors. Each totem represents one of my children by my wife, Angeni."

"The woman in the portrait?"

"Yes. The Upper Realm would call her my life-mate, although her life was unfortunately much shorter than mine. Our children were longer lived, but even they only lived a couple hundred years. Their children, and their children's children, and on and on are listed on their totems. For the first few generations, I played an active role in each child's life. But eventually I had to remove myself from the picture. It became too hard to explain, too awkward for my descendants to understand, especially as the Human Realm forgot about magic and embraced science. But I watched, and I waited.

"As the years passed, the lines began to consolidate, the great-grandchild of one line meeting and marrying the great-grandchild of another line. I didn't stop these unions. They were too far removed to pose a genetic risk, and it seemed that individuals with fae ancestry were drawn to one another.

"Over the last few centuries, someone began targeting my descendants in the Human Realm. There were some suspicious deaths, timely accidents that prevented the birth of new members of my line. Eventually, there were only two branches left, but they had ancestors in all twelve of my children's lines. When your parents met and fell in love, it was a chance to bring everything together. My hope nearly died when I discovered a plot on their lives. I was too late to prevent their deaths, but the assassin who staged the car accident didn't know your mother was pregnant. I pulled you from her womb and brought you to the Upper Realm, to Curuthannor, knowing he would be able to hide and protect you, until you were ready to hear the truth, and able to protect yourself."

Lord Garamaen paused, giving Rie a chance to pull her thoughts together. She took a deep breath, inhaling the purifying scent of rosemary and welcoming its cleansing touch.

"How did my parents die?" Rie's voice was quiet, hiding her internal struggle to understand and believe all that Lord Garamaen had said. It wasn't that she thought he was lying, her sixth sense shouted that he was telling the truth, but it didn't seem possible that she was essentially royalty amongst the greater fae.

"Their car was pushed over the side of a bridge, rammed by another vehicle. I pulled your mom from the wreckage first, hoping I could revive her, but my efforts failed. Her soul had already fled. She begged me to save you. She loved you, even though she barely knew you."

"So you saved me. Why? And why didn't you keep me?"

"You're the last of my line, and have the potential to be the greatest of my descendants. It wasn't certain, of course, but you have the blood of all twelve of my children running through your veins, and the potential to match my skills and abilities. I couldn't risk the assassins finding and targeting you. I wanted you to grow up without living in fear, at least until we knew if you had any magic. You may be the only person in all nine realms capable of stepping into my shoes, of becoming Sanyare."

"But I'm human."

"You are human, but as I told King Othin, you are also sidhe. You have magics that no human has ever possessed."

"Like what?"

"Each of my children was born with a different primary gift, a legacy of my own fae powers." Lord Garamaen began to walk the circle, touching the face of each plinth as he passed.

"The oldest was Siseka. She was profoundly skilled in precognition. She could tell to the minute when and how a person would die, whether the harvest would be enough to pull the tribe through winter, and where to stage an ambush on our enemies to have the greatest possible success. Within a few years of reaching her majority, no tribe dared attack us, knowing that Siseka would predict and outmaneuver their raid efforts. She brought peace and prosperity, negotiating treaties and ultimately becoming tribe shaman after her mother's death. I was so proud of her.

"The next born were my warriors. Fraternal triplets, if you can believe. Honovi had incredible strength. He could uproot a mature tree with a single pull. Payatt was faster than human, nearly as fast as a blood sidhe." Garamaen smiled, clearly lost in his memories. "There was this one time, when he was just a toddler, he spotted a herd of horses on the plains, and decided to have a race. Not only did he catch up with the horses, he passed them and kept running. We found him a day later curled up next to a foal, being tended by the mare. Those horses loved him like their own." He paused, gaze focused in the past. Shaking his head, he returned to his story.

"And then there was Nina. She contained the power to

withstand any pain and channel her anger into precise and vicious fighting. We call it berserker now, but when she fought, there was no stopping her. She was beautiful in battle, absolutely breathtaking. In combination, these four alone could defeat an army.

"But then we added Takoda. He was everyone's friend, able to charm his way into the hearts and souls of anyone who met him. He ended up with more than a hundred children of his own, by various mothers."

"That doesn't sound like magic, that just sounds like a man who knew his way to a woman's bed," Rie regretted the words as soon as they left her mouth, afraid she might have offended the man who represented her only biological family. "Sorry," she mumbled, even as Lord Garamaen laughed.

"It's true, he was a bit of a player, as the humans would say. But in his case it was more than that. He had the strength of charisma, a spirit magic that draws people to follow, sometimes against their better judgment. It's a subtle thing, but I think you've experienced it. Like with your pixies, or even your new friends in the Shadow Realm. You should have been turned over to King Othin immediately, yet they defended you, and even the Shadow King gave you asylum."

"He had an ulterior motive."

"Really?"

"Well, I think so. I don't know quite what it was, but my Conscription into the Shadow Guard was a ploy of some kind, a scheme against King Othin, I think."

"I see. Well there's another skill to add to your repertoire, and that of your ancestors. Truthsage was Yaholo's skill. But he was born after Rowtag, my fire starter." He patted the statue of a young man on the cheek. "He was a troublemaker, that one. I tried to capture the mischief in his eyes, but the stone doesn't do him justice."

"You carved these yourself?"

"Of course! By the time I had the idea, they had all passed on."

Rie looked more closely at the statue nearest her. Nina. The detail in the carving was stunning, the woman bearing a thin scar across her cheek that did nothing to mar her beauty. With almond shaped eyes, and full lips, Rie was sure she would have received more than her share of attention from the men of her time.

"The statues are beautiful."

Garamaen shrugged, taking the compliment in stride. "Thanks. After Yaholo, the twins were born, Una and Nashota. Like the Shadow Court heirs, they had complementary gifts in soulspeech and soultouch. They could speak with the souls of the departed and help them move on to the appropriate afterlife. Their skills were highly valued by the grieving families who wanted to make sure their loved ones were taken care of. But they also ensured that the malicious souls weren't allowed to haunt the living.

"Aran was next, his ability to create light without heat. You might say we benefited from an early form of electricity, although without danger of electrical fire. Then Kai came next, an energy master, and finally Kaga, our little historian with postcognition."

"So twelve children with twelve different abilities, all stemming from your own powers?"

"You got it."

"You have twelve magical abilities from," Rie paused, counting back over everything she had heard, "four different magical disciplines."

"I am what some call an Origin Sidhe. Before the splitting of the realms and the settling of the worlds, my kind existed on a single planet. But as you know, we are a long-lived people with few births, but fewer deaths, except from war. As our world became more populated, and the struggle for resources more profound, war was a constant in our lives. To end the violence, we opened the portals and spread out across the dimensions.

"Imagine if my children were full-blooded sidhe, and lived for thousands upon thousands of years, as I have. Their children, and their children's children, would be born and raised together. It was very crowded. So they left and settled in their own dimensions where they felt the most comfortable. Those with fire magic, for example, gravitated to the Summer Court, while the dark elves with their sensitive eyes and communion with the soul, traveled to the Shadow Realm. Eventually the realms became specialists in their magics, concentrating their abilities in one area instead of many. I'm one of the last with multi-disciplinary talents."

"Why did you choose the human realm?"

"I fell in love." The words fell from his lips with a shrug, a simple statement of fact. "I loved Angeni, with all my heart, all my soul. There was no one before her, and no one since. I have continued to live for my descendants, but you are the last."

"What exactly does it mean, that I am your last descendant, apprentice, and heir?"

"It means that, if you accept your heritage, you will live and train here with me. It means that you are no longer bound by the rules of the treaty, and will be allowed to travel to any of the realms at any time, for any reason. It means that you now have a target on your back from anyone who might want to see the treaty, and the Truthseeker, dead."

"Oh." Rie thought over the implications. She could learn more from Lord Garamaen than she ever would in any of the Universities. He was the source of her abilities, the man who could give her a history and a home. But there would be danger and responsibility. She wasn't sure she wanted or needed that kind of life. But he seemed to believe she could handle it, had waited for her to be strong enough to survive, and tested her with a journey to the Shadow Realm.

"I won't force you into this," Lord Garamaen said, interrupting her thoughts. "You can stay here without becoming Sanyare. You are my child. But I'd like it if you gave it a chance." His lip quirked to the side, not quite a smile. Hope shone bright in his eyes. Once again, Rie's sixth sense kicked in. He was being one hundred percent honest, the truth shining brightly in every cell of his being.

"I've been waiting for a proper heir since the last of my children died over three thousand years ago. I watched as my lines diluted and changed, losing their magic, and then as they consolidated again and became stronger." Garamaen's sandaled feet crunched the gravel as he returned to face Rie. He reached out with both hands, asking without words for Rie's acceptance.

"I've waited for the right combination to find each other, to bring about a child that would be stronger than any in the past, even my immediate children. I've hoped for a child to continue my work and make life meaningful again. If I'm being totally honest, I've wanted a daughter who holds something even more, a piece of Angeni left in her soul. You have it. I see it in the way you hold yourself, the way you stay calm and face every challenge without hesitation. You think through a problem, and you deal with it. Even when there are terrible consequences, you don't panic or break down. You have a strength of spirit I've never seen before. You are my heir, even if you choose not to take the title of Sanyare. You are my heir."

Rie felt a hot tear track down her cheek. She wiped it

away with a quick hand. Had she ever cried before? She didn't know.

She reached for Lord Garamaen, carefully placing her hands in his.

"I don't know if Sanyare is for me, but I can at least give it a try," she said, choking on the words as the tears continued to fall.

"Welcome home."

TO BE CONTINUED...

NOW AVAILABLE!

TURN THE PAGE TO START THE NEXT
INSTALLMENT OF
THE SANYARE CHRONICLES

CHAPTER 1

Goosebumps rose, candle flames guttered. The tiny hairs on the back of her neck lifted, and Rie shivered. She felt like she was being watched.

Two skulls rested on a nest of elder tree leaves, their empty gazes mocking. Rie narrowed her eyes, daring the bones of her long-dead ancestors to judge her. She tried to picture the muscle and skin on top of the bone, tried to imagine the faces that stared back at her.

She was not scared. Nope. Not scared at all.

The crunch of gravel made her spin in her seat.

"Just me," said Lord Garamaen, who preferred to be called Greg but was also known as Sanyaro, or the truthseeker of the nine realms. He found a seat in the rocky border that lined the path from the clearing to the house.

Rie nodded, returning to her task. She only had a few moments before the deepest dark of night turned to the light of day and the opportunity to reach the Daemon Realm closed. She couldn't fail again.

Rie clenched her eyes closed and envisioned the two women before her. Una and Nashota, Greg's twin daughters. They'd mastered the magical abilities of soulspeech and soultouch, the same abilities Rie sought to harness in this test.

But in six months of training, Rie had yet to successfully call on any of her supposed magical abilities. She couldn't light a candle or intentionally summon a premonition. Day after day, they trained. Day after day, she tried one skill after another. And day after day, she failed even the simplest of tasks.

Today represented the first attempt to call on the souls in the Daemon Realm. At Rie's request, they had avoided it until now. Her testing in the Shadow Realm had been bad enough, seeing and feeling the death of a bird. She really didn't want to experience the death of a sentient being.

Greg finally forced the issue, believing the skulls would act as a built-in connection to his long-dead children, a connection he'd strengthened over the centuries with repeated use. That connection should make it easier to magically cross the veil and call upon Rie's ancestors.

Rie grimaced. Centuries dead, and Greg still kept the bones of his children with him. It was almost as bad as a taxidermist who stuffed every pet he'd ever owned, but worse since they'd been human.

"Focus," Greg repeated. "Your thoughts are wandering."

Right.

"Find the frequency, amplify it, and call the soul to you," he encouraged.

Rie scrunched her eyes tighter. A discordant buzzing noise built in her head, growing louder as she concentrated. Nearly unbearable, Rie fought the discomfort and searched for the connection to the skulls.

The buzzing separated into two distinct sounds within Rie's brain.

She grinned. This might work. Almost there.

She let the vibrations pulse through her body,

selecting one at random. She could feel the wavelength moving like a string on an instrument. She pulled the string toward her. With a snap, Una stood before her.

"This is a surprise," Una said in the common tongue. The woman's voice sounded soft and lilting, the cadence unfamiliar to Rie's ear although she understood the words. She looked exactly like Rie expected. Greg's memory, and his skill, had captured everything from the gently pointed ears to the dimple in her left cheek in the bronze statue that honored her in the sacred circle.

"Who have you brought, Father?"

"Meet your many-times great-granddaughter and my named heir," Greg replied. "She is just beginning to harness her abilities. Perhaps you could give her some tips on soulspeech?"

Rie connected with the second skull and pulled. Nashota arrived.

"Yow!" the woman squealed. "That was unnecessarily rough."

"Sounds like she needs more help with soultouch, than soulspeech," was Una's dry reply.

"She's new."

"She can stop pulling now. She's about to attract the wicked souls I was working with," Nashota chimed in.

"How goes the counseling?" Greg asked.

"Catch up later. She's still pulling!"

A third soul popped into existence next to Nashota. He snarled, his incorporeal form lunging toward Rie. With the finesse of a thousand years' practice, Nashota pulled a spear out of thin air and whacked the soul across its head with a resounding crack, pushing him back and away from his target.

Rie felt tension on the line to Nashota, as if she had gone fishing, but caught a great white shark instead of trout. It shivered and shimmied and lunged back and forth as more souls pulled their way through the veil and into the Human Realm.

"Drop the connection," Greg commanded.

Mentally flailing, she tried to let go, tried to push the souls back through the veil to their rightful place in the wastelands of the Daemon Realm. She failed.

Like the apparitions of Una and Nashota, the souls were gauzy white and incorporeal. They floated in the air, their howling, grimacing faces distinct but the rest of their body flowing from one form to another. They lunged and swirled, shoving against one another in an effort to get past the twins.

Gods damn it all. Her first success would end in catastrophe.

"Rie, you have to let go now," Greg urged. "Disconnect from the Daemon Realm. Una and Nashota can remain, but the others must not get through."

"I'm trying," Rie ground out.

She hardly moved, yet sweat beaded on her forehead. Greg acted like there was nothing to it, like the connections could be made and broken with ease. Nothing that she tried worked. It was as if, now that the ability had been woken, she couldn't shut it down.

One of the souls, a woman, slid toward Rie like a snake with a human head. The manic grin on her face promised pain. Rie rolled out of range just as Una knocked the woman back into the crowd.

"The Moirai are not going to be happy about this!" Nashota yelled.

Greg stood and dusted off his pajama bottoms with his hand. He walked over to the mass of souls and began sending them, one by one, back to the wastelands where they belonged. He made it look so easy, just a touch and they disappeared.

Rie swallowed her fear and stood. She kept an eye on

the shifting mass of disembodied heads. "They're just ghosts," she told herself. "Nothing to fear."

She could do this.

"Did you teach her nothing before calling us?" Una asked.

Greg ignored his daughter and addressed Rie without pausing his efforts to return the souls. "These aren't just ghosts — the afterimage of the body's spirit — these are *souls*, and not just that, they're the souls of the wicked and damned. They want one thing and one thing only: to once again have a body," Greg said.

"And you've brought them here to the Human Realm, to a land that has given up magic and left itself wide open to possession. Put them back. Now," Nashota commanded.

Rie swallowed hard.

"I don't know how." Strained frustration leached into her voice.

Her hands itched for her missing khukuri blades. For nearly a century she'd relied on her physical abilities, trained to fight with fists and knives. Now she was being asked to use abstract ideas and intangible magics to perform tasks she'd never imagined she could achieve.

The connection with the Daemon Realm still vibrated with the pressure of more souls trying to break through. She mentally pushed and pulled at the line, trying to cut the connection, but it only stretched with her efforts. She didn't know how to sever it.

"Tell me what to do!"

"Father, what were you thinking, allowing someone so inexperienced to call on us," Una demanded.

"She is untrained, yes, but she is my apprentice and heir. She must learn."

"Sink or swim isn't the way to teach control."

A few of the souls darted forward, only to be pushed

back by one or the other twin. When they weren't harmed, some of the others grew more bold.

A group of three new souls rushed Nashota. She spun the spear. Pushed them back. Ducked under a clawed hand.

Una, meanwhile, fought with two small knives held in reverse grip. Any soul that found a way around Nashota, found itself sliced instead. But they couldn't send them back. The best they could do was herd them toward Greg, and there were too many for him to deal with alone.

They kept coming, all slathering to reach Rie.

"What do I do?" she cried.

"Sever the connection, Rie. Push the souls out of this realm. You can do it."

He touched another soul and it disappeared. The rest of the swarm spread out around him in ripples of angry mist, trying to flee the area before he could reach them. The twins struggled to keep them contained.

"How?" She needed to stop this. Needed to help. They were fighting her battle, cleaning up her mess. She was better than this.

"How would you cut a rope? Or a ribbon?" Garamaen asked. His voice remained surprisingly calm given the chaos around him.

"Father! Now is not the time," Nashota called. "We cannot let the souls escape."

Rie backed away as a soul found its way around Una and toward her, his scarred face twisted into a mask of anger and pain. A tendril of whatever substance it was that made up his body reached out toward Rie. With a quick flick, the tendril pierced the skin of her wrist.

She shook her hand, trying to dislodge the unwanted connection. The mist, or whatever it was, pushed its way into her arm. She could feel it slide beneath her skin, wriggling its way past her elbow like a parasitic worm.

Her muscles seized. Her brain clouded. Her body was being invaded. She couldn't do anything to stop it.

"Get it out! Get it off!" she screamed. She swiped at it with her other hand, but the soul used the contact to set more hooks in her skin.

"Help!" she cried. She had no control, no defense against the thing inside her. It wouldn't be long now before the soul embedded itself completely.

"Shield yourself!" Greg's voice boomed through the clearing.

They'd started with shielding. They'd practiced. In her panic, she couldn't remember a word of what he'd said.

"Imagine a wall, a barrier, an impenetrable steel plate," Garamaen instructed. "Build a fortress in your mind. Enclose your soul in an armored safe. Protect yourself on the inside as you would on the outside."

Bricks. Imagine bricks.

The mental wall crumbled, cracked, and broke.

Fire.

The soul pushed through the flame like smoke on the wind.

"I can't!" She leaned her head back, trying to get away from the thing climbing up her neck. It did no good when that thing was on the inside. It just kept coming.

Greg waded through the crowd of souls, sending them back with each swipe of his hand. Not fast enough. He wasn't going to make it. The soul had nearly disappeared into her skin. His laughter bubbled up through her own lips.

"Too late," the voice that was hers but not hers said. "Mine now."

Greg shook his head, his expression filled with disappointment and resignation. He looked deep into Rie's eyes. Frowned.

"No," he said.

A single word relayed all of the bitter discouragement felt by everyone in the clearing. Rie had let every single one of them down. Had failed so miserably, she didn't deserve another opportunity. She was a disgrace.

A tear dripped down her cheek while the alien soul inside her smiled.

Greg lifted his hand. Touched her head. Everything went dark.

***

Sanyare: The Heir Apparent Now Available!

PIXIE TAMER
A SHORT STORY PREQUEL TO
SANYARE: THE LAST DESCENDANT

It's Nuriel "Rie" Lhethannien's twenty-fifth nameday. She should be celebrating her rise to maturity, not sweating in the training hall. But life isn't fair, and humans aren't equal to the elves, at least not in the High Court.

After losing a practice bout to the one man she wants to trust, Rie is thrown into the most challenging test of her life. Will the rewards outweigh the risks?

Sign up for my newsletter to get your FREE copy! http://www.meganhaskell.com

PLUS

Tell me you've read *Sanyare: The Last Descendant* and I'll send you two FREE deleted scenes from Daenor and Braegan's point of view. Each month you'll receive an email from me with the latest news, events, and giveaways, including a free snippet from my latest work in progress and a chance to win a signed print copy of one of my books!

PLEASE REVIEW!

An author's career is built with the support of readers like you, and reviews increase an author's or a book's visibility in the marketplace. So if you enjoyed reading *Sanyare: The Last Descendant*, please consider leaving a brief review on Amazon. Every review helps!

ABOUT MEGAN HASKELL

Legend has it, I was born with a book in my hands. When I was a kid, my mom would ground me from reading in order to get me to do my chores. To this day, I can readily ignore the real world in favor of the imaginary one lurking between the pages of my current addiction. My dad — also an avid reader — introduced me to Tolkien in my late elementary years, and I never looked back. I love escaping to worlds where magic and monsters are real, especially stories with kick-butt heroines and dangerously attractive heroes.

Despite my voracious book appetite, I didn't start creative writing until I was working as a number cruncher in a big accounting firm. With an hour commute by train every day, and a demanding left-brain occupation, I needed a mobile creative outlet. A pen and paper are about as mobile as it gets! As the pages filled, I moved onto a tiny laptop, and a writer was born. Now I create my own fantasies!

I currently live in Southern California with my wonderfully supportive husband, two daughters, and a ridiculously energetic dog.

Sanyare: The Last Descendant is my first published novel. I also have a short story prequel, *Pixie Tamer*, available now on Amazon. You can also get a FREE copy of *Pixie Tamer* by subscribing to my newsletter at www.meganhaskell.com/newsletter-subscription.

Special Thanks

This book would never have been finished if it wasn't for my hugely supportive family and the small army of individuals who helped prepare the manuscript.

To my husband: I never would have started writing if it hadn't been for your support and encouragement. You've been with me through this entire process: you went above and beyond to give me time to write and never complained when I ignored you in favor of the story in my head. When it came time to publish, you listened to my debates about cover, price, and platform, helped with my website, and generally put up with my blabbering about an industry you have no interest in. Thank you. A million times, thank you.

To my critique partner, Christy: You've been a godsend over the last year, helping to get Sanyare into decent shape. Thank you for your patience and participation. I'll return the favor, I promise.

To my beta readers — Allison, Daphne, Eve, Oz, and Scott: Thank you for your support, encouragement, and most importantly, your critical feedback. I couldn't have done it without you.

To my editor, Laura Taylor: You were the first published author to support and believe in my writing. Thank you for polishing Sanyare until she gleams.

Last, but not least, to my readers: Thank you for reading Sanyare: The Last Descendant. I hope you love Rie and her story as much as I do. Now, you can continue her journey in *Sanyare: The Heir Apparent!*